REFINED TASTES

"What does blood taste like to you, *monsieur?*" Sade asked.

"Like blood. Doesn't remind me of anything else."

"Does not each victim have his or her own essence? A tingle on the tongue, a spicy burn passing down the throat. A shimmer of herbs pressing against the palate. A bitter rush sparking an involuntary wince. *Ou* a sublime sweetness that the taste buds savor."

"You get all that when you feed?"

"Ah, *Monsieur* Bridgewater, when you were mortal you probably feasted on fast food and TV dinners. *Alors* it is time to expand your appetite so that you are not just feeding but savoring."

Other *Leisure* books by Mary Ann Mitchell:
DRAWN TO THE GRAVE
SIPS OF BLOOD

Quenched

MARY ANN MITCHELL

LEISURE BOOKS NEW YORK CITY

To John

A LEISURE BOOK®

April 2000

Published by

Dorchester Publishing Co., Inc.
276 Fifth Avenue
New York, NY 10001

ISBN 0-8439-4717-9

Prologue

Fog dampened every surface, sinking into clothing and through flesh to chill the bones of the San Francisco inhabitants. Day bowed out to allow night's darker citizens to walk the streets, moving freely in each other's shadows. Homeless huddled under a freeway overpass setting up their bedrooms on cement sidewalks. One man swept the sidewalk with a flimsy broom, losing straw with every pass, but cleaning away the day's trash, dumping it at the curb. Slices of cardboard rested atop mounds of blankets, clothes, and personal property that the man had collected into his Safeway cart. He had separated himself from the homeless crowd half a block away in order to retire for a decent night's sleep.

"Lookit old Sam across the street. He's going

to wear himself out with all that tidying up. I can hear him huffing and puffing from here." The black man spoke the words with a smile on his face. He liked Sam, but like the others on the block thought Sam to be an eccentric. "Cliff, how much dirt you think he manages to eliminate with all his effort?"

Cliff rubbed his red beard and thought awhile. In the midst of his meditation, Cliff set his hands flat on the ground and lifted his behind, twisting his neck to the side, allowing himself to check the sidewalk on which he sat. Relieved, he plopped his rear back down on the ground. "I'd say he ain't accomplishing much."

The black man scratched his crotch and leaned back against the overpass wall.

"But he sure gives himself a workout each night, don't he? Cliff, if you ever see me, myself, and I, Emory Lansing, doing something like that, call the police and have me locked up."

"Shit, I couldn't do that."

"I know you'd miss me, but living with a nut is no life."

"Shit. I ain't got the change to call the police, and if I walked up to a cop to complain, he'd probably throw me into a cell."

"Lucky for you that you'll never have to face that tragedy. I mean having me put away in a loony bin. Jail you'll manage on your own. But I come from good solid stock. Nobody in my family ever goes bonkers. Had an old aunt that used to like to go down to the local bodega in Harlem topless on hot summer afternoons. Wasn't nuts, though; just too lazy to get completely dressed for such a short trip."

"Hell, man, when it hits the nineties in New York, I wouldn't blame a nun for going topless."

"You get to the shelter today?"

"Naw, managed to scrounge up some change and buy myself a burger down at the Mac's."

"Hell, you missed a great Jerry Springer Show. Eleven a.m. each weekday I'm down at the shelter, front seat, sniffing the beginnings of lunch preparation, goosing my appetite with some heavy repartee. I love that show. Best thing on the air. And I think it's good for society. These people get to go down to a television studio and work out their grievances within the confines of a well-refereed setting. Those Springer bouncers are better than those refs over on the boxing shows. Nobody gets hurt. Occasionally some babe complains about a broken nail, or scratch, but on the whole, it's a real safe way of airing your disagreements. A couple of times after a commercial I see a guest with a Band-Aid stuck to his nose or forehead, but it don't get any worse than that. Sometimes I get so excited I'm whooping and cheering 'Jerry' with the audience. You know what I mean?"

"Yeah." Cliff gave out with an uncomfortable chuckle.

"How many times you seen the show?"

Cliff shrugged and rubbed the side of his face against his camouflage jacket.

"No more than a handful, I bet. You gotta come down to the shelter with me and catch the action. I tell you, when they start swinging and the babes start ripping each other's clothes off, I damn near piss my pants."

A few cars still sped by, but otherwise the mood was quiet. Most of the homeless snuggled under rags and cardboard, replenishing the day's lost energy. All except for sleepy-eyed Cliff and loquacious Emory.

"You know, I made a few dollars today myself," said Emory. "Didn't waste it on any Mac, though. Naw, I'm thinking more in terms of French cuisine."

"They sell French fries at the Mac," quipped Cliff.

"Hey, give me a break. I need to dream of something. Ever have those French snails?"

Cliff shook his head and adjusted his woolen cap further down on his forehead.

"Me neither, but I read an article about them once in one of those food mags."

"You read *Gourmet*?"

"Hell, I don't remember the name of the mag. It was the first one I picked up when I got to the library. Hid behind it, hoping the librarian wouldn't bust me. It was pissing cats and dogs that day, and I wanted to dry off a bit. The librarian let me hang out long enough for me to read about these bugs in a shell. Starve the shit out of them for a few days, then toss some garlic and butter over them in a hot saucepan, and you got a real French meal."

"What about that long thing they eat?" asked Cliff.

"You got a dirty mind."

"The bread. The bread."

"Oh, yeah, you need some of that to dip into the sauce."

At the end of the block a man in a wheelchair tried to maneuver onto the sidewalk. He kept slipping back onto the street, almost spinning out of control into the midst of traffic.

"What's that?" asked Emory.

"Some cripple."

Emory slapped Cliff on the side of the head. "Didn't your mamma teach you to respect the disabled? He looks like he needs some help. Come on, let's go down and help him onto the sidewalk before some car smashes into him." Emory stood and looked over his shoulder at Cliff. "Come on, get your white ass up off the ground and do a good deed. It'll make you feel better."

"I don't feel so bad now. All I need is some sleep." Cliff slowly got to his feet, almost falling over halfway, except that Emory grabbed one of Cliff's arms to give him balance.

The two men hunched their shoulders against the clammy cold fog and walked in the direction of the man in the wheelchair.

"Wait up, man. We'll give you a hand," yelled Emory.

The wheelchair came to a stop against the back end of an old Lincoln town car.

Emory checked the sloped sidewalk and couldn't see any reason for the difficulty in maneuvering the wheelchair.

"Something wrong with your wheels?" Emory moved toward the seated man, and with one hand on the man's knee, squatted down to check out the wheelchair.

"I don't see any problem. Cliff, you used to run a bicycle shop. Come over and check out these wheels."

"Bicycles and wheelchairs ain't the same thing, Emory." But he obliged his friend and also squatted next to the wheelchair.

"What am I supposed to be looking for, Emory?"

Suddenly Emory was swept backward into the arms of a dark hulk that gnashed its teeth before burying them deep in his neck.

Cliff never made it to his feet, because the man in the wheelchair dug his fingers into Cliff's voice box, exploding the fleshy cartilage.

Part One

Chapter One

Wil came out of the bathroom still wet from his shower. His tattoos shimmered in exotic colors all up and down his legs. His long, dark hair glistened, and his chiseled face still showed evidence of water droplets.

"Okay, your turn. If you don't want to take a bath, how about I sponge you down at least?"

"I don't need any sponging."

"Dad, you telling me your fingers don't feel like they're sticking together?"

"I'll lick them clean." Keith drew his tongue up and down his right index finger.

"Come on, I'll wash off that stale blood before I slide you under the bed."

"I want a proper coffin. Can't be a decent vampire without a real coffin."

"We can't afford one."

"Sure we can. Some guy told me they sell them over the Internet real cheap."

"And to where will it be delivered?"

"To this damn room, of course."

"Great. People notice us already because of the wheelchair. We have a coffin delivered, and they'll be wondering who we killed." Wil glanced around the room to make sure everything was in place before they both retired for a few hours. He noticed that the window shade had slipped up, and went to pull it down.

"I don't know why you bother. Here we are in a cloudy, rainy city in a sixth-floor room of a twelve-story building facing a brick wall. A brick wall that we can actually reach out and touch. How much sunshine you think will make its way inside this dump?"

"One should always practice good habits."

"Practice them where it's needed, idiot. I'm living with a son who's sucked off kids, beat people with whips, humped an old lady who killed his father, and suddenly he's worrying about good habits. Your S and M friends worry about doing good?"

"Don't have any friends anymore."

Keith tsked. "I feel sorry for you."

"I don't expect pity from you, but you should take some responsibility for how our lives have turned out. It was you who introduced me to Marie. And she's the one turned us both into blood-sucking vagrants." Wil pulled the bed-spread down on one side of the bed and the sheet down on the other side to make a tentlike effect that would prevent bright sun from hitting either of them while they slept. "Dad, since we're so dependent on each other, maybe we should try to be more affectionate toward each other."

"Don't start slobbering kisses on me." Keith held up both his palms as if fending off his son's affection.

"No, Dad. It doesn't have to be kisses or hugs. Just a kinder way of speaking to each other. If we could put the rancor behind us, we might be able to figure out this vampire life."

"Death," Keith corrected.

"We'll be striving in dumps like this one until the end of the world." Wil walked back into the bathroom and came out with a wet washrag. "Marie's son-in-law hinted at there being something like a training period for vampires." Wil grabbed one of his father's hands and began wiping it clean. Keith didn't bother to fight him. "Unfortunately for us, nobody stuck around to orient us to this . . . condition." Wil dropped his father's hand and while deep in thought, turned toward the bathroom.

"Hey, aren't you going to clean my other hand, too? My legs may not work, but both my hands do."

Wil finished the job and threw the washrag across the room, where it landed on the tile-covered bathroom floor. He bent his knees and prepared to lift his father out of the wheelchair.

"Wait! Before you tuck me in, could you do me a favor? Spread a little more of the soil under the bed."

"There's enough there already. Besides, I brought only a limited amount in the suitcase.

17

Once that's gone there's no more home soil for us."

"I was thinking, maybe you could spread some extra where my legs rest."

"We've already tried that, and you haven't regained any use of your legs."

"Maybe you could rub some soil on my legs and the bottom of my feet."

"We've done that also. I don't even know whether there's anything to this home soil business. I read about it in a couple of fiction books and thought, just in case this author knows something or it could be something, I figured I'd try using it. So far there's been no proof that we need the soil."

"We've never tried sleeping without it, Wil."

"Are you volunteering to try?"

The old man looked down at his paralyzed legs, and when he winced, Wil knew that his father had attempted to move them. Wil cringed in sympathy. *It's true*, he thought, *neither of us would be in this position if I hadn't been playing games with the vampire dominatrix.*

"I'm sorry, Dad."

"I just want to be able to move around again on my own two feet. Why the hell couldn't I heal up the way you did? You were badly burned, you said, and now there isn't a scar on you. At least not from the burn."

"I don't know why you didn't heal completely. Maybe the injuries were so bad that your body just couldn't mend all the damage. I promise to keep researching, and if I do find a cure, I'll do everything in my power to see that you're made

18

whole." Wil scooped his father up into his arms. He had already swept the bedcover back in order to smoothly slide Keith under the bed. He heard his father sneeze. "Dad, it's psychological."

Keith rested both his hands across his chest and set his facial expression in a stubborn glare. Wil simply brushed the bedcover down over the mattress, hiding his disgruntled father from view. He heard another sneeze that he could have sworn sounded forced. As he shut off the lamp's dim bulb, he heard his father start humming the nightly dirge.

Adorable sorceress, do you love the
    damned?
Tell me, do you know what is irremissible?
Do you know Remorse, with the poisoned
    arrows,
For which our heart serves as target?
Adorable sorceress, do you love the
    damned?

> "Irreparable"
> *Les Fleurs du Mal*
> Charles Baudelaire

Chapter Two

"Damn! Why the hell do you want to bring me to a place like this?" Keith's stomach felt dyspeptic. It always seemed to happen when he needed refueling. Instead of heading down the alleyways of San Francisco, Wil guided the wheelchair into a fetish club.

"Dad, it's your birthday. I thought we'd do something special. They're supposed to put on some impressive plays here, and best of all, the audience gets to participate."

Black appeared to be de rigueur. Some people wore leather, some spandex, and a fair number of females were covered in lace or sheer gauzy nylon and silk, but the attire was all black. Phony nails elongated stubby fingers, and pale makeup blended female and male faces into a shiny, reflective crowd under halogen lights.

Keith's wheelchair caught on a fuchsia ribbon of netting that slid down the bar onto the floor. His body jerked and he mumbled a curse.

"Take it easy, Dad." Wil lifted father and chair off the netting.

"Damn trap they've set."

"I simply missed seeing it." Wil stood tall, looking for a table.

A woman's hands wrapped around Wil's upper right arm.

"I had to check. After seeing that feat of strength, I couldn't resist." A ribbon of blond curls circled a very pretty face. She ran her tongue across her lips and closed her eyes while kneading Wil's upper arm.

"Is she orgasming or what?" Keith asked.

"Dad, must you insult everyone?"

"No insult," the girl muttered. "The cripple is right," she said, moving her crotch into Wil's right hand.

Keith watched his son's fingers rub against the sheer metallic material clinging to her body. "Boy, we come here so you can get laid?" he said.

Wil pulled back from the girl. "I've got to find a place for my father to sit."

"He already has one," the girl said, waving a hand at the wheelchair. "Besides, he shouldn't be a cripple. He's a mutant. A freak. Why hasn't he healed?"

"You're right; he doesn't deserve to be crippled, and he shouldn't have to listen to ignorant people like you." Wil grabbed hold of the handles on the wheelchair and started pushing his father toward the center of the room.

"She doesn't know what kind of freaks we are. Maybe we should take a stroll out in the alley with her and show her."

"She's just an ignorant girl, Dad." Wil kept moving through the tight crowd.

"Yeah, exactly why we should educate her."

"Here's a free table." Smoothly Wil moved his father next to the table.

"Ain't no chair."

"I'll squat."

"Long as you don't try sitting on my lap."

"Can I get you guys drinks?" a waitress asked.

"Honey, I could really use a drink. Matter of—"

"We'll have two red wines," Wil interrupted.

Keith looked at the waitress. Her face looked chiseled, though too made-up. When she turned from the table, he noticed she wore shorts that seemed to dig into her crotch and allow her round cheeks to bulge out under the satin-black material. As she walked away, he saw that her calves were covered with swollen, knotted veins. Keith used his right shoulder to brush some dripping saliva from his chin.

"I didn't mean to hurt your feelings."

Keith looked over to see Goldilocks back accosting his son.

"It was my feelings you hurt, not his," said Keith.

The girl glanced over at him and paused a few moments before curtsying and giving him an apology.

Keith leaned toward the girl and said, "Come closer, little girl."

"Cecelia," she hissed. She walked a few paces closer to him.

He could smell her blood, see the gold rings piercing her nipples below the thin sheer material of the metallic dress. He reached out to touch one of her breasts, but his son swept his hand away. Cecelia chuckled.

"Maybe you should move away from us," Wil told her.

Cecelia's expression became serious. "Would you send me away just because you don't want to compete with your father?"

"Listen, you don't know anything about us. Believe me, it would be far better for you to walk away now."

The waitress placed two wineglasses on the table and a bill. She waited.

"Can we pay you later?" Wil asked.

"I need the money now. People here make quick contacts and then disappear."

Wil pulled some bills from the back pocket of his jeans and slowly started counting.

"Here, Cyn. Keep the change." Cecelia had reached inside one of her boots and pulled out a twenty-dollar bill. The waitress took the money and walked away.

"Hey, we can pay for our own drinks," Wil said, continuing to count out his roll of dollar bills.

Cecelia wrapped her hands around his and forced them closed.

"Save them, baby, you may want to play some

games in the arcade." Her head motioned toward a back room, blinking with lights and filled to capacity. "The game room is the perfect place to use your spare change."

"Spare change! She's insulting you, son."

"She's right, Dad." Wil tossed the roll of dollar bills onto the table. His dad retrieved every one of them, shoving them into the side pocket of his polyester pants.

"The cripple is frugal," Cecelia said.

"Don't call my father a cripple. His name is Keith."

"Mr. Bridgewater," Keith corrected.

"And your name?"

"Wil."

"Since you don't have much money to blow in this place, why don't you join me at a late-night party I'm going to?"

"Sounds good to me," Keith said, hoping to have the girl as the meal he badly needed.

"No," Wil said.

"You are the stupidest jackass I've ever seen." Keith lifted one of the wineglasses. "Do you think this stuff is going to last us until tomorrow night? Child, if you know of a party, we're with you."

"It's a blood party," she said simply.

"You mean an S and M party, don't you?" Wil reached for the remaining glass of wine.

"S and M, blood, whatever you want," she said, passing a hand across Wil's genitals.

"Why don't we go now," yelled Keith.

"We're not going, Dad. You're making a mistake inviting us to a party like that," he told Cecelia.

She pouted and moved closer to Keith. "Think you could talk your son into going, Mr. Bridgewater?" She smiled and touched her hand to Keith's shoulder.

"I'll damn sure try. If he don't go, though, I'm up for the party."

"It's an invitation for the both of you. Can't accept one without the other." She brought her left index finger to her mouth and bit down. She used the finger to rub her blood across Keith's lips.

He wanted to snap at her hand like a rabid dog. The smell. The whisper of the coppery blood staining his lips and feeding his tongue. Only once before was he ever this hungry. He watched as she squeezed a few drops of blood from the bite onto his tongue. The room seemed flooded with the scent of blood. He closed his eyes, and a veil of red blood covered his vision.

He remembered the first time that he awakened from his deathlike sleep. Famished for blood and yet surrounded by blood. Blood clung to his clothes, to his skin, wrapping him in a filmy shroud. He opened his eyes and saw a human form lying beside him in bed, cuddled close, soundly sleeping. His teeth immediately tore into the still body's cheek, shredding muscles and nerves in a quest for blood. But his son was able to fight him off, leaving Keith dangling over the edge of the bed, his legs totally useless.

"Dad, you all right?"

Wil's face floated in front of Keith, almost appearing severed from his son's body.

"Are you okay? You look like shit."

Again Keith wanted to sink his teeth into the smooth unscarred cheek, but knew his legs would keep him from succeeding.

"Hell! Get out of my way. Dammit, I'm getting the hell out of here."

Keith scooted his wheelchair around Wil and directed himself to the exit, ramming into anonymous shins and knees on the way. At the threshold he was stopped by two powerful hands that caught hold of the chair's armrests.

"Monsieur Bridgewater? Unexpected. I hope this doesn't mean your family is traveling with you."

"Mr. Sade, you understand all of this. Why can't I walk? Why didn't I heal like a true vampire?"

"Perhaps you are not a true vampire," Cecelia whispered in Keith's left ear.

"Please, let us not wax about the *fantastique.* Ah!" said Sade, letting go of the armrests in order to stand tall and face Wil. "Just the *personne* I did not want to see ever again."

"Let's get the hell out of here, Dad."

"No! Wait! Mr. Sade, at one time you promised to help me with your mother-in-law."

"Obviously I failed."

"But you can still help me, can't you? You can make me walk."

"A Christ I am not, *monsieur.* Although I did spend four years with the Jesuits at the Louis-le-Grand school, and the *correcteur* did at times attempt to reshape me into an imitation of

Christ. However, I have remained steadfastly in the devil's brigade. *Un vieux de la vielle.*"

"I've been abandoned by Christ, Mr. Sade. If the devil wants my soul in return for giving me back the use of my legs, then he can have it."

"He already does, *monsieur*. And I think he grabbed it long before you met Marie."

"Then we should all go to the blood party," Cecelia said.

"*Mon enfant*, she always makes snap decisions for which she must pay dearly."

"You're with Sade?" Wil asked Cecelia.

Next to Cecelia's ear Sade spoke low but loud enough for Wil to hear:

"Adorable sorcière, aimes-tu les damnés?
Dis, connais-tu l'irrémissible?
Connais-tu le Remords, aux traits empoison-
    nés,
A qui notre coeur sert de cible?
Adorable sorcière, aimes-tu les damnés?"

Cecelia smiled and said, "Baudelaire."

"*Oui*, she is mine, *monsieur*," said Sade.

"Dad, come on, you don't want anything to do with these people." Wil grabbed the handles of the wheelchair and pushed past Sade.

"Dammit, I want to stay and talk to Mr. Sade," yelled Keith, almost flinging himself from the wheelchair.

"But wait, you have to come to the party with us," called Cecelia. "It's where you belong. Where our kind belong."

"Our kind?" Wil stopped but refused to let go

28

of the chair, preventing his father from turning back toward the club.

Cecelia smiled and lowered her lashes. Her right hand beckoned him to her, but he refused to budge.

"Such a stubborn blood-sucker. Of course I know that you're a vampire and your father . . . he's a mutant of some sort."

"Mutant, my ass!" Keith attempted to fight Wil's grip on the chair. He wanted to confront the bitch.

"I want nothing to do with anyone who keeps company with Sade," Wil said.

"I could say the same thing in reference to your father. But I've taken a liking to you. More than a liking. I lust for you."

Roughly Sade pulled the girl back.

"The games *la petite fille* likes to play may not suit you, *monsieur*. As I recollect, you did have a limit. She . . ." From behind, Sade placed his hands on the girl's breasts. "Has no limits. She is *une parfaite* student."

Keith stretched to look over his shoulder. Sade's jaggedly cut white hair fell full down to the man's shoulders. His blue eyes glittered, competing for attention. And the lips, parted so slightly, crinkled into barely a smile. The girl in Sade's arms submitted to his touch even as he explored the intimacies of her body. And her body looked sensually plump, with the paleness of her skin allowing the faint blue network of veins to peep through. She did not suffer the hunger that drove Keith. She looked sated, sated and willing to share if demanded of her. Sade

29

obviously made sure the young vampire did not want for the elixir that they mutually craved.

Sade could end Keith's hunger and paralysis. Keith remained sure of this even while his son pushed his wheelchair out onto the street.

Chapter Three

The mother and son walked down the damp street. It had been raining earlier in the evening, and the chill in the air prevented the sidewalk from drying completely. A good son, he held his mother's arm, helping her to maneuver around and over the cracks, holes, and debris of the sidewalk. A woman in her late seventies, his mother had not aged well. Arthritis swelled the joints of her hands, and diabetes caused an unhealing wound on her foot that gave her a limp. Her body was trim, but almost half her skin was covered with eczema. She clung to her son's arm as tightly as the twisted joints would allow.

The son remained patient with her frail health. He never rushed her or scolded her for taking too long. He had returned to live with her when he lost his job fifteen years earlier. Not that he hadn't worked since, but the jobs now were all temporary. At fifty he couldn't expect to change his own lot, but only to inherit the family house once Mother joined Dad in the cemetery. His hair was almost all gray, and his bushy eyebrows only hinted at the blond of his youth. His slender, tall body leaned into his mother, helping to carry her weight. Dressed in a black turtleneck and a khaki jacket, he fancied himself handsome. The contrast of the colors with his olive complexion certainly gave him an air of sophistication.

"You remember I have an appointment with Doctor Phillips tomorrow, don't you?" Her voice did not carry well, but her son had attuned himself to it.

"Yes, Mother. At seven-fifteen in the morning."

"Awfully early, don't you think?"

"We're usually up and around by then."

"Up, maybe. But at that hour, I'm just barely getting around. You called the car service, didn't you?"

"Sam offered to drive us."

"That weasel. Are you sure you can trust him to remember?"

"Told him we'd take him for lunch at his favorite pizza place."

"Maybe since you mentioned food, he'll show. The appointment is important. If Sam's not on time, you may have to call a cab, and not that horrid one we used several months ago. Taking us for a tour of San Francisco, as if we were

32

tourists who didn't know our way around. Why you gave him a tip at all I don't understand."

"I gave him fifty cents to show him what I thought of him and his driving. Didn't want him to think I had just forgotten. Don't worry, Sam will show up."

They were close to home, an old Victorian built at the middle of a slight hill. Mother could no longer manage on her own. She left the house only with someone. Tonight they had been visiting one of her old friends, a woman she had known since grammar school. The two girls had dropped out of school in the seventh grade. Each had managed to obtain jobs with a clothing factory. The mother's husband, may he rest in peace, had worked briefly at the factory also. He had worked there long enough to fall in love.

"Mom, be careful of this curb, it's damaged. Don't know why the city can't keep the streets in better shape. Look at that man in the wheelchair over there. He's having a hell of a time crossing that street. Thank God there aren't many cars out tonight."

"When I see someone like that I treasure the fact that I can still use my two legs. Luther, what if I should lose a leg because of this damn wound?"

"You'll always have me, Mother. Besides, the wound seems to be stabilized, and hasn't gotten any worse in the past month. Think I should go over and help that poor man in the wheelchair?"

"I'd say yes if I were feeling stronger, but I

don't think I could even stand in one spot without your assistance."

Mother and son huddled closer together, thankful for each other. They passed the man in the wheelchair and didn't look back.

Just before starting up the final hill for home, the mother asked that they stop a few minutes so she could catch her breath. They lingered long enough for the wheelchair-bound man to catch up.

Luther noticed that the disabled man looked angry. Of course he had probably seen him and his mother walk by. A flush of guilt soured Luther's placid contentedness. He had to say something to the disabled man. He had to explain why he hadn't helped.

"Sorry, sir. I saw you needed assistance back there, but Mother can't really stand for very long on her own, and I was afraid to leave her."

The disabled man glared at Luther.

"Don't say anything, dear. The man may not want your pity," the mother said. Suddenly her son was snatched from her grasp. She wavered, looking for something to hold onto. After several slow laborious steps, she reached out to touch the brick wall of a bank.

"Luther," she cried, and after balancing herself carefully, she looked behind her. No one was there. The disabled man and her son had disappeared.

It is the Devil who pulls the strings that
   move us!
In repulsive objects we find enticing lures;
Each day we go down one more step
   toward Hell,
Without horror, through the darkness
   which smells rank.

"To the Reader"
Les Fleurs du Mal
Charles Baudelaire

Chapter Four

Cecelia listened to the slapping of flesh, the moans, the groans, the whispers, and the lapping of tongues. All background noise in her world. The blur of flesh no longer registered as lascivious, merely folds and creases pressing against themselves, she thought. The whippings melded into embraces. Piercings offered a fresh entrance into another being. Vises charged flesh long numbed by the repetitious bruisings. Flames blistered and burned already soiled flesh. Open cuts fed the damned and the near-damned.

She consciously avoided looking for Sade. His smell, still fresh in the room, indicated that he remained at the party. He took blood promiscuously; he ravaged human flesh and savored the pain and fear. Coitus only enhanced his appetite. He could never find peace, never share again with her the novelty of her training. The innocence of her soul.

"Mistress Cecelia." A white-haired woman of twenty curtsied. "I have missed you, mistress, and am ready to do your bidding."

The woman wore a red shift that covered her body completely, but hid nothing of her flesh. The dark hair at her pubis contrasted sharply with the dyed hair on her head. Her slender body almost looked boyish, except for the small breasts that peaked in fat hard nipples. Her head, bowed deeply, hid her features. She waited and would remain waiting until given direction.

"Harlot, where is your charming playmate?" Cecelia referred to the young boy the woman led around on a leash, a boy of thirteen, fourteen, who walked in a drug-induced daze.

"He is no longer with me, mistress."

Silence. The woman would explain no further if not asked. But Cecelia didn't care about the boy, didn't care about Harlot. She brushed aside the woman, who immediately fell to her knees, kissing the hem of Cecelia's gold dress. Cecelia, the queen of Sade's kingdom, pulled the material from the woman's hands. She would have spat on the woman, but didn't care enough to do so. A slight, she knew, that would wound Harlot deeply.

"Never will you hold him, Cecelia. He will continue to love me forever." The voice Cecelia heard was that of Liliana, Sade's niece, and the only love he had permitted himself. A girl Cecelia's own age when turned into a vampire. Occasion-

ally the sprinkle of soft sobs interwove with Liliana's words. But Liliana no longer existed in material form. The niece's body had been ripped apart by vampire mutants; however, her spirit continued to haunt Cecelia's mind.

Cecelia needed a distraction, a new toy. Wil would be ideal if he would only separate himself from that loathsome father. She had never seen him in the club before. Would he come back? Not if he listened to his father. Then again, Dad seemed really obsessed with Sade.

She sniffed the air. Sade was nearby. A cursory glance across the floor in front of her revealed only naked bodies attempting contortionist positions in their quest for the unique. She spun around and found him standing behind her, his arms crossed, his expression placid.

"I was looking for you," she said.

"I know, *ma fille*." He waited.

"I was thinking of those two men we ran into tonight at the club. Remember the young man and his wheelchair-bound father?"

"Of course I remember."

"They seemed to know you from somewhere."

Sade's blue eyes looked dull.

"How do you know them? Did you make them vampires?"

"*Ma fille*, would I create flawed vampires?"

"The young man was not flawed."

"In his own way he is. Forget the two men, *ma fille*. Neither is safe to be around."

"Why?"

"You are bored, *ma petite fille*, and want to

rush into trouble. Do *les attentions* I pay you not satisfy *ta soif*?"

"You never share your blood with me anymore." Her voice rose and hardened as she spoke.

"Ah! But I often bring you *un cadeau*."

"You bring me men that satisfy your own sick interests, partners in sexual acts that frequently turn my stomach. You've seen more than once that I can't drink from them after the crude play we've engaged in."

Sade uncrossed his arms and rested his right index finger against her cheek.

"Your purpose is to serve, *ma fille*. And if you find pleasure while doing so, then it is a gift from *moi* to you." He rubbed her cheek with the back of his hand. "You cannot demand from me. But a smile." His thumb ran across her painted lips. "Instead of a frown." His other fingers rubbed her forehead. "Could possibly seduce *moi* to gift you with a prize."

"I want Wil," she demanded.

Sade used his hand to push full force against her face. She fell sprawled across a vibrating mass of flesh. Sade reached out a hand to her. She did not take it.

He leaned over her, his face close to hers. His breath smelt of earth, moss, blood, and sex. The mass of flesh sprouted arms that fumbled over her body. Sade's voice held her in place.

> "C'est le Diable qui tient les fils qui nous
>   remuent!
> Aux objets répugnants nous trouvons des
>   appas;

Mary Ann Mitchell

*Chaque jour vers l'Enfer nous descendons
  d'un pas,
Sans horreur, à travers des ténèbres qui
  puent."*

"And you are the devil," she said.
"And it is your strings that I pull." He forced
her head into the mob of people and set her lips
upon a purplish penis that throbbed boldly,
forcing itself inside her mouth.

Chapter Five

"Hardly enough blood in this idiot to satisfy one of us, never mind the two of us."

"Dad, you were supposed to snatch the old lady."

"I'm supposed to survive on a crone? Well, drinking her blood would have been like drinking poorly stored old wine. Her blood would have been vinegar."

"I would have taken her blood. I always grab the strongest of the victims and leave you the weaker, since you don't have my mobility."

"I didn't want to touch her. Did you notice she was covered with some sort of rash?" Keith shivered at the memory.

Wil shook his head and kicked the dead man's weighted body into San Francisco Bay.

"What do we do now?" asked Keith. "I'm as

hungry as I was before. We could have had that blonde morsel at the club. Vampire or not, she seemed willing."

"She belongs to Sade." Wil circled his father's wheelchair.

"And he could help me. Damn, don't you care about your own father?"

"Sade made Marie a vampire. Everything that's happened is ultimately due to Sade." Wil continued circling his father's wheelchair. "He's the one responsible for your being in this chair."

"No!" shrieked Keith. "You're responsible. You and your perverted appetites. That damn bitch did this to me to have a clear path to you. She knew I didn't approve. If you had never come back, if you never had been born . . ."

A spray of water lightly touched Keith's face.

"If I hadn't been born, then Mom would still be alive. Forgiveness is out of the question, isn't it, Dad? I may as well leave you here to fend for yourself." He knelt in front of his father and looked him full in the face. "Should I leave you here? Do you care at all?"

"Of course I do. I need someone to help me get around." Keith looked down at his paralyzed legs and slammed the palms of his hands on the chair's armrests.

"No, you don't, Dad. You do quite well on your own. I'm merely a memory that you'd like to forget."

Keith looked his son in the face. "You're a crutch, boy. My crutch. And like any cripple I have to accept you. And I'm your penance, boy.

A debt you'll be paying until the end of the world."

Wil stood and turned his back on his father.

"I could leave you here," Wil said. "I could toss you into the water, weigh you down, and have you live out your time with the fishes."

"Dead! I'm not alive! Neither are you. We're two dead people with no grave to go to. We need each other for company. We need to hate each other so we don't have to hate ourselves."

"I hate myself." Wil turned and faced his father. "I don't hate you, old man. I've never hated you. I hate myself because I can't make you love me." Tears streamed down Wil's cheeks.

"Pathetic shit. Wheel me back up to the road so we can finish off the night with a good feed. And I don't want an old biddy. I want young. I want healthy."

Chapter Six

"What the hell is that?"

"What?" The middle-aged man's voice sounded gruff.

"That rag you're reading." The younger man scratched his scalp, causing his oily black hair to release a shower of dandruff onto the shoulders of his pea coat.

"It's a magazine I picked up on the next seat."

"Left by some weirdo just for you to find." The young man snuffled.

"Jerry, this happens to be a medical magazine."

"With all those pussies showing." Jerry chortled. "That ain't nothing but a girly rag."

"It's printed for gynecologists."

Jerry opened his mouth to laugh, and sprayed the centerfold with his spit. "Mike, you're not living in the real world, are you?"

"This is as real as I'm going to allow my world to get."

The BART train pulled into the station, and the two men huddled together over the magazine. A young man pushed an old man in a wheelchair into the car.

"Wow! Look at those bazooms. Suppose they're real?"

"Nah. You can tell by the shape and the fact that they're sitting too high up." Mike outlined the model's breasts with his index finger. "Dated a broad who got herself a set of these. Went back to work too soon. She was one of these topless dancers. Well, the stitches hadn't completely healed, and one night the right one come flying out, landing in the audience someplace. She never saw the silicone sac again. Some lonely guy probably took it home to rub up against it."

"Oh, man! What a sicko!"

Mike nodded in agreement.

"Hey, look at the two guys over there, Mike." Jerry bobbed his head in the direction of the wheelchair. "They don't look too good. Think they've been out begging?"

"More likely brawling. The young guy's a mess. Got a tear in his shirt and a spot of blood up near his right shoulder."

"Yeah, but they look hard up, and that old man don't look like he's got much more time in him. Think we should slip them a few dollars?"

"It might be an embarrassment all around. What if they refuse it?"

"They look pretty independent. Hey, I've got an idea." Jerry reached into the inside pocket of his coat and brought out a twenty-dollar bill. "We only got one more stop to go. What if this should slip out of my pocket and land on the seat?" He let the bill fall in between himself and Mike. "They'll think they hit the jackpot." Jerry chortled, feeling immensely generous and satisfied that he had just set some good karma into action.

The old man watched Mike and Jerry. Spittle flowed out the side of his mouth and down his chin. The poor old man didn't know enough to wipe the spit away, probably didn't even know it was there.

Mike and Jerry looked at each other and shook their heads.

"Don't want that to be me when I'm old," Mike whispered to Jerry. "Just let me go fast. Don't want to slowly fall to pieces."

"Know what you mean."

They were coming into their station. Jerry nudged Mike and both checked to make sure the twenty was visible on the seat between them before rising.

Once on the platform, they heard the doors shut and the old man shriek. They turned back to see the old man waving his arms and reaching down to the wheels as if he wanted to get away from his young companion. The young man held firmly onto the handles of the chair.

"Think he's his father?"

"Don't know," said Mike. "But he's a saint for sticking by that old man."

The train pulled out of the station, and both watched the old man give them the finger.

46

Ceaselessly beside me the Demon writhes;
He swarms around me like impalpable air:
I swallow him and feel him burning my
   lungs
And filling them with an everlasting guilty
   desire.

"Destruction"
Les Fleurs du Mal
Charles Baudelaire

Chapter Seven

Sade fingered the late-nineteenth-century vibrator. A British antique, the mechanical massage device had been designed by the physician Joseph Mortimer Granville, a dear friend who'd frowned on Sade's use of the machine. They would argue for hours about the appropriate use of the vibrator. Granville believed that the vibrator could ease the pain of male skeletal muscles. On the other hand, Sade believed women could find sexual satisfaction apart from the clumsy manipulations of husbands and lovers.

On several occasions he had found Cecelia using the device, and she always glowed afterward. Proof that the device would be of no harm to women, except for those pregnant, where uterine contractions could be induced.

He slipped the vibrator back into its velvet-lined case and put it back on the mantelpiece. He looked around the room. They hadn't bothered to stock any of the rooms with furniture, and this room seemed especially empty. A pitifully old and faded Persian rug lay on a badly bruised hardwood floor. The rug and the poorly reproduced Tiffany lamp had been left by the prior residents. Two old beanbag chairs cluttered the distant side of the room. Both had been found in the basement. The girl had absolutely no taste. He never sat on the chairs. He tried to ignore them the best he could. If he were sure San Francisco would not bore him, he would refurnish the entire Victorian house, although the narrow hallways made him feel claustrophobic. Still, the rooms were comforting because they were so dark. The houses had been built in tight clusters, thereby resisting the glare of the sun. An unconscious vampire's prolonged exposure to the sun could cause serious damage. The house needed paint inside and out. The living room walls seemed to be cream-colored, but he guessed that at one time they had been white.

He left the room and climbed the stairs to the second floor.

"Cecelia," he called, but no one answered.

As he neared the top of the stairs, he could hear Cecelia having a conversation. The words were muffled, but an ear to the door solved that problem.

"I can't, Liliana. He'd never allow it. It would be the same as if I created new vampires. He would squash me."

Sade sighed and shook his head. Cecelia's conversations with the invisible Liliana had become more frequent. And even though he knew that his soul and all other vampire souls were bound to the earth, he did not believe that any could reach into the living world. When their bodies were destroyed, vampires suffered an eternal limbo, bound to the soil and air of the earth. Right now vanquished vampires surrounded him, but neither he nor they could reach one another. Actually, there were none he would want to reach. The voice of Liliana could only sadden his wicked heart.

A long crack swept across the hallway ceiling, splitting when it reached the dusty chandelier. The tattered hallway carpeting bunched into dirty balls of yarn. His residence at the Bastille had been better equipped than this American horror.

He faced his own room at the opposite end of the hall. He had managed to fit the room with several classic antiques, all European in origin. His casket rested atop a whitish-gray marble table that had once been used as a Christian altar. A tinge of pink ran through the marble and could be seen most clearly in the lamb frieze on the front of the table.

He heard Cecelia sobbing behind her locked door. She still met his demands; only her mind did not seem strong enough to accept this eternal existence. A stubborn girl who rejected his lame solace. Even he had to admit it was lame. He himself sparkled in this dark cruel world. He had been meant to join forces with Satan.

He remembered what Baudelaire had written, and pronounced the lines aloud to share with whatever or whomever was listening.

"Sans cesse à mes côtés s'agite le Démon;
Il nage autour de moi comme un air impal-
    pable;
Je l'avale et le sens qui brûle mon poumon
Et l'emplit d'un désir éternel et coupable."

Chapter Eight

Wil walked through the dingy lobby of his hotel, relieved that his father had decided to stay in and sulk. The floor looked like badly stained bathroom tile, and the paint on the walls peeled off in chunks. He guessed that at least six coats of paint had been on the walls, given the multitude of colors showing through. A few folding chairs had been spaced out in the lobby close to old-fashioned round standing ashtrays.

The manager, Pete, sat with his left elbow leaning on the desk and his head resting on his left fist. A new paperback absorbed all of Pete's attention until an eighteen-year-old male shouted at him.

"Hey, what's Old Man Jones doing sitting on the vestibule steps?"

"Is that piece of shit still sitting there?" Pete slammed a glass ashtray on top of the book to

52

save his place. "I told him to get the hell out of here, and that includes the vestibule. The old drunk will make us look seedier than we are."

"Why don't you just take him up to his room?" the teen asked.

"Because he don't got a room here anymore. Hasn't paid his rent in months. Let him go sleep in one of the local alleyways."

"Give him a break, Pete," said Wil.

"You want to talk rent money?"

"We're paid up."

"Barely." Pete stood. His blue oxford button-down was spotted with sweat, and the buttons were ready to pop over his beer belly. He sported an old-fashioned crew cut that was mostly white. His complexion appeared ruddy, whether from sunburn or alcohol was hard for Wil to tell. When Pete rounded the desk, the teen stepped quickly out of his way.

Pete opened the inner glass door and assaulted Jones with curses.

"Sad, isn't it," the boy said. "If I had known, I never would have said anything."

Wil looked into the boy's deep-set blue-gray eyes. The truth or not? Wil couldn't tell. There was deception surrounding the kid, but Wil could never distinguish truth from lies. The boy's cherub face and shoulder-length sandy-blond hair gave him the aura of an innocent, but Wil was willing to bet the kid hadn't been inno-cent since the age of two. Growing up with a prostitute mother and lots of paying customers had aged the boy.

"How's your mother, Tim?" asked Wil.

Tim shrugged. He never talked family, even though he still lived in a one-bedroom with his mother.

"Your mother mentioned she was going to retire," said Wil.

Tim smiled. "Forced to retire. Ma's in her mid-forties; how much money you think she can make a night?"

Wil wanted to reply that it depended on what she did, but allowed a kinder bone in his body to overrule the spite.

"You see that bastard out there again, you tell me and I'll call the police," Pete said, walking back behind the desk to continue reading his paperback. He thought for a second and added, "There's twenty bucks in it for you."

"Yes, Mr. Connors," the teen answered.

Wil figured for twenty bucks Tim would help eject his own mother without even thinking of the consequences to himself. The kid had no job, unless one counted the fact that his prowess serviced several girlfriends, girlfriends old enough to buy him gifts and take him to dinner. Wil had been there, except that he hadn't been particular about the flavor of his meal ticket.

"How's your old man?" asked Tim. "He ain't been looking so hot lately."

"Feisty and sour as ever." Wil moved away from Tim and toward the desk. "Pete."

The manager grunted but didn't look up from the book.

"Pete, how much cash you got behind the desk?"

Instantly Pete looked up. Apprehension worried his eyes.

"Got your attention," Wil said. "You planning on renting out that room Jones lived in, or are you turning it back into a broom closet?"

"You're such a shithead." Pete returned to his book.

As Wil reached for the glass door, Tim called out his name. He turned to see what the boy wanted.

"While you're gone, should I look in on your old man?"

"What?"

"The other day he asked me into the room to keep him company for a while, but I had something else to do, so I turned him down. Didn't mean to hurt his feelings. Being wheelchair-bound and everything, he must get kinda lonely sometimes. For a few bucks, I wouldn't mind baby-sitting him for an hour or two."

"No, he doesn't need any baby-sitter. He needs to learn self-control."

Tim's puzzled expression forced Wil to add, "Whatever you do, don't let yourself be alone with my father. He's . . . you know, an old man, and sometimes gets a bit peculiar. Wouldn't want to burden you with one of his attacks. Okay?"

"Sure."

"The old man's horny," said Pete, still looking down at his book.

"What?"

"He tried to get that young chick next door to

you in his room too." He finally looked up at Wil. "She complained to me about it the other day."

"Aw shit!"

Chapter Nine

The smell of wet, bloody earth stings the inside of her nostrils, blazing into a walloping headache that spreads from mid-brow to temples. Flesh deteriorating into carbonous clumps, bones falling loose from their sockets, hunger swelling into a pregnant cry that is unable to escape. Fingers touching air, grasping onto her own palms, cutting out semicircle wounds that need rest to heal. And over all this Liliana calls. Liliana begs to return.

Cecelia catches a breath too soon. Her sleep is not complete.

"Cecelia, bring me back. Bear me in your womb. Nurse me at your breast." Liliana's voice echoes inside the casket, ricocheting off the sides, bouncing against the lid, smothering finally in the earth on which Cecelia rests.

"Bleed life into me. Caress the soul that can no longer wait. I am numb. There is no pain, no happiness, no flesh to bite back the screams I cannot yell. Cecelia, you can give me the semi-life I need. Existence without salvation."

Cecelia chokes and sputters, writhes in the sodden earth that soaks her skin.

"Cecelia, don't leave me in this vacuum. Spare me the misery of impassiveness. Cecelia! Cecelia! Cecelia!"

Cecelia's arms pushed out against the lid, hands touching taffeta, body springing up, lifting the casket's lid. Too soon, she knew, but the lid flew up, exposing her to the living world.

Cecelia sat poised, waiting for the hint of Liliana's voice. She looked down at her hands and found her fingers blackened from decay. Nails seemingly growing against withered flesh. Veins inelastically running between knuckles spotted with earth.

She woke before her body had time to prepare for the new day. Instead she looked as she did during every sleep: partially decayed, completely dead. Death without oblivion, without what Liliana needed. Never would her mind be wiped free, memories swept away. Like Sade's niece, Cecelia would never find peace. If her body were destroyed, she would still remember.

"Liliana, I will help to birth you with your uncle's semen. With your uncle's love. Then free me from your power. Leave me to play and forget the inevitable non-ending."

Cecelia's hand touched the edge of the casket, and as she drew her hand away from the wood, she saw the thin layer of flesh she had left behind. A whitish-gray that turned instantly to dust. Her flesh was still too soft, too infested with decay. Lying back down upon the earth inside her casket, Cecelia waited for the healing, for her flesh to become solid, for her bones to mend. She waited for the smell of redolent rot to ripen into sweet flesh.

Chapter Ten

"Damn! I've had enough of your gluttony." Wil slammed the door behind him.

His father sat spread out in the wheelchair, his pants baggy, his undershirt yellowed and torn, his feet bare and lifeless.

"What the hell are you talking about?" said Keith. "You just walked out the door fifteen minutes ago, and here you are back, accusing me of one of the seven deadly sins."

"One? You're guilty of them all, old man. Matter of fact, I think you're capable of coming up with new ones."

"You telling me you think I'm God?"

Wil shook his head.

"It was God who invented those sins. God created evil, son. He created us." Keith spun his chair around so that he could face away from his son.

"You've been trying to get some of the residents inside this room."

"So what! I'm alone. I need help sometimes."

"Bullshit! There's a saying, 'Dogs don't shit and eat in the same place.' And you're trying to do both." Wil grabbed the handles on the wheelchair and turned it around so that his father was forced to face him. "Man, I don't know what they'd do to us if they found out what we are. You know how Sade did away with his mother-in-law? He cut off her head and burned it in the fireplace. Doesn't that sound like fun, Dad?"

"We don't have a fireplace."

"Naw. They'd probably burn us in one of those trash cans in the alley."

"Nobody's going to do any burning."

"Old man, we kill people. We suck the blood from their veins. You don't think this might piss some people off?"

"Who's going to get peeved because I decide to snack off that wannabe gigolo kid? You think his mother is going to report him missing? Hell, no! She's going to party till she drops. And that prostitute next door . . ."

"She's not a prostitute, Dad."

"She's not? Hell, why's the headboard on her bed banging against our wall at all hours? Think she's got a massage button revving up her mattress? More likely some stupid dick fucking his brains out. He can probably pick up something not so used for a few bucks less down at Union Square. He ain't gonna miss her."

"And what about the bodies?"

"You're in charge of sanitation." Keith's left leg began to shake violently. His left foot spasmed. "Shitty legs. They don't do anything but spite me." Keith placed his two hands on his left thigh, trying to steady the vibrating appendage that balked at his temper tantrums.

"Calm down, Dad, and it'll go away." Wil took in several breaths, steadying his own nerves. "All I'm asking is that you not eat in the room."

"You taking on the job of kitchen police?" Keith's voice trembled.

"You know what I mean. Don't *kill*." Wil paused, realizing that his voice was too loud. He changed to a soft whisper. "Don't kill anybody in our room. We agreed that we would feed at least several miles away from where we sleep. Now I find out you've been trying to break the agreement."

"I have a wimp of a son who keeps feedings to a minimum. What the hell do you expect me to do?"

"The more people we kill, the greater the chance we'll be caught. Don't you understand that?"

"I'm going to walk someday. I'm going to get up on these useless legs and walk, but I need to feed first. Blood will bring back movement in my legs. Starvation only prolongs the wait."

"You don't know that."

"I believe. You don't know what it feels like to be stuck in this chair."

"I know what it feels like to take care of an obstreperous old man."

Keith wheeled himself forward and grabbed hold of Wil's cotton T-shirt.

"I'm here because of you. You have no right to complain about my behavior. If you had been living sanely, I wouldn't be in this chair. Marie did this to me because she wanted a clear path to you, except she didn't want to let me go easy, so she gave me enough of her blood to keep me in a limbo." Keith let go of his son's T-shirt and chuckled. "And evidently enough to make me a vampire."

Keith rubbed his numb legs.

"We're going back to that fetish club," he said. "I want to talk to Mr. Sade. He knows what I should be doing and probably doesn't have any qualms about draining half the city in the process. And if you don't take me back, I'll have Tim or that floozy next door take me. Maybe even snack on one of them on the way home."

Keith leaned back in his chair and smiled.

"Know what I'm going to do when I can walk? I'm going to start my own harem and make my own slaves. Hey, I can offer them eternal life, the best damn bribe there could be."

"And how will you control them?"

"They'll depend on me to teach them how to exist as a vampire."

Wil laughed hysterically.

Keith scowled and said, "By then I'll know all that Mr. Sade knows."

"Old man, you're such a fool. You won't be able to use Sade. He'll use you. I'll take you back to the club. Hey, maybe Sade will take you in and wheel you around the city. That would give me less to worry about. Finally free from each other. Sounds like a good plan. Want to go tonight?"

A knock on the door prevented Keith from answering immediately. Wil opened the door and faced Tim's mother, a woman in her forties who could easily pass for fifty, holding a plate of home-baked brownies. With makeup embedded in every wrinkle of her face, she somehow looked comical. The lipstick was the darkest red Wil had ever seen. The clotted eyelashes swept up at an extreme angle, making her blue eyes appear too large for her face. Her clothes were tight even on her emaciated body.

"Hi, Wil, is your dad home?"

Keith groaned.

Wil invited the woman into the room.

"I ran into your son downstairs in the lobby just about a half hour ago," he said.

"The punk," she muttered, and laid the plate on the old stained dresser that stood to the right side of the door.

"They all are," grumbled Keith.

"I brought the brownies I promised. My sister makes a batch every other week and always drops off a bundle with me before delivering them to the local markets. It's not much of a business. Doubt it even pays for itself, but she's hoping that will change."

She turned to Wil. "Your father has been telling me how much he likes brownies, and I knew he had to try my sister's. They're absolutely drop-dead," she said as she popped a sugar-coated morsel into her mouth. "Look at me, eating the brownie I brought for you, Keith. I'm afraid I'm not going to be able to hang around like you suggested. I have . . ." She thought for a moment. "An old friend visiting today, and I have to spruce up a bit before he comes."

"A customer," muttered Keith.

"I don't know what you mean, Keith. I've known the gentleman for years."

"Always good to have return clientele, Sondra."

"What is your father trying to say, Wil?" She glanced at the brownie plate, obviously deciding whether or not to take the brownies back.

"Take the plate and brownies with you, Sondra," said Keith. "It's you I want, not that sticky crap."

Sondra's shoulders relaxed. "Oh, my, so sorry. It must get lonely sitting in this room all day. But Wil does take you out a bit. I've seen you two a few times down at . . . Anyway, I certainly will come another day and sit with you for a while. I didn't realize. I'm so embarrassed. I should have known that the company would be more important than some sticky whatever."

Wil and Sondra laughed.

"I can't stay today, but I promise I'll make time for you another day," she said.

"How much will it cost me?" asked Keith.

Sondra huffed, and her whole body stiffened before taking in several deep breaths. She looked at Wil and said, "I guess being disabled sours some people's disposition."

"No, it wasn't the disability that did it. More like innate with my father."

Sondra looked over at the brownies. "You wouldn't happen to have a plate so's I can transfer the brownies?"

Wil shook his head. She took one last look at the brownies, sighed, and resigned herself to having one less dish in the cupboard. She said her good-byes and left.

After closing the door, Wil turned to his father and said, "Tonight, it'll be."

Madam, forget such fears, and be my pupil,
And I shall teach you how to conquer scru-
  ple.
Some joys, it's true, are wrong in Heaven's
  eyes;
Yet Heaven is not averse to compromise . . .

Tartuffe
Molière

Chapter Eleven

"Choose your weapon, *mademoiselle*." Sade opened a cherry oak box and presented the contents to a young naked woman. "Several of the *prestiges* were selected for me by my dear departed Renée."

The woman giggled.

"*Pres . . .*" Unable to pronounce the word, she giggled again and said, "Silly, those are dildos."

Je puis vous dissiper ces craintes ridicules,
Madame, et je sais l'art de lever les scrupules.
Le Ciel défend, de vrai, certains contentements;
Mais on trouve avec lui des accommode-
    ments . . ."

"You sound so sexy," she said in complete ignorance.

"Ah! And this one is called an *étui*." He lifted out a circular wooden sheath, which he presented to the woman. She took the object in her long fingers and lightly tapped it with her pale blue fingernails. Finding that the top was removable, she opened the sheath and emptied out a small handful of pins.

"You certainly don't expect me to put something like this inside of me. What if it should open?"

"*Non, non,* Mademoiselle Felicity. This is not for you, but for me."

"Huh?"

"When I enter Mademoiselle Harlot with my *rapière,* I want you to probe my anus with . . ." Sade drew a long, chunky piece of wood from the box and brought it to Felicity's lips, whereupon she kissed it.

"Please hurry," said Harlot. She knelt naked on a bare pink mattress that was spotted with flourishes of white carnations. Her long white hair hid the details of her features, but the definition of her buttocks seemed emphasized by the fact that they rose straight up into the air. Her wrists and ankles were tied with silk scarves to the metal posts of the bed.

"Your sister needs *punition,* Mademoiselle Felicity. Perhaps the bindings are far too loose or her position much too comfortable." He placed the cherry box carefully on the night table and handed the wooden sheath to Felicity, who began to lick and suck the tanned wood. He lifted a broad paddle from the bed and spanked Harlot until her buttocks glowed like a ripened red apple. He threw the paddle across the room and mounted Harlot from behind. Both shrieked so loudly that Felicity almost dropped the sheath.

"Now," he shouted at Felicity. "Now, *mademoiselle. S'attarder* will only fuel my anger for sweet revenge on both of you."

Felicity hurried to perform her task, but hesitated when she noted the shape of the sheath and the size of the ingress.

"Perhaps I should lubricate this thing with something."

"Use your spit, *femme. Dépêchez-vous!*"

Quickly Felicity spat into the palm of her right hand and used the spit to coat the wooden sheath. Something sharp pricked her palm.

"I think this dildo may have splinters."

"*Dépêchez-vous!*" he shouted while hurriedly humping Harlot.

She licked his hole to add lubrication and then speared him full force with the phallus. Shivers seemed to pass from Sade into Harlot as they both jolted in sync to the rhythm set by Felicity.

"Suck *les burettes*," Sade cried.

Taking a wild guess, Felicity scooped her head between his legs and caught a testicle in her mouth. Shortly Felicity was rewarded when Sade withdrew from Harlot to drive his penis into Felicity's mouth, where she happily drained the milky sperm from him.

Chapter Twelve

Tim counted out the money left by Mrs. Galloway, the middle-aged wife of an elderly doctor who could no longer satisfy his wife, not that he ever did. She spent lots of time telling Tim how poorly her husband functioned in bed. He often thought she did this to assuage her own guilt about bedding a boy younger than her own son. Not that she hadn't bedded her own flesh and blood. Mrs. Galloway shared stories about taking her young son to bed when he was four or five, not to sleep, but to play with his body. She liked exciting the child. Of course, she never had *real* sex with him. It was only play that she and the boy both enjoyed.

"Old pervert," muttered Tim. He knew about those kinds of playtimes, when fear caught in the victim's throat. When tears seemed to feed the adult's hunger instead of softening a heart.

She had left him some extra money today. Because he had been exceptionally good, or was she feeling exceptionally guilty? No matter. He rolled off the wrinkled yellowed bedsheet and slapped his feet atop the grungy carpet. The room reeked of an expensive perfume she had dabbed on before leaving. She never bothered with a shower when she visited his room at what she called "the Hell Hole Hotel." He guessed she feared the breeding mold that lined the cracks between each tile in the bathroom.

When he stood, he faced the bureau mirror. He noticed that his hair seemed flattened on one side. Had he actually nodded off for a while? Maybe it was later than either of them had suspected. He checked the night-table clock. Little Ben showed that it was merely fifteen minutes over her usual departing time. Must have been a quick nap with a heavy head.

As he headed for the bathroom door, his mother entered the room.

"What the fuck are you doing?" she asked.

"That's what I was doing. Now I'm headed for the shower."

"If you're going to start making money, then you should start paying your way."

"Later," he said as he closed the bathroom door.

"Don't you later me. I've worked hard to support you all these years. I think now I should get a little back." She kicked open the door.

Tim stood in front of the toilet, his steady

stream never abating until he was finished. He shook his penis several times.

"Whatcha' want me to do, Mom, keep you in prunes in your old age?"

"I'm far from old."

"Yeah, that's why you're so scared. I see you check your hairline for grays. I watch you smooth on slimy creams to cover and plump the skin. Know what? It don't work. You look older everyday."

"You little bastard. I should have put you up for adoption the minute you slid out from between my legs."

"On that we can agree." Tim bundled an old towel under his arm.

"There aren't any fresh towels, unless you've suddenly moved your ass into gear."

Tim made a point of shaking out the formerly balled-up towel in his mother's face before sweeping back the shower curtain.

Oh yeah, he thought, another reason that Mrs. Galloway refused to bathe here. He stared down at the scum hardened onto the sides of the tub. Several roaches scuttled down the drain as he stepped into the tub.

"That old man Keith in a wheelchair . . ." she said. "Know who I mean?"

"Only one wheelchair in this place."

"I think he's got the hots for me."

Tim swept the shower curtain across the rusted bar. Water splashed, drowning out anything else she had to say.

The hots, he thought. The old man had to be in his seventies, maybe older. Tim had never tried his own sex before, but hell, if money could be made, he was willing to try. So far, Tim's mother hadn't gotten a cent off him. Tim figured he could continue like that for at least the next couple of months. Eventually she'd be too broke to let it ride.

Sondra pulled back the curtain and announced that she had a date due in fifteen minutes.

"They're called johns, Mom. You haven't had a real date in years." At least not since his last uncle had given them both the heave-ho out of his residence in Dublin, California. Tim had been about eleven at the time—that would have been seven years ago. And every year since things had gotten worse for him and his mother. Initially she had had a real job at a supermarket, but she was too embarrassed to keep that job. She hated seeing people she knew. Worse, she hated the meager salary. Somehow she acquired a pimp and worked nights. Once, when she thought he was asleep, Tim followed her. He rode the BART without her knowing and shadowed her down some rough-looking streets. He figured out what Mom did for a living.

Was that when he lost respect for her? Naw, he thought, he had never respected her, not after seeing the pummeling she accepted from his father. Dear old Dad died just the way he would have wanted to. In a bar brawl over an underage female.

"Come on. Come on. I don't want you here when he arrives," she urged, holding out the used towel he had slung over the bar.

He shut the water off and spread out his arms so she could dry him off. Sondra dropped the towel to the floor and walked out of the bathroom. Wasn't always like that. Not, at least, when he was a scared little boy.

He stepped out of the tub and picked up the towel. Serve her right if he hung around. The johns were always uncomfortable with sons hanging round. When he was a child, he used to hide in his mother's bedroom closet and listen, until one night when he became brave enough to peek out. Holy shit! He'd scared the daylights out of that john. Thought he was being set up for blackmail. After that Mom would lock him in his bedroom. However, when they moved into the current dive, there were no longer working locks on the doors. Except for the front door, and that had a tendency to stick more than lock.

"Get the hell out of here," Sondra yelled from the living room. Tim walked back into the bedroom and pulled on a black T-shirt, eschewed the underwear, slipped into black jeans, and searched under the bed for his running shoes. He had two pairs: one nifty and spot-free; the other stained, with a hole on the right shoe where his little toe pushed out into the open air. He didn't expect to hit it big tonight, so he went for the ratty shoes.

Maybe he'd stop at the old man's room and keep him company for a time. Could even feel him out, so to speak, and see just how far the old man wanted to go and how much he would pay. As long as he didn't have to be the receiver, he could probably close his eyes and forget what sex was massaging his winkie-dink. He couldn't believe he still thought of his penis as a winkie-dink. His mother had baptized it with the name while playing with him in the tub.

Winkie-dink. He shook his head. Some guys have a Bruno, a Rex, or even a Scimitar. He had a winkie-dink. Thank heaven the organ didn't reflect the name. His was fat, long, and indefatigable.

Proudly Tim sauntered into the living room, where his mother instantly pulled open the front door and threw him out, pushing and shoving him into the hall.

Winkie-dink, he thought.

—You smell bad, said the little girl
—We'll all smell bad, said the first old man
When we're dead.

The Neighborhood of Saint-Meri
Robert Desnos

Chapter Thirteen

Cecelia stroked the left side of Sade's cheek with the back of her hand.

"*Ma petite*, what do you desire?"

Her voice became childish and high-pitched. "A baby."

The expensive brandy in Sade's mouth turned sour. He shoved the drink away from him and looked into her eyes.

"*Pourquoi?*"

Cecelia pushed in close to him, blocking out the rest of the club, which didn't even notice them.

"Liliana wants back."

"*Et* you intend to birth her?"

"Yes." She kissed him on the cheek before turning to his lips.

"*Non, ma petite. Jamais*. She is gone, and I will

not have her back." He pressed two of his fingers against Cecelia's lips and forced her back down onto her bar stool.

"But you love her."

"I will not be tortured by love. I deal with physical pain and pleasure, *ma petite*. Love I have abandoned."

"She's with us now, urging us to give her life."

"*Non, ma petite*. She is inside your head. She is weighing your thoughts down with guilt because you allow it. Liliana hated the semi-life I gave her. She would never want to return. Her grandmother, on the other hand . . ."

"It is Liliana." She raised her voice, demanding to be believed.

"Liliana would also know what you seem to forget."

"What is that?"

"Two vampires cannot bring life into their dead world. At least one of the pair must be mortal in order for life to take hold. The progeny of two vampires aborts itself in quite painful ways, *ma petite*. It starves from the dead blood that circulates our bodies."

"But a mortal can—"

He placed his left palm across her mouth.

"I am the one who delivered you into this eternal semi-life. I will guide you. Protect you. Even supply food for you such as . . ." He turned her head slightly so that she could see the mortal bartender. After bringing her head back to face him, Sade continued. "At a price. A *cher* price, *ma petite*. Your soul and existence belong to me. You will take no *servantes*. *Jamais* share your blood with anyone. And always return to me. Depart from me only as I wish."

"Which will be never," she said sulkily.

"I destroy those that I grow tired of, *ma petite. Et* I believe I feel a yawn coming on, so be wary."

Sade dismissed her with a wave of his hand.

Cecelia crinkled her nose in disapproval.

Sade responded by quoting Robert Desnos:

> *"—Vous sentez mauvais, dit la petite.*
> *—Nous sentirons tous mauvais, dit le pre-*
>   *mier vieillard*
> *Quand nous serons morts."*

Chapter Fourteen

Already he searched the club for new flesh. She watched Sade eye a slender teen who wobbled in her high heels, and she breathed deeply to calm her fears. Yes, he would have her tonight, and perhaps he would kill her, depending on his hunger.

Harlot crossed the room. Headed for me or Sade? Cecelia wondered. She felt relieved when Harlot rubbed up against Sade's linen suit. Sade seemed pleased. Lucky for you, little girl, she thought, watching the teen move into a larger group of friends.

Cecelia looked at the bartender. Sade had implied that he could serve the bartender up as a meal. Cecelia didn't want food, she wanted love. Physical love. Someone who could be a daddy. The bartender was gay, very gay. He didn't experiment with different flavors.

"Where's Sade?" a man's voice asked.

Cecelia turned to her right and saw Wil. Still a hunk, she thought, but an infertile one, she reminded herself.

"He's right over there on the bar stool." She pointed in the direction where Sade had been sitting.

"Is this something new? Now we can become invisible?" he said.

"I don't know where the hell he's gone. I thought you didn't like him."

"Don't. Dad expects Sade to work miracles. 'The lame shall walk.' That kind of thing."

On cue, Keith jostled his wheelchair against the back of Wil's legs.

"Where the hell is he?" Keith demanded. "Can't she tell you? I'm not going back to the residence until we've found him. Maybe we should move around the club."

"If you can squeeze yourself in between the people in this crowd, then go ahead. I'm staying here at the bar."

"Goldilocks got you again?"

"No, I'm tired of pushy old men who can do nothing for themselves."

"Rut to your heart's content, son, but be sure you're here when I want to go home." Keith inched his way across the room, ignoring the glares and even the suggestions of assistance.

"So do you want to fuck?" Cecelia asked.

"I thought you belonged to Sade," said Wil.

"When he doesn't have anything else to do."

She put her arms around his neck. "You could console me."

"Here in the middle of the bar?"

"Wherever. I've done it everywhere."

"And you sound happy about it."

Cecelia slipped a hand under his T-shirt, searching for his nipples, finding the jagged rings that pierced them. She moved her body against his and felt him harden. She pulled back just enough to raise his T-shirt up above the nipples. Once she tasted his flesh, she felt her own juices wet her thighs. She stretched upwards to assist him in removing his T-shirt. The definition of his muscles attracted surrounding glances, she noticed. Mine, she silently said, as she smoothed her palm down his abdomen and below the band of his jeans.

"You've got an inny," she whispered.

"It's no secret," he said.

"Let's see if we have any secrets." She undid the button of the jeans and unzipped the zipper. The scrape of the zipper turned another head toward them. A vampire no doubt, she thought, else the woman now staring at Wil's bulge never would have heard the sound.

"Not here, Cecelia. You know that."

The bartender had slipped from around the bar to remind her that sex was not permitted in the main room of the club. Or perhaps he just wanted to get a little closer, she thought. Feeling selfish, unable to share, she didn't argue with Felipe the bartender. Instead, she took Wil's hand and led him to a door marked "Management." On the door was a giant condom ad. The door opened easily—it hadn't been completely closed. Most people were in too much of a hurry to wait for the lock to catch. Not her invited guest, she thought; he leaned against the door to make sure it had closed all the way.

"How anal!" she said.

"What?"

"How do you want to give it to me?"

"Let me count the ways."

The hall light was dim, and periodically the bulb would go out, then immediately come back on. She smelled the blood that splattered the walls and the jism that caked the floor.

A kid whose face was covered with zits came staggering out from behind a curtain. He was rubbing his neck, smearing blood all over his shoulder. He wore tight black latex with gashes in the material up and down his legs. His shirt had been latex too, except now he held it shredded in one hand. His bare feet slapped the floor with an almost drunken gait. Behind him a female appeared with exceptionally long nails that curved in toward her palm. Painted a swirling grayish-white, the nails looked like baby snakes. She wore a caftan that could easily be lifted off or slipped back on. The folds of material swept around a voluptuous figure that undulated to a sexy rhythm. A black lace veil hid her face. Cecelia noted that the veil had a spot of blood.

"Some cold water should get that out." Cecelia touched the tip of the veil, causing the woman to back up a pace.

Still holding Wil's hand, she continued to walk

down the hall. Black velvet curtains hung in doorways, making it difficult to figure out which rooms were occupied. Finally she took a chance on one.

Her favorite room happened to be available. Covered with vinyl lemongrass tiles, the walls added an exotic air to the room. There was no window, and the pillows on the floor in black, white, red, and gold added a hint of color to the blank room. No gadgets cluttered the place. It allowed two, three, or more bodies to explore with only their talents and gifts.

Wil went to kiss her mouth, and she turned her head away, while sliding the wraparound dress down her body. He smiled, looking satisfied by what he saw.

"You mean Sade is already bored by this?" he asked. He followed the curve of her breasts, the sweep of her hips, and stopped where the delicate gold chain hung down between her legs. He touched the chain and she felt the vibration excite her clitoris.

She slid her hands inside his jeans and slowly lowered them down over his hips. By the time the jeans had fallen around his ankles, Cecelia knelt before him, her mouth almost touching his cock.

"How did you meet Sade?" he asked.

She reached out her tongue barely in contact with the drop of semen that bubbled up at the tip of his penis. At first she tilted her head as if she would catch the drop; changing her mind, she pulled back and splayed her body across several black and gold pillows.

"I'm his housecleaner's daughter."

"You're what?"

Cecelia furrowed her brow and repeated, "I'm his housecleaner's daughter. My mother picked up after the vampires. Of course, she didn't know they were vampires, although she always seemed to suspect that Louis was a dirty old man."

"Shit!" Immediately Wil reached down and pulled up his jeans, closing them in haste. "Shit! Shit!"

"What the hell's wrong with you? You have a prejudice against domestics?"

Wil looked around on the floor, lifting pillows, tossing them across the room.

"If you're looking for your shirt, we left it on the floor near the bar."

"Shit!"

"You're a great conversationalist. Hope it gets better after we've fucked."

Wil exhaled loudly and went to step around Cecelia, who grabbed his right leg. She had to be careful, because his strength might be equal to hers, or even greater; after all, he was not a mortal.

"Shit! Let go of me, dammit." He reached down and violently shoved her away, forcing her body to slide up against the far wall.

"What the hell happened here?" she shrieked as he brushed aside the curtain and departed.

Chapter Fifteen

Out on the barroom floor, Wil searched for his father. As he passed the bartender, his T-shirt slapped him in the face.

"Hey, that was a quickie," Felipe quipped.

Wil noticed his father by the game room, where the old man was attempting to seduce a girl of no more than fifteen.

"Enough," Wil said as he rested his hands on the handles of his father's wheelchair. "We're getting out of here."

"Maybe you are, but I haven't found Sade yet. I thought you were busy with Goldilocks."

"She's the housekeeper's daughter."

"What housekeeper . . ." Suddenly Keith smiled in recognition. "Small world, hey?"

"We should have guessed since Cecelia was with Sade."

"So what?"

"I'm about to puke if we don't get out of here." Wil's right leg shook faster than the beat of the background music. He yanked the wheelchair backwards and headed for the exit. He saw Cecelia two feet from the door, the wraparound loosely tied, anger and pain marring her pretty features. She rushed at him with a daggerlike object. He couldn't tell whether it was a knife or simply a letter opener, but he moved quickly out of her way, since the object seemed to be pointed directly at his heart.

"Son, are you that rusty at satisfying a woman that she comes after you with a knife?"

A blinding movement wrapped around Cecelia's arm, and briefly Wil made eye contact with Sade.

"Whoa, I ain't going nowhere," Keith said.

Ignoring his father, Wil pushed the wheelchair out onto the street.

He curled up on the bed next to his father's dead body. Wil slept under the influence of the smell of blood, the smell of death and decay. How long he had slept, he didn't know. All he could remember was his father taking a chunk of flesh from his cheek, his dead father frantic with blood lust.

"Dad, hold it," he said.

Red blood vessels colored his father's eyes with the look of evil. There was no recognition in those eyes, only a ravenous hunger that stared out at him. Blood dripped down his father's jaws, and flesh, his own, dribbled out between his father's lips. Dad's hands clawed at the blankets until his legs were free. Then he clawed at his useless legs. Screaming in frustration, his father's voice caught in a paroxysm of coughing.

Sliding his ass across the floor, Wil didn't stop until his back was against the bedroom door. A violent seizure possessed his father, causing the mattress to shake and the springs to squeak. Wil waited, sucking and biting on his thumb like a child.

Finally his father seemed to pass into a passive stupor and lay with his eyes staring at the ceiling. No muscle flinched. No nerve jolted. Wil wondered whether his father was now really dead. It took several minutes for Wil to recover the courage to approach his old man.

"Dad?" Wil gawked at the dead body, but then the old man's mouth began to move, began to suck at air.

"Hungry." The raw voice was almost unrecognizable as his father's.

"Dad, I've just fed, so I can share some of my blood with you if you promise to tame the frenzy."

His father reached up and tried to grab at his son's throat. His eyes followed the rivulets of blood running down his son's cheek.

"You can have some if you contain the violence. Remember, we need each other now. We can't afford to destroy one another."

Wil finally soaked a towel with the blood from his wound and allowed his father to suck on the cloth. By the time his father tamed down, the towel had been chewed to bits.

Over the next few days the men learned to feed from each other without depleting their store of blood. Soon they realized that they needed fresh, live blood in order to thrive. His father's skin appeared to be covered with whitish-gray scales. Gradually bits of his flesh sloughed off. He couldn't walk, and his legs shook uncontrollably when his temper flared.

Wil found that his own movements were becoming sluggish. His reasoning ability slowed. Perhaps fresh blood would ease these problems. Where to look? He hated the idea of killing. He remembered Marie taking small amounts of blood. Perhaps if he could find a donor or someone as warped as he had been . . .

Wrapped in several layers of clothing and a broad-brimmed hat, Wil made his way on foot to Sade's home. If Sade still dwelt there, he could be of help. If not, then there might be some information stored away in the house that could reveal the vampire's secrets.

As he approached, he noticed an old Ford parked at the front door. The hood was still warm. Someone definitely was at home. He knocked on the door, and within thirty seconds a middle-aged woman answered. She stared at him as if he had something to tell her.

"I'm looking for a Louis Sade. Is he at home?"

"Hasn't been for weeks. I hoped you had a message from him. I don't know what to do about the house. He and his niece seemed to have abandoned it. Is this about a bill?"

"I'm due something from Mr. Sade, but it's not money."

"Thank God! I've been waiting for the bill collectors to come. Every other day I stop by to make *sure the house is still okay. I'm their housekeeper, or was. I'm not sure of my status, except Mr. Sade was so good to me when my daughter died that I feel I owe him. My name's Matilda." She almost curtsied as she introduced herself.*

"I'm a neighbor," Wil cautiously said. "He was supposed to supply me with information and, well . . . My life and my father's have been made very difficult without it."

"I wish I could help, but I don't really feel comfortable searching Mr. Sade's desk, and certainly I couldn't allow a stranger to do so. I still don't go into the upstairs rooms."

Wil nodded. The pulse in her neck seemed to skip a beat. Arrhythmia.

"I do remember Mr. Sade mentioning you one time when he was commenting on the way my father and I live. You see, my father is paralyzed from the waist down and certainly can't clean, and I spend most of my time taking care of him. He suggested that I use your services. Actually, one of the things he did give me was your name, and like a dunce, I forgot it. But he did highly recommend you."

Her fingers fidgeted with the lacy pocket of her apron. Her hands were red, raw from hard work. And the veins seemed more pronounced than he had ever seen on another human. She also smelled of blood from menstruation or a wound. He could not decide.

"Since I assume you have less work to do here than normal, would you mind coming to our home and cleaning up a bit? I'll pay whatever Mr. Sade does."

"Mr. Sade pays me too much. I often feel guilty, but he does have me run funny little errands sometimes. Usually I limit myself to tidying up the house and leave. I don't believe I'll be doing errands for the next people I work for. I found my own home life suffered. My daughter . . . She became involved with the wrong crowd. We think, my husband and I, that her boyfriend had something to do with her death. Only seventeen. One more year and she would have graduated. You know, we were worried about what she'd do after high school when we should have been keeping track of what she did in high school."

"I'm sorry. If you're still in mourning . . ."

"I'll always be in mourning, but I stay active. Where is it that you and your father live?"

"I'm poor at giving directions. Why don't you follow me in your own car?"

"I'm afraid I won't be able to start this soon."

"No problem, but at least let me show you the way for the next time you can come."

"Tomorrow I have a free day. That's when I did errands for Mr. Sade. I suppose it would be easier if I followed you this afternoon and maybe took a look at the place to give you an idea about what I'd charge."

"I would appreciate that."

"So you killed the girl's mother; big deal. You're just screwing her in more than one way, that's all."

Wil's father's hoarse voice removed Wil from his reverie.

"We both killed her."

"Hey, when she leaned over to prop up my pillow and I smelled rich coppery blood, far better than the shit we'd been sharing with each other, I lost control. Anyway, you didn't bring her home to clean our house."

"No, I didn't."

Chapter Sixteen

Red bicycled up and down the streets of San Francisco, trying to stick with the flat areas, especially those places where tourists hung out. The streets were either too crowded or too deserted. What he needed was a woman returning from the local pub or from some adult education class, preferably carrying packages to give her less maneuverability. Damned if he wanted a repeat performance of last night's embarrassment.

The woman had looked as if her mind were thousands of miles away. She couldn't see him coming along on his bike, and besides, she had been walking pressed up near the wall of the office building. Easy mark. Red went up to her and pleasantly asked for her purse. "Huh?" she responded, still lost in her own world. He repeated his request. She looked at her bag as if she just remembered she carried one. Then she lunged at him while he straddled the bike. God, it hurt. He worried he wasn't going to be able to get it up when he got home to Ginger. But he needn't have worried. He fucked her three times last night just to prove his mettle.

His head itched from the woolen cap he wore. Had to wear it, though; otherwise people would see his red head coming a block away. The pedal caught on the torn cuff of his jeans. What the hell, he thought, maybe he should go home and fuck Gin some more.

He turned his bike around and started for home until he spied a pretty young woman exiting a cab a half block away. He slowed to almost a halt and waited to see which way she would go.

Instead of going into any of the doorways, she began walking in his direction, and the cab took off for its next fare.

Yeah, baby. Her legs were long, and with each step her long skirt parted, revealing a good portion of each thigh. Her braless breasts bounced in sync with her gait. Her bag hung casually over one shoulder. Not a monster of a bag either, but one tending toward the small. Easy to loop it around his arm and get away. This time he'd be sensible and give her a hard punch in the stomach before grabbing her bag. *Won't be any fight left in her then.*

Red sped up and at the last minute steered into the woman's path.

Whap!

Grab!

Out of there!

He didn't bother to look back; he knew he had hit her hard enough to not only immobilize her, but also to take the breath out of her. His cockiness didn't slow him down. He sped across an intersection and turned a sharp corner.

He hadn't expected an old man in a wheelchair to be lazily rolling along, but there he was, and Red veered right to try to miss him, thus losing his balance and falling over.

"You okay?" a voice called out.

"Him? What about me?"

"Dad, he swerved to avoid you and he did."

"Barely."

Red had to get back on the bike and take off. He had left the woman only a few blocks away.

A man in a T-shirt helped Red up and snatched the bag out of his hands.

"You don't look like the type that carries handbags around."

"It's my girlfriend's. Give it back." Fuck the bag, Red thought, just grab the bike and get the hell out of here.

Red grabbed the bike, but the man swiftly kicked it from his hands.

"Hey, man. What you think you're doing?"

"Stopping a thief." The man opened the purse and took out a wallet. "What's your girlfriend's name?"

"Okay! You can keep it or give it back to her. I don't give a damn, just let me take my bike with me."

"Wil, you were always pissed at me because I never bought you a new bike," the old man said.

"That one looks almost new. Bet it was stolen out of a shop today."

"Shut up, old man," said Red. "You sure don't have any use for a bike." When in doubt cocky it out, Red advised himself.

"Do you know that this is my father?" said the man named Wil.

"So what? I have one too. And they're not all they're cracked up to be."

The man named Wil nodded, conceding a point.

"We were looking around for a place to have a midnight snack. Want to join us?" Wil passed the handbag to his father.

"Nah, fuck you." Red stretched out an arm to reach the handlebars.

"Think you're going to find some more easy prey?"

"You guys aren't cops." Red lifted the bike. "Why don't you mind your own business?" Red swung a leg over the saddle of the bike, and Wil kicked the bike from beneath him. "Okay, keep the bike. I don't have any cash, though." Red turned his jeans pockets inside out. He was smart enough to have sewn a money pocket inside his right boot.

"We don't want your bike." Wil reached out and grabbed the hat off Red's head.

"Man, you want my hat? Crazy pair of fuckers."

"We want you. I bet the nickname's Red," the old man said, barking out the color.

"I'm not into that kind of stuff. The pickups I make are only with females."

"Males. Females. They both taste about the

same. Although maybe the females have a bit weaker flavor." The old man sucked his lips, trying to recall the taste.

"You guys ain't getting a taste of me. I save that for Ginger."

"Ginger can't suck it from you like we can, son." The old man moved closer.

The homophobic Red was sure the old man was heading for his dick. He took two steps backward and bonked against a wall. Wil hadn't moved, but seemed tensed.

"Beat it, or I'm calling the cops," Red said.

Wil laughed, and the old man bumped the wheel of his chair against Red's leg.

"Fucking creeps!" Red didn't expect the old man to be a problem, but the guy called Wil looked fit. Red would have to put all his energy into downing Wil and hope the old man didn't trip him up. Red decided to run up the hill. If he stayed on flat ground the wheelchair might have a chance.

Red lunged head-first into Wil's solar plexus. He felt his legs being lifted off the ground. Shit, he thought. Wil flipped him over and Red hit the ground with a hard thump. He must have directly hit his spine, because the pain traveling down the center of his back prevented him from getting to his feet. He'd never live this down. Raped by an old man and his son. Hell, he hoped they killed him.

I folded you to my breast like a dove
Which a little girl smothers without knowing it.

   "Love, Disdain, and Hope"
   Guillaume Apollinaire

Chapter Seventeen

Cecelia lay still, sensing the coldness and dampness of the casket. Not her own, but his. For the first time, Sade had invited her to spend their sleep time together. But she couldn't sleep. Neither could he. When she shivered, he responded by holding her closer. He hadn't allowed the decay to set into his body. Was he waiting for her to go off first? He had added some of her soil to his own box, promising that this small amount of earth would keep her safe. Sincere? His voice, his actions, his eyes. He hadn't punished her for the scene she had made at the club. How unlike him to be able to keep his temper, she thought.

She reached down and rubbed her hand over his privates. She didn't want sex. She wanted a response. He didn't push her hand away, but he didn't bloom the way he used to when she touched him.

"Dormi, ma petite."

Sleep. No, she couldn't. She didn't trust enough. Having him near, she played at being exhausted lovers trusting each other with their vulnerability. Played, but didn't believe. How much of her dirt was here? A handful, perhaps less. She'd noticed that hardly any was missing from her own casket. A small scoop that could have been impressed on the soil. After all, she hadn't seen him taking the soil.

"Il te faut une bonne sommeil, enfante," Sade whispered.

"Oui," she sighed, burying her face into his silky poet's shirt. He smelled of earth, the strange combination of decay and life. But she enjoyed the softness of the material that covered his chest, and rubbed her cheek roughly against it.

"Cecelia, why are you wasting time? Spare me this long wait. He cannot help you to bring me back." Liliana's voice seemed loud enough that Sade should have responded in some way, but he didn't. "He fears me, Cecelia. He runs from the innocent and corporal love we had shared. Find a mortal youth to bed and bring me back."

"Do you hear anything, Louis?"

"Only the scuttle of an insect or two that share our bed, *m'enfante*. Is that what keeps you awake?"

"You know better, Louis."

"Oui. If we stay in this casket together, neither of us will rest." She felt his arm tighten around her. "But we should try."

"You mean to destroy me," she calmly said.

"*Mais non! Toujours* I am afraid to allow you to part from my side. The voice you hear condemns me."

"No!"

Sade hushed her.

"The voice demands that you be disobedient to me. It calls out for a freedom that the spirit can no longer have."

"A child. I can have a child and bring Liliana back."

"Are you sure you are not being tricked, *ma petite*? Are you so sure that this is my niece? *Ciel!* It could even be my mother-in-law plotting her revenge."

"I know the voice, Louis."

"Why would she come to you to be brought back?"

"I think she saw me as a child, a bored child. I meant her no harm, and she knows that. Yet she can also understand how I feel, since we both changed at the same age."

"Do you feel my arms wrapped around you, *ma petite*?"

"Yes," she answered, savoring the pressure of his embrace.

"I am with you, not merely a vacuous voice making promises or threatening."

"She has never threatened me, and she has made no promises."

"Ah! *Mais* you hope to banish that voice when a child is born. *N'est-ce pas?*"

He was right; she decided she did hear the scuttle of two insects, one close to her ear. The other sounded like it pounded on the lid of the casket.

"No answer, *ma petite*. Truth is hard to deny. We will rest a while longer. Do you still hear the voice?"

"No. The insects you spoke of. Only the insects."

She thought she heard his voice crack as he spoke.

> "*Je t'ai prise contre ma poitrine comme une colombe*
> *Qu'une petite fille étouffe sans le savoir.*"

Chapter Eighteen

Jerry woke to a dark, dingy room. He turned over onto his left side and recognized Sondra. Shit, he had paid double to spend the night, and what the hell did he do? Sleep. He decided to take a piss before returning to bed to get his money's worth.

He swept back the red cotton blanket. The woman really took her job seriously, he noted, judging from the black sheets and red blanket. Too bad she didn't realize that her skin against the black looked sallow. She wasn't a blooming rose anymore, but she was serviceable. He scratched the top of his bald head. He would have had a semicircle of white fuzz from ear to ear, except that he regularly shaved his head. His chin was smooth also, with only a mild case of five o'clock shadow. His skinny legs and arms contrasted sharply with his bloated trunk. In his genes, he knew. The whole family looked like olives walking around on toothpicks. Sometimes his member got lost in the folds of flesh, but not this morning. Christ, he really needed to piss.

He sat and let his feet rest on the filthy carpet. He'd probably come down with athlete's foot again, but he didn't know where his socks were and couldn't waste time looking for them. He stood and paused, trying to recall where the bathroom was. He was damn sure it wasn't connected to this bedroom. There were only two doors in the room: an exit door and a closet door that stood open, the spillage of contents resting against the bottom of the door.

Aren't that many rooms, he thought; should be easy enough to spot the bathroom in the tiny hallway. His bones creaked a bit when he started walking, and when his hand touched the doorknob, he heard a rustle coming from the bed. She'd have to wait; he had to take care of a necessity.

The bathroom faced the bedroom, and Jerry scuttled quickly onto the cold tiles. He didn't bother to close the door—she had seen everything. He ushered out a sigh as he evacuated his bladder. He flushed the toilet, but didn't bother to wash his hands. Back in the small hall, he suddenly felt peckish. He knew the kitchenette marred one wall of the living room, and he started for it. He hesitated when he heard a low throaty snore that did not come from the bedroom.

He peeked around the doorway molding and saw a kid stretched out on the pull-out sofa. The kid was naked except for a bit of material draped across his chest. Looked like the kid had gotten warm during the night and pulled off his T-shirt while still sleeping.

Jerry started thinking seriously about getting the hell out of there. Where the hell were his clothes? They had started fooling around as soon as he had entered the apartment. He had only been worried about ripping his clothes, not about where they landed. *Damn bitch!* He'd make her get up and look for them.

A sneeze came from the bedroom, and then Sondra stood in the doorway, wiping her nose with the back of her hand.

"Morning," she said, smiling, forcing laugh lines to cluster around her sleep-encrusted eyes.

"Who the hell's in the living room?" Jerry whispered.

"He's a kid I took in."

"What?"

"He had no place to go. I felt sorry for him. Thought of him as kind of a younger brother."

"So you gave him the keys to your digs?"

"Yeah. He's quiet. Runs errands for me. Earns the roof over his head."

"You've never told me about a boarder."

"He's not a boarder. He's like family in a way."

"Go find my clothes. I'm getting out of here before your sonny boy wakes up."

"I said he's like a brother."

"Sondra, am I supposed to believe that you bring a young stud into your home and treat him like a brother? We've known each other for a couple of months. I got a good idea of what's been going on here. Not that I give a damn; just I don't like surprises in the morning."

"Tim," she called.

"Yeah, Mom," a sleepy voice answered.

"Perhaps he doesn't quite think of me as an older sister," she explained to Jerry.

"You never told me you had a kid."

"He usually disappears when I have company, and you're the first company that I've had in a long while that stayed overnight.

"Tim, find this man's clothes. Seems he doesn't remember where he dropped them."

"I bundled them and put them on the chair," Tim said.

"He cleans up after me too. There's only one chair in the living room. Should be easy to find."

"Hell, I'm not going out there naked."

"My son's not gay."

"I don't give a damn what he is. I'm not walking out naked in front of a stranger."

"I was a stranger once." She smoothed her palm against his cheek. "Besides, he's probably fallen back to sleep already." She walked into the bathroom, closing the door behind her.

"Bitch," he cursed. He stood tall, pulled in his gut, and walked into the living room, remembering how he looked like a fat olive.

Instead of being asleep, the kid had propped himself up on one arm and seemed to be waiting for Jerry's entrance.

"Morning. I'm Tim."

Jerry nodded while heading for the chair.

"Hope I didn't wake you when I came in last night," Tim said.

Jerry cleared his throat and picked up the bundle.

"Staying for breakfast?" asked Tim. "I can run down to the Jack in the Box and get us something."

Feeling awkward, Jerry murmured about being late for an appointment.

"Better take a quick shower then. You smell . . . You know what I mean."

"I'll stop by my apartment," Jerry indignantly replied, heading back to the bedroom.

"Oh, hey, wait." Tim pulled the white strip of cloth from across his chest. "Got cold last night, and I didn't feel like mussing through the bureau in the bedroom, so I borrowed your undershirt. Warmed up later on, though." He held out the undershirt and waited for Jerry to take it.

"That's okay, kid. You can have it."

"I don't want it. I can afford my own."

Jerry didn't want any trouble, so he snatched the undershirt out of the kid's hand and continued on his way to the bedroom. When he entered the bedroom, he couldn't figure out why he hadn't just gotten dressed in the living room and made a run for the door. Spotting his watch on the night table made him glad he hadn't.

"Didn't get your money's worth, you know." Sondra leaned against the door of the bedroom.

"That's okay," he said, slipping on his boxer shorts.

"No, it's not. I owe you a free one."

Jerry didn't say anything.

"You are coming back, right?"

Jerry zipped up the fly on his pants.

"You suddenly go deaf?"

Jerry pulled on his shirt and found he had difficulty doing the buttons.

"Don't see why you should be pissed with me, just because I take care of my boy."

"This how you take care of him?" Jerry asked, checking the time on his watch before putting it on.

"He's got food and shelter. He could be one of those kids wandering around on the streets, kicked out by his mom. Give me that much credit."

"Sondra, I don't have children. Know why?"

" 'Cause your dick's too wimpy?"

"Because I respect kids too much to cheat them out of decent lives." Jerry shook out the jacket to his suit. He'd have to take the suit into the cleaners before he could wear it again. He didn't bother to put the jacket on, he simply slung it over his right shoulder.

"Hey, Jerry." She cuddled up to him. "You've got my number."

"Do I ever." Jerry pushed Sondra away and walked back into the living room.

"Like some coffee?" Tim asked, standing naked in the kitchenette, his flaccid penis showing signs of awakening.

Jerry looked back at Sondra, draped in a mauve polyester robe, and shook his head.

"Tim, get some clothes on. You know you shouldn't be walking around naked."

"Don't bother on my account," Jerry said, and left the apartment.

Chapter Nineteen

Sondra picked up Tim's pillow and threw it at him.

"Damn you! You lost me another customer," she yelled.

"Since when did your johns start spending nights here?"

"He paid some good money to stay over."

Tim shrugged. "You probably could earn the same amount in an hour when you were younger."

"Shithead! Don't give me your lip."

"What'd you expect me to do? Sleep on the sidewalk?"

"Could've bunked in the lobby."

"Right. Pete would have been thrilled to have the company."

"What about that old man in the wheelchair

111

and his son? They'd probably take you in for the night. We should arrange something for the next time."

"Mom, you got high hopes." Tim poured out a cup of coffee. "Want one?"

"Black. I need to get my head straight." Sondra flopped down on the mattress of the pull-out couch. "That's what we'll do, we'll set it up so's you can stay with Keith and Wil. They won't mind. I've been bringing the old man brownies and promising to spend some time with him. Maybe we can work something out."

"I think he's paralyzed from the waist down, Mom." He brought two mugs of coffee over to the bed and handed one to his mother before flopping himself down on the mattress.

"I didn't mean sex. Although the son may be amenable."

Tim laughed. "He's not going to want to spread your legs. You'd be the one he'd be doing the favor for, not the other way round."

"Get some shittin' clothes on. We're going up to see Wil and Keith now."

"What about you, Mom? You're going to scare them with that smeared makeup and wild hair."

"I'll take a quick shower. You just get dressed."

He knew what a quick shower meant. She'd spend at least a half hour in the bathroom, rubbing on the scented soap, using a loofah to smooth her skin, powdering her dried-up body, and painting her face. Tim decided he could make himself a fairly decent breakfast while he waited.

There were two eggs in the carton, which had a sell-by date of a month ago. He picked them up and did a delicate juggling act with them. Since they hadn't smashed, he figured whatever happened with the eggs was fate. He cracked them open over a bowl, added some milk and pepper, and whisked the mixture together.

By the time Sondra came out of the bathroom Tim had eaten, had dressed, and had just finished returning the last cushion to the couch. Proud of himself, he smiled at his mother.

"What'd you do?"

"Cleaned up." He waved his hands around the living room.

"What's that pile in the sink?"

"I'd say it was yesterday's breakfast, last night's macaroni-and-cheese pot and dishes solidly soiled, and a couple of dishes that have been used this morning."

"Smells like eggs in here."

"None left, but we've got some Belgian waffles in the freezer. Want me to toast one or two for you?"

Sondra rubbed her tummy. "Yes, I would, and I'd like some of that fancy maple syrup you brought home."

Sondra went into the bedroom to dress, closing the door behind her.

By the time she came out, Tim had the waffles and syrup on the coffee table along with some watered-down orange juice. Sondra sat down and feasted.

"Want me to go up and talk to Wil and the cripple while you eat?" Tim asked.

"Don't call him a cripple to his face. He's very sensitive. Can you handle it without causing any hard feelings?"

"Sure. A cinch."

"Don't curse or become angry if they turn you down."

"Naw, I'll leave that up to you when I come back down and tell you what happened."

"Don't get in a snit simply because I'm trying to teach you good manners." Sondra poured a generous helping of syrup over the waffles. "Remind the old man about the brownies and my promise to spend some time with him. I'll probably never get around to sitting with him, but he doesn't have to know that. Oh, and the young one, Wil. Tell him that I'd be *extremely* appreciative if he could let you stay over once in a while."

"Yeah, right," Tim said.

Since the elevator often broke down, Tim normally took the stairs. Wil and Keith were only two floors above his own. Pete was cheap and kept the stairway dimly lit. Bulbs functioned on every other floor, but even in this light, Tim could read the graffiti on the walls. Funny how many words rhymed with Pete, Tim thought. Upon reaching Wil's and Keith's landing, Tim opened the door to the hallway. Brown doorways dotted the beige walls.

Tim knocked lightly on Wil's and Keith's door. He waited a minute and then knocked harder. He vaguely heard some cursing from inside.

Maybe now wasn't the time to be asking favors. What the hell, he thought, and knocked again.

The door swung open, and the cripple sat to the side.

"Hi," Tim said brightly.

The old man seemed flustered, at a loss for something to say.

"Mind if I come in?"

The old man actually smiled and waved Tim in.

"Hope I'm not interrupting anything."

The man shook his head eagerly.

"Seems my mother has a favor to ask. And it has to do with me. Wil here?"

"Wil's out. Hurry, tell me what you need."

"A place to stay once in a while. See, when my mom has her johns stay overnight, I make them uncomfortable."

"And I'm sure you try your damnedest to make them feel at home."

"Not quite. Anyway, she was wondering whether on those nights I could sleep here."

The old man's hands fidgeted, his nails picking at the plastic cover on the arms of the wheelchair. "Would I know beforehand?"

"I could try to tell you and Wil. That is, if Mom tells me."

"No, no. Just tell *me*."

"You don't think Wil'd like my staying here?"

"Don't want to bother him with details." The old man rubbed his numb thighs with his liver-spotted hands.

"You okay? I mean, if there's anything I can do to make you more comfortable . . ."

"Oh, you could, but Wil is due back any

115

minute. If he weren't, we could get to know each other much better."

Given Tim's experience, he decided that meant sex. "It would depend, of course, on what you'd want to do. I mean, I don't take it."

"I'm looking for a giver, Tim. Don't worry about that."

"Want me to come back sometime when Wil's not here?"

Tim watched the old man bite down on his own left index finger. He bit so hard that blood dripped from the finger.

"I guess it's been a long time," Tim said.

The old man licked the blood off his finger and said, "It always feels like ages."

Wil walked into the room. "What the hell is going on here?"

"I just came up to ask a favor," Tim said.

"Did my father ask you to come up?"

Tim looked at the old man, whose face was contorted into an elaborate wince.

"No. My mother sent me. Seems she wants—"

"Always looking to blame shit on me," said Keith. "I'm just doing the neighborly thing inviting the young man in. His mother sent him up here for the dish she lent. Remember, the one she left with those delicious brownies?"

"You liked them?" Tim asked. "I always find the chocolate too bitter. Aunt Tess scrimps on the sugar in the batter. She lightly sprinkles them with powdered sugar, but that's not the same as having lots of sugar right in the brownie."

Wil walked over to the dresser, picked up a full plate of brownies, dumped the brownies into a trash can, and handed the plate to Tim.

"Our secret." Wil winked at Tim.

"Sure." Tim laughed. "If only Aunt Tess would listen."

"Anything else?" Wil asked.

"That's all the woman left here," said Keith. "What else could she possibly ask for? Let the poor boy go. He doesn't want to be cooped up with us." Swiftly Keith made for the door and opened it.

"Thanks," said Tim, feeling awkward and silly with the soiled plate in his hand. "Bye. I'll be seeing you later." Tim directed the last comment toward the old man.

"We both look forward to seeing you again, son." Keith waved Tim through the doorway.

Thinking he hadn't completed his assignment, Tim halted on the threshold.

"Mom says to tell you that she's extremely appreciative."

The puzzled look on Wil's face made him cringe. He had to give the entire message, though; any extra money Mom could make fed and sheltered the both of them.

"For what?" Wil asked.

"She wants you to know that she could be extremely appreciative if you stopped by downstairs. She doesn't charge a whole lot."

"Thanks, but I'll be passing on that and the brownies."

Even though Tim had expected just such an

answer, he felt disappointed, but he nodded and went out into the hall.

The door immediately closed behind him.

At least he had salvaged something. Now he knew that the old man was turned on to him.

Chapter Twenty

"Sondra's really something," Wil said.

"Yes, but I think you could have been kinder." Keith backed his wheelchair to the front of the door.

"Kinder?"

"Yes, that crack about her brownies. We may not appreciate them; still, she went to a lot of trouble to see that we tasted them."

"Come again? She didn't make the damn things. Her sister cooks, not Sondra. All Sondra had to do was deliver them."

"She made an effort. After all, why would a woman come up here to hang out with us two? Besides the fact that she'd probably like to get laid by you. What is it with you and older women? Have you ever been to bed with anyone close to your age? That's right, Goldilocks, but she came after you with a knife."

"Or a letter opener. I couldn't see it clearly." Wil lay down upon the bed and opened the day's newspaper, which he had just bought in the lobby.

Keith sighed, seemingly bored. Inside he was riled up. His grand opportunity had walked out the door. Tim would be such an easy mark. Maybe he could control his own hunger enough to use Tim for the long haul. Keith had never taken blood from a victim without killing. With Tim, he could try. Money would be the holdup. Tim would expect cash for whatever he did. Wil and Keith rolled their victims, and occasionally Wil got a temporary job. That gave them enough money to afford the room in which they rested and some extra cash for clubs and transportation. *How much would Tim expect?* he wondered.

Clubs! Shit, that's exactly the kind of situation for which Tim would be most helpful. Wil never wanted to stay any place where Sade showed up, but the kid . . . What did Tim know about Sade? Nothing. And perhaps Goldilocks could entertain the kid while he and Sade plotted.

Yeah!

"Is Pete on the desk downstairs?" asked Keith.

"Yeah, he never seems to go home. The bastard's too cheap to hire more than an occasional relief man."

"I think I'll go down and talk to him."

Wil lowered the paper.

"You get along with Pete?"

"We talk."

"Figures." Wil went back to reading the paper.

Keith sneered at his son and opened the door. He'd have to control himself. He was feeling his usual peckish self, but he couldn't wait to ask Tim to take him to the club. Perhaps even tonight. He pressed the down button for the elevator.

"Damn thing better be working."

"I agree. I'm sick and tired of going up and down the stairs," commented Franny from behind him.

Franny lived next door to Wil and Keith. Several times Keith had tried to have her come into the room. Always she sullenly walked away shaking her head. *Thinking "old pervert," no doubt.* She certainly appeared to be ripe and swollen with juices. Not obese and not thin; she was just right in Keith's eyes. She had to be a C cup, even though her breasts were probably only thirty-four inches. Her waist tapered over blooming hips with a relatively flat tummy and a high ass. Her legs were always naked almost up to her crotch. He wished she'd bend over just once. Best of all, she used very little makeup. Her eyes, face, and lips were tastefully tinged with realistic hues. And her blood flowed smoothly through her veins. The pumping of her heart sounded regular and steady. He didn't know which would be better, fucking her or drinking her blood.

He smiled at her and she smiled back, but kept her distance.

"I think I'll give up and take the stairs. What are you going to do? Is there something I can get for you?"

"Give it another minute or two. I think I heard some noise coming from the shaft."

"Damn elevator always takes so long."

"Yes, but isn't it better than hiking down those stairs?"

"The exercise is good for me. Only I don't like leaving you here by yourself."

"I must say I appreciate the company. Sometimes I get a little nervous riding the elevator alone."

"Don't worry. The worst that could happen is that you get caught in the elevator for five minutes. Just start pushing the bell button like crazy. Pete hates the sound of that bell. Some of the kids do it to annoy him. But the elevator won't drop or anything like that." She smiled to herself. "I guess this isn't making you feel any better. Now I feel compelled to ride down with you. What about your son? Isn't he willing to ride down with you?"

"Not home. Thank you for waiting with me." Keith's voice was soft and meek. "I definitely hear it coming now."

"The old clang and rattle. I can understand how that would make you nervous."

Keith hoped he was winning her over. Hoping that someday she would trust him enough to allow . . .

The doors to the empty elevator opened. Keith pulled back to allow her to enter first. Such a gentleman, he thought; besides, he got a good view of her ass.

"The lobby?"

"I'm stopping at Tim's apartment first."

Franny pressed the two buttons, and the doors slowly closed.

"I wish Tim would find a job. I've even suggested to Pete that he hire the kid. He can't keep living like his mother. It's not right," said Franny.

The elevator balked and moved and jolted to a halt.

Heaven, Keith thought.

"Wouldn't you know, I go ranting on about the elevator, and it stalls with us on it."

She reached across Keith to ring the emergency bell and Keith twisted round his wheelchair to trip her. Franny fell clumsily into his lap and into his waiting hand, which quickly tore at her throat.

Chapter Twenty-one

"Hey, Pete, what's up with the elevator?" asked Edwina.

"It'll come down. Take it easy. Haven't you ever heard that old cliché, whatever goes up must come down?"

"I've been waiting fifteen minutes and nothing's come down."

"Shit! Is that damn thing on the blink again?"

"I've been sitting for at least twenty to twenty-five minutes, and I haven't seen the damn thing come down. Looks like it's stuck on one of the higher floors, or maybe in between," said Jones, who had managed to get enough money together to at least snag himself a seat in the lobby instead of huddling on the outside steps of the residence.

Pete looked at the two elderly people. Edwina must be at least eighty-five years old and fifty pounds underweight. Couldn't ask her to go climb the stairs to the sixth floor.

Jones only paid for a seat in the lobby. Jones's old room was still empty, but business was business, and Pete was not going to overlook the few dollars' difference. He could have Jones climb the stairs and see whether the kids had been up to mischief again. Maybe find that the doors had been jammed open.

"Jones, how would you like to spend overnight in your old room?"

After Jones had come back down to report that the elevator was definitely stuck between two floors, Pete had called the repair people.

It took the repairmen an hour to get to the hotel and ten minutes to get the elevator running again. A tall, slender repairman stood at the elevator doors in the main lobby waiting for the slow-creeping elevator to return. His partner had gone into the back office with Pete to settle up the bill. He checked his watch once; he was due home for his kid's birthday party. Two years old. He remembered cradling his infant son in his arms at the hospital.

Finally the elevator doors opened. Instantly he saw an old man covered in blood, a woman lying at his feet.

"Help me," cried the old man. "And help my daughter, please."

The workman rushed onto the elevator, immediately kneeling down next to the young woman while the old man maneuvered his wheelchair to the side and the elevator doors closed again.

Keith arrived at his own floor. The wheelchair skidded on the blood, but he managed to block the doors from closing with the repairman's body. He rushed down the hallway to the door to his room, but the knob wouldn't turn. *The asshole's locked me out.* He pounded his fist on the door, hoping only his son would respond. He heard the lock click. One look down the hall and he knew he had left a trail of blood.

"What the hell happened?" asked Wil.

"Quick, you gotta mop up, else they'll see the wheel marks."

Wil yanked his father into the room and proceeded to clean the tiled hallway. He swept the blood across the elevator floor, eliminating the skid marks from the wheelchair. He tossed the repairman's body back into the elevator, and the doors slowly closed.

Back in the room, Wil tried to pull answers out of his father.

"Listen, I recognized the woman next door, and there seemed to be some sort of maintenance man."

"My guess is he's the elevator repairman."

"How the hell did you manage to get on the elevator with those two?"

"Franny felt sorry for me and the guy was trying to help."

"Help Franny?"

"Me and Franny. Like a gentleman, he assisted her first."

"Giving you the opportunity to attack him."

"I was waiting for the elevator. Franny comes by, waits with me. We get on, the doors close, and boom, the elevator stops between floors. It had to be fate."

"What about the repairman?"

"Kept me waiting a damn long time. Must have been in that elevator an hour and a half. If I had been claustrophobic, I would have been tearing my hair out. Eventually the doors open, and there stands this guy. I ask for help, and he gets right on. I push the up button, and the doors close."

Wil had just finished cleaning the room and the wheelchair, and Keith watched his son check out the room for any bloodstains. Keith sat calmly in the bathtub telling his story. The bathwater now ran clear.

"Think you could dry me off now? Think I could borrow one of your shirts? You just burned up my last clean one."

Like a child, Keith passively sat while his son dried and dressed him and returned him to the spotless wheelchair.

When a knock came at the door, his son jumped. Keith figured the knock was inevitable. The police would be questioning everyone in the hotel. He was right. The police did a cursory job interrogating him. They were more interested in Wil. Wil had two good legs and looked pumped. How could an old invalid take on two people or even one?

"Mind if I check on some friends?" Keith asked the police detective.

"Can't have people wandering around at a murder scene," the detective answered.

"I only want to go down and check on Tim and his mother, Sondra. He's young, and she's rather scattered. I'd like to give them some support." Keith felt his son's eyes suddenly on him. Wil even had to ask the other detective to repeat a question.

"That's commendable, but we'd like you to stay right here for now."

"Franny was so sweet. A little racy, but sweet," Keith said, sadly looking up at the detective, who was finishing up the notes from the interview he had done with Keith.

It's little that you know of woman's heart,
Or what that heart is trying to convey
When it resists in such a feeble way!

Tartuffe
Molière

Chapter Twenty-two

Sade winced at the sight of the book Cecelia was reading while she sat on one of the beanbag chairs.

"*L'education de Laure ou le rideau levé.*" Sade yelled out the title in surprise and disappointment. "*Ma petite,* how can you read such garbage?"

Cecelia gave a single peek over her book, but immediately returned to reading.

"Honoré Gabriel Riqueti, Comte de Mirabeau, was an ass."

"Did you know him?"

"Ugly man. Pockmarked from smallpox. *Un cousin éloigné.*"

"You and he are related?" Cecelia looked up from her book, interested in the proximity of history.

"Distant, I said."

"But still related. Did you meet him? Talk to him?"

"Briefly. *Et* at the time I did not know it was he. We were imprisoned at the Vincennes at the same time, although I did not recognize him. The commandant's punk stole my promenade privileges. I was confined to my cell while Mirabeau paraded about the courtyard. As if the indignity of being referred to as Monsieur Number Six was not bad enough. Imagine, I was called by the number of my cell."

"I'm sure you complained. To Mirabeau about the walks, I mean."

"*Oui*. I told the Comte de Mirabeau what I thought of him. The crass villain had the gall to threaten my life."

"Doesn't sound as if you were in much danger. Why was he imprisoned?"

"*Lettre de cachet.*"

"Same as you. So neither of your families trusted you to roam around free. You should feel some empathy for him."

"For Mirabeau! *Jamais!* The scoundrel, a deputy of the Third Estate, accepted money for *débauche*, from the King and Queen. The fools of the Assembly converted the Church of Ste. Geneviève into a tomb for him and other French heroes. Quickly they removed his body from the church when evidence of payments were found among the King's papers."

"I think you're just pissed because he took walks and you didn't."

Sade watched as Cecelia screwed her face into a most unappealing expression.

"The man came from an insane *famille*," he said.

"Obviously," she said, pointing at Sade.

Sade bristled. "His grandmother died insane; one of his brothers and one of his sisters had spells of insanity."

"Louis, so do you."

"*Mais non!* Besides, you should not be reading that *pacotille*. I did not teach you French so that you could fill your mind with such filth. Best that you stay with English and read Richardson. Read *Clarissa, Grandison,* or *Pamela*. With Richardson's works as inspiration, I wrote *Aline et Valcour, Juliette,* and *La philosophie dans le boudoir*."

"They were inspired by the works of Samuel Richardson?"

"*Oui*. Is it not obvious? I perhaps did not share the same optimistic morality as Richardson."

"You sure didn't." Cecelia went back to her reading.

"Cast away that trash, *ma petite*." Sade grabbed the book from her hands and flung it out the open window.

"That's a library book."

"A book by Mirabeau does not belong in a *décent* library. It is no loss but a blessing if some stray *chien* relieves his heavy bladder on it.

"Besides, you have promised to rehearse the lines from *The Self-Styled Philosopher* with me. Tonight there should be many new faces at the club as I assisted in getting out the publicity for entertainment. I believe we left off where *La*

Présidente announces to Ariste that she too is a philosopher."

Sade took the stance of the rationalist philosopher and began:

"You, Madame! And of what school? Stoic, Epicurean?"

Cecelia lazily leaned back into the beanbag chair and answered:

"Oh! My word, the name makes no difference. I have ten thousand *écus* of income, and I spend them very pleasantly. I have good wine from champagne that I drink with my friends. I am in good health. I do what I please, and I live and let live. That's my creed."

"That's all very well said, and exactly what Epicurus taught."

"Oh! I can assure you that no one has taught me; all of that comes straight from me. For the past twenty years I have read nothing but my wine list and the menu for my supper!"

Sade noticed that Cecelia repeated the lines with too much gusto. Temptation gnawed at him to stop this farce and set Cecelia straight about the origin of whatever knowledge she had. Instead he continued:

"On this basis, you ought to be the happiest woman in the world!"

"Happy me! I am in need of a husband after my own taste. My *Président* was an imbecile. He was good only in court; he understood the law, but that's all. I want a man who understands how to love me, who occupies himself with me alone. . . ."

Sade regretted choosing this play. Cecelia seemed to relish the lines.

"You will find a thousand of them, Madame, and . . ."

"I know that I am not pretty, but ten thousand *écus* of income as a wedding present are worth more than the attractions of a Clarice; and although love be rare in this age, one ought to get it for ten thousand *écus*!"

Breaking away from the play's dialogue, Cecelia closed her eyes and asked, "Do you suppose wealth could bring love? Certainly my beauty has not prevented you from putting our relationship at risk."

"What is our relationship, *ma petite*?"

"I know you believe it to be the joining of two hedonists."

"And you, *ma petite*, what do you believe?"

Cecelia opened her eyes and stood. "We're preying animals making believe we're human. But we no longer experience the human emotions we once did."

"You are sorry to be vampiric?"

"No. I want the strength and power. I don't like being a minor actor in your plays, Louis. And . . ."

Sade watched her shake her head. She started for the doorway, but he grabbed her arm.

"And you want to cause me pain by bringing back someone I did love. You think that will free you from the voice and cause me to soften. *Jamais*. Once I did bend for the sake of my Liliana. Even then I did not break. I did not allow my domination to be weakened. I destroy what I cannot control. Remember the burnt remains of Marie's skull. The remains that I dumped onto your lap when I returned to the car as we fled the Eastern Coast."

"What did you do with those remains?"

"She will not return. I have assured myself of that."

"How?" Cecelia asked.

"She sleeps safely in a place where I can watch her. Nothing for you to think about, *ma petite*."

"Meaning it's none of my business."

"*Oui.*" Sade let go of her arm.

"She'll come back someday for her revenge. She'll come back the same as Liliana will. They don't need their old bodies to haunt you." Cecelia left the room, leaving the parlor door ajar.

Sade wondered why he bothered to tolerate Cecelia. She teethed as if she were an infant. Power slowly grew inside the girl; however, she did not know how to use it. Did she really hear Liliana? he wondered. If she did, could he destroy Cecelia? His beautiful niece, Liliana, torn to shreds by mutants. His stomach heaved until he recalled his mother-in-law, Marie, and the way he made her pay for all the years of misery.

He would keep Cecelia. She reminded him of the care he should take in producing new spawn. Cecelia was not his delicate Liliana, but she also was not the shrewd, wizened Marie. He did not feel threatened by the girl, merely impatient, but he must have patience, for she could still bloom into a treasure. She had done so physically. If only her temperament were more amenable to the life they shared.

Mary Ann Mitchell

He walked to the window and saw the book she had been reading lying in the alley.

Muttering to himself, he said:

"Que le coeur d'une femme est mal connu de vous!
Et que vous savez peu ce qu'il veut faire entendre
Lorsque si faiblement on le voit se défendre!"

Chapter Twenty-three

"Wow, what a kinky place. Lots of weirdos hanging around. Can't believe you asked me to take you to this joint."

"Tim, this is a special club. A fetish club. People here have unusual tastes."

"Like the guy over there with his pants ripped up the sides."

"I'm sure he had them specially designed for him," Keith said.

"He looks like a fag."

"He probably is. Ignore him. There are lots of young, attractive women here. I leave you free to prowl, boy, but remember, don't leave without me."

"Nah, why would I do that?" Tim looked closely at a woman wearing a flesh-toned leotard. Or was it a leotard? he wondered. Certainly the old man could find his way home.

"I'll give you the money I promised tomorrow," Keith reminded him.

"Fifty bucks isn't a whole lot, you know."

"It's what we agreed upon."

Given a frontal view of the leotard-wrapped body, Tim realized the woman was a man. "This place is really freaky. You sure anybody is what they look like? Maybe I should pick up a guy 'cause it'd really be a woman."

"Don't simplify. You'll get into trouble."

"Why don't I roam around with you for a while?"

"No one's going to bother you. Just say 'no, thanks' and they'll go away."

"You sure about that?"

The old man looked perplexed. "I can't be dragging you all over the place. I'm looking for someone specific, and we have private business to discuss. Anyway, I thought it had entered your mind to go both ways. At least that's my impression."

Yeah, that was the impression Tim had intended to make, except that he had figured the old guy probably wouldn't be able to get it up. Although thinking about his own dick inside the old man's stale mouth gave him the shivers.

"I'll go over and sit at the bar, Mr. Bridgewater."

"Money?"

Now that the old man mentioned it, he could use extra cash. He didn't expect to pay his own way on this outing. "Broke. Maybe you could give me a few bucks for the bar. Not to be subtracted from the money you owe me, of course."

"Of course." The old man dug deep into his pants pocket. He pulled out a handful of bills, which he counted at his side, below the armrest. "Here." The old man swept several bills at Tim and put the rest of the money in his pocket.

"Thanks." Tim watched the invalid roll away from him.

At the bar Tim was sorely disappointed to find four bucks in the palm of his hand.

"What the hell can I get for four bucks?"

"Mineral water," answered the bartender without officially being asked.

"Why are you with that invalid?"

Tim heard a feminine voice. But it could just be some guy in hormone therapy, he thought.

"I can go in the men's room and get myself some water right out of the tap," Tim said.

The bartender leaned toward him. "The men's room is only for customers."

"Give him a beer," the feminine voice said.

"He's too young."

"Felipe, you don't give a shit about how old the customer is. Hell, you know lots of kids are drinking booze, and it's being bought for them by people with fake I.D.'s. Give him a beer and put it on Louis's bill."

"If you weren't so pretty . . ." Felipe reached out to rub the woman's cheek, and she pulled away.

Curly-headed blonde with blue eyes. She looks real, Tim thought.

She smiled at Tim. "You didn't answer my question."

"Hi, I'm Tim."

"Cecelia," the woman said. "I'm surprised to see that someone like you travels with the invalid and still lives."

"Mr. Bridgewater is crusty, but he wouldn't hurt a fly."

The bartender placed the beer in front of Tim and made a quick swipe for Cecelia's cheek. Tim noticed that the bartender's move was half-hearted and missed Cecelia by a good distance.

"You're not a fly, Tim."

Tim sipped his beer, hearing what she had said. He chuckled and came away from the glass with a slight foam moustache on his upper lip. "I would hope humans get even better treatment than flies."

"Why would you presume that?" she asked.

"I'm an optimist." Tim thought that an odd thing to say, considering the way his own life had been going so far. He decided he was more a liar than an optimist.

"How did you meet the invalid?"

"Mr. Bridgewater. Invalid sounds . . ." Tim tried to think of the right word.

"Crass," Cecelia suggested.

"Yeah, that too." He picked up the beer and tried to look cool even after he spilled some beer on his shirt.

"A wise guy," she muttered.

"I hope you mean that in a good sense," he said.

"Sure. I find you entertaining. Still, you haven't told me how you know . . . Mr. Bridgewater."

"Lives in the same building I do."

"He lives with his son?"

"Wil? Yeah. They have one of the smaller digs. Basically a single room with a bath. Don't seem to need a kitchen. Guess they go out for most meals."

"I know they do."

"How do you know them?"

"From this club. Mr. Bridgewater seems to be becoming a regular. Son didn't seem as interested in the place."

"Strange. The old guy, Mr. Bridgewater, seems so out of place here. I bet he's the oldest person here."

"You'd lose."

"There ain't people older than Mr. Bridgewater." Tim pulled in his gut and stood tall. Through the sheerness of her gown he could tell she actually was a babe. Unless she had had one of those major jobs done.

"What's the matter, Tim?"

"Would you tell the truth? I mean, are you a girl?"

"Always have been."

Tim didn't want to believe Cecelia lied. He wanted to get laid.

"I'd invite you to have a drink with me, but . . ." He held up the four dollars and shrugged.

"Don't worry about impressing a girl, do you?"

"Money isn't the only way to impress a woman." Tim moved closer to her. He noted she didn't budge. It'd be fun bedding someone his own age for a change, he thought. "I got a lot to impress you with, and I know how to use it." Tim grinned.

"What a unique pickup line."

"Bartender, give her a drink. What would you like? We'll put it on—what's his name again? Louis's bill."

"She doesn't go for alcohol, buddy." Felipe swept off the counter with a damp rag.

"Are you one of those healthy people who doesn't drink alcohol or eat meat?" Tim asked.

"I stick with a liquid diet," she said.

"Watching your weight, huh?"

"No. I prefer a liquid diet." Cecelia raised her cold hand and settled her fingers atop his carotid. "Healthy. Probably quite potent too."

Tim moved closer to her.

"You sizing me up for a lay, honey?" He spoke an inch away from her left ear. He breathed in her scent and noted that she didn't seem to sweat. Instead of feeling warmer near her body, he got a chill.

"You've already sized me up. Why can't I do the same?"

"Nothing to hide, baby." Tim stretched out his arms and swung his pelvis forward toward Cecelia. Shock hit him when she grabbed his genitals and lightly squeezed. His confidence flagged; not his dick, though.

"I really shouldn't leave Mr. Bridgewater."

"Going somewhere?" she asked.

The answer caught in his throat. Was she making fun of him? The people around him seemed to be leaning in to hear his reply. Shit, she made him look like an ass.

"I think you're blushing," she whispered in his ear. "Or is a single beer too much for you to handle?" She pulled away from him. "Felipe, another beer." She looked at Tim. "We can go off and discuss this problem, Tim, and we don't have to leave the premises."

. . . He orates till he feels
Suddenly on his rear a couple of kicks,
Then he kisses his fat partner and turns
   cartwheels.

The Clown
Paul Verlaine

Chapter Twenty-four

Louis Sade had to be here. Keith had seen Goldilocks when he and Tim first entered the club. The lights appeared to be dimmer than usual. He overheard people discussing a play that had been performed earlier in the evening.

"Can't get it back up?" a slender, silver-haired male joked with the owner, who fiddled with the lighting switches. The thin owner, dressed in retro 1970s leisure suit and gold chains, thumbed his nose at the patron.

"Excuse me. I have to get through." Keith forced his way through a group of people to sit near the owner. "Sir, I'm looking for Louis Sade." Keith pulled on the owner's jacket.

"Probably off signing autographs."

"Or drinking his fill on his fan club," the silver-haired man added.

"Where would he be doing that?" asked Keith. The smell of blood permeated this area of the club. He quickly looked around. A couple seated at a nearby table had cut themselves on their forearms and were squeezing their blood into separate crystal liqueur glasses. When there was enough for a taste, they exchanged glasses and drank each other's blood. Keith's mouth felt parched.

"Dammit! Where the hell is Louis Sade!"

"Behind door number . . ." The silver-haired patron waved his index finger in the air. "Ooops! No number. Oh, well, try the door marked 'Management.' "

Keith spun his wheelchair in the direction in which he had been pointed.

"Don't say thank you. It was my gift from me to you." This was punctuated by a kiss.

On the way Keith checked the bar. No sign of Tim. That kid had killed his fifty bucks.

Keith pushed open the "Management" door. Blood, sex, and vomit assaulted his sense of smell. A long row of curtains hung from door-ways on either side of the hallway before him.

"Louis Sade!" he yelled, and began pushing aside curtain after curtain. Most rooms were empty; a few had pairs and threesomes exhibiting their sexual prowess.

One revealed the sight of two men and a woman. The young man's head rested on the thighs of an older man and a young woman's head bent over the young man's neck, lapping at droplets of blood. Goldilocks stopped to look up at Keith; Sade merely put a finger to his lips to signify silence, and Tim swooned within both their grasps.

"He's mine," Keith insisted.

"*Monsieur*, we share as families do. No one person belongs completely to any other."

Goldilocks and Tim were naked. Sade was dressed in a black linen suit, his feet and chest bare.

"He came with me, and he's leaving with me, so tell Goldilocks to stop sucking up his blood." Keith wheeled himself into the small room. He saw that the threesome had spread themselves across a pastel-blue silk coverlet draped over multiple pillows. "Hey, get yourself up," he said, shaking Tim's shoulder.

"How rude, *monsieur*. The gentleman certainly was enjoying his time with *la femme*. I, *monsieur*, was invited. I don't remember anyone telling me that you would appear." Sade looked at Goldilocks.

"I didn't invite him," she said. Her pale white skin glowed a pinkish hue from the feasting in which she had just engaged.

Keith smelled Tim on her. The boy's blood, the boy's semen, the boy's sweat, all played the air with stifling intoxication. Tim's body hinted at rot and decay from the arms in which he rested.

"Give him back to me." Keith prepared to drag Tim away from the other two.

"*Monsieur*, you are too old for tantrums as I am too old to tolerate them." Sade pushed Tim into the woman's arms and stood over Keith in what seemed like one sweeping movement. By the shoulders of Keith's shirt Sade lifted the old man from the chair. Keith heard the material rip and felt death meld with his own flesh as Sade's flesh came into contact with his own.

"Marie left you unable to walk, *mais* I shall leave you without a head if you persist."

Keith heard Tim groan several times.

"Tim, you all right?" Keith asked while still staring into Sade's frozen gaze.

"Shit, that was the best fuck I ever had. What the hell are you two guys doing here?"

"The boy's conscious now, Mr. Sade. No sense in making him wary."

"Is this an audience?" Tim asked, leaping out of the woman's grasp.

The woman applauded and Sade tossed Keith to the floor.

"*Monsieur*, you can crawl back into your chair."

Keith felt Tim's arms scoop him up and help him back into the wheelchair.

"I didn't come to fight with you. I . . . Tim, why don't you and Goldilocks go back out to the bar."

"Naked? Man, you're the one's out of it. You and this guy can take your argument somewhere else."

"The boy is right, *monsieur*. We have intruded upon these two lovers." Sade smiled down at the woman. "We can move out to the bar."

"No!" shouted Keith. "I need privacy to talk."

"*Solitude*. I don't believe we have any important *affaire* to discuss. At least nothing of importance to me."

"I beg you, Mr. Sade. You couldn't save me before, but you could help make up for it now."

"Are you attempting to put upon me *un sentiment de culpabilité? Pourquoi?*"

"You tortured my son."

"*Et* you care? No, *monsieur,* I do not buy that. You torture your son on a daily basis. I merely tested his limit for physical pain and released him. On the other hand, you break him down emotionally and wait for him to heal before breaking him down again. I don't seek complete destruction, only a *unique* moment of passion."

Keith felt Tim dressing next to him. If the boy would get out, he could speak freely. Goldilocks lounged on the silk-covered pillows.

"You see how that woman left me," Keith said, indicating his legs. He became aware of Tim's sudden interest in the conversation. He turned to look at Tim. "You look dressed to me now. Here." Keith reached into his pants pocket, took out the stash of bills, and handed them all over to Tim. "Get the hell out of here."

"There better be more than four bucks here." Tim seemed satisfied after counting out what he had in his hand. "Yeah, I'll be outside waiting for you." He didn't bother acknowledging the woman or the stranger; he simply swept the curtain back and disappeared.

"How can I get you to help me, Mr. Sade?" asked Keith.

"You can do nothing. However, I have been bored recently." He glanced down at the woman. "You might be *un divertissement.*"

Mary Ann Mitchell

"You help me to walk again and I'll tap dance for you every night."

"Nothing so *vulgaire, s'il vous plaît.*
". . . *Il pérore et se tait tout soudain,*
Reçoit des coups de pieds au derrière, badin
Baise au cou sa commère énorme, et fait la
    roue."

Syphilitics, fools, kings, puppets, ventrilo-
    quists,
What does Paris the whore care about
Your souls and bodies, your poisons and
    your rags?

Parisian Orgy
Rimbaud

Chapter Twenty-five

"Roof rats."

"What?"

"You've got roof rats."

"Come on, all I have is some scuffling noises in the attic." Hank made a face at his best friend, Mark.

"I'm telling you, you have roof rats." Mark's T-shirt felt two sizes too small on him. That always happened right after he had worked out at the gym.

"Last night I hear a lot of scuffling noise up in the attic. Some sounds of running, and then *boing*, whatever it is hits his head on the recessed lighting fixture. Everything is quiet."

"Check to see if the rat had a concussion?"

"Doesn't have to be rats. Sadie would be pissed if she thought we spent big change on a house with rats." Hank looked over his shoulder toward the front door of the house to make sure Sadie hadn't come outside.

"My cousin had roof rats and had a hell of a time getting rid of them."

"But he did get rid of them?"

Mark shrugged.

"My cousin died from a massive heart attack; the house went into probate and was sold."

"The rats scare him to death?"

"No. He died skipping rope."

"What?"

"He was doing his aerobic exercise in his living room while he watched television."

"Had nothing to do with the rats?"

"No, Hank. They weren't turning the rope for him. He liked working out alone. Always was a bit of a hermit. Never would consider going to a gym to work out. Maybe if he had, he could have gotten help, and it would have saved his life." Mark wore wool socks under his work boots and his feet were sweltering.

"The rats didn't try to eat his body, did they?"

"One taste of him and they probably would have spit him back out. Calling him dour is an understatement."

"What do I tell Sadie?" Again Hank checked to see if his wife had come out.

"What does she think is up there?"

"A cute squirrel."

"Squirrels are rodents."

"Yeah, but at least they beg for food and have bushy tails. That she can tolerate."

"Enlighten her. Tell her squirrels are rodents.

She'll still think it's cute, and you can honestly say there are rodents in the attic instead of the other R word. Rats." Mark thought about how oblivious Sadie could be.

"But if I call in a pest-control guy, he's going to spill the beans."

"Whoa! My cousin didn't call anyone in. He got a book out of the library. Told him more than he wanted to know about rats."

"I'm not going up to the attic searching for rats. Hell, I can't even stand up straight when I'm up there." Hank shook his head.

"Oh, come on. Some rat poison. A few traps. You can even use the fireplace tongs to pick the dead animal up. No problem."

"Things stink. What if I can't find a dead body and one manages to decay in the walls? You know what that would smell like?" Hank placed his right hand atop his distended belly.

"Sadie's in charge of cleaning up. Send her up there." Mark hoped this flippant comment didn't get back to Sadie, since she could be sensitive about a joke.

"I wouldn't ask Sadie to do something like that. Hell, she's already got the kids so squeamish I can't even take them fishing."

"Now that's an idea. Send the kids up there."

"As what? Sacrifices? Mark, you're not being much help."

"Hi, Sadie." Mark watched Hank's wife walk down the few steps leading from the front door. Her body was slender but luscious in a sensual way. Her breasts were not large, but shaped exactly the way Mark thought breasts should be shaped. Her tummy still remained taut, even after three kids. Her tanned legs were long and shapely in her cut-off jeans. Best of all, she had the tightest pussy he had had in years.

"Hank, what are you and Mark busy talking about? Am I missing out on something?"

Mark liked keeping her on edge. Gave him a special power over both Sadie and Hank.

"We were talking sports," Hank said, smiling lamely at his wife. "Sports and . . . Mark thinks we have rats."

"What the hell are you talking about?"

"You know. Those noises coming from the attic. He thinks they're roof rats and not squirrels."

"Could be squirrels. Of course, they're rodents too," Mark added.

"Go dunk your head and stop causing trouble," Sadie said.

"Don't blame me if one night you're sleeping and you feel ticklish movements crawling up your arm, and you open your eyes to stare into the eyes of a hungry rat."

"Go home, Mark." Sadie grabbed hold of her husband's arm. She seemed to be comforting Hank.

"Just trying to do a good deed for friends."

"If you want to do a good deed, why don't you walk across the street and help that man in a wheelchair? He seems to be lost."

"I will. Maybe he's going my way, and I can have some protection on the way home."

"You'll be over next week to watch the game?" Hank asked as Mark headed for the curb.

"Like clockwork." Temptation nagged at Mark. He wanted to remind Sadie of their Friday afternoon date in bed, but why ruin a good deal by letting her husband in on the secret? He waved and crossed the street.

The man in the wheelchair seemed to be holding a map of San Francisco. Didn't even know which way to hold the map.

"Got a problem?"

"I'm trying to find my way back to my hotel."

"Don't know much about the hotels, but if you have two cross streets I can direct you."

Suddenly Mark noticed a dark figure in the doorway of the building in front of him.

"Bon soir, monsieur." A man came out of the shadows. He wore a dark linen suit without a shirt and expensive-looking sandals. "I overheard the conversation you have had with this gentleman. Perhaps I can assist." The man smiled and flashed white teeth, pale skin, and glowing hair.

"What the hell . . ." the crippled man said.

"You don't sound like you'd know San Francisco any better than I do," said Mark. "What's that? A French accent?"

"Oui, monsieur."

"Dammit, you're supposed to grab him." The old man appeared to be grumbling to himself.

"Always wanted to visit Paris," said Mark. "Never had enough money to do it up right. I want to go classy. The Concord. The Ritz. The best food. No cheese and stale bread for me. I bet you could give me some cool recommendations."

The Frenchman spoke:

Quenched

"Syphilitiques, fous, rois, pantins, ventrilo-
  ques,
Qu'est-ce que ça peut faire á la putain Paris,
Vos âmes et vos corps, vos poisons et vos
  loques?"

"Guess I should learn some French before I worry about affording the plane and hotel," said Mark.

"But then you may never get there, *monsieur*. The plane and the hotel would keep you from the sparkling life you would find in Paris."

"Life!" The old man in the wheelchair threw his map on the ground.

"Ah, *monsieur*. You should not litter, for it may attract attention." The man in the linen suit picked up the map. "May I invite you both for a drink?"

"I'm always up for a cold one," said Mark.

"Et vous, monsieur?" the man said, turning toward the invalid in the wheelchair.

"It ain't done like this," warned the old man.

"How is it done in your country? Was I too forward, *monsieur*?"

"You were supposed to grab him." The man in the wheelchair became agitated.

"Do you know what he's talking about?" the Frenchman asked.

The younger man shrugged.

"Excusez-moi, monsieur. Je m'appelle Louis." Sade made a slight but courteous bow.

"Mark." He put his hand out, and Louis hesitantly shook it.

"This is worse than being with Wil," said the invalid.

"Why don't we walk down to a *petit café* I have found and talk? We may even be able to assist you," Louis said, directing his last words toward the invalid.

. . . flatter them, gratify them with pleasing
   lies;
No matter what indignation fills their heart,
They'll swallow the bait and you'll be their
   friend.

   The Funeral of the Lioness
   Jean de La Fontaine

Chapter Twenty-six

"It is totally unnecessary to rip open the neck, Monsieur Bridgewater. A look into the victim's eyes can slow his intellectual processes. A mere nip is all that is *nécessaire*. You . . . *mange comme un cochon*."

"What was all that foreign stuff? Why can't you just speak English?" Keith wiped the sleeve of his shirt across his lips.

"*Parce que* some words sound so much better in French, especially for your ears."

"My ears can't comprehend a damn word in French."

"That is the problem. You must use your brain, *monsieur*."

"What are you going to do with the body?"

"I have had many *domestiques, mais* I have never been one."

Here's how it works:

Each package will carry a FREE 10-DAY EXAMINATION
privilege. At the end of that time, if you decide
to keep your books, simply pay the low invoice price
of $11.25, no shipping or handling charges added.
HOME DELIVERY IS ALWAYS FREE!
There's no minimum number of books to buy,
and you may cancel at any time.

AND AS A CHARTER MEMBER,
YOUR FIRST THREE-BOOK
SHIPMENT IS TOTALLY FREE!
IT'S A BARGAIN YOU CAN'T BEAT!

✂ CUT HERE

- -

Mail to: Leisure Horror Book Club,
P.O. Box 6613, Edison, NJ 08818-6613

YES! I want to subscribe to the Leisure Horror Book Club. Please send
my 3 FREE BOOKS. Then, every other month I'll receive the three newest
Leisure Horror Selections to preview FREE for 10 days. If I decide to
keep them, I will pay the Special Members Only discounted price of just
$3.75 each, a total of $11.25. This saves me between $3.72 and $6.72
off the bookstore price. There are no shipping, handling or other charges.
There is no minimum number of books I must buy and I may cancel the
program at any time. In any case, the 3 FREE BOOKS are mine to keep—
at a value of between $14.97 and $17.97. Offer valid only in the USA.

NAME:_____

ADDRESS:_____

   CITY:_____ STATE:_____

   ZIP:_____ PHONE:_____

LEISURE BOOKS, A Division of Dorchester Publishing Co., Inc.

"But I'm an invalid. What do you expect me to do?"

Louis shrugged.

"What would *you* do, Mr. Sade?"

"*Quelle désordre!* I would not have made such a mess. The brutal wringing of the neck as if you were a chicken farmer."

"He fought me."

Sade knelt down in front of Keith.

"Look at my eyes, *monsieur*. Are these the eyes of a brutal man?"

Keith scratched his head.

"Answer me!"

Keith almost leaped from the wheelchair. "I wouldn't trust them," he said.

"That's only *parce que* you know me. Do they not invite you into my soul?"

"I'm not that kind of guy," answered Keith.

"Cooperate, *monsieur,* or I will leave you here." Sade stood, and appeared to be much taller than he really was.

"You've got big blue eyes with a touch of angst. Or maybe a certain innocence. You look to me for warmth, and I feel almost sure you could respond in kind."

"You are no longer human and can recognize a fellow vampire. If you were mortal . . . ah, that would be different."

"So you're telling me that you get your meals simply by looking into people's eyes."

"*Et* exerting my power over them."

"I don't have that kind of power."

"*C'est effrayant*, but you do. You were made in

violence. No one cooed you into the fold. You have missed the seduction, *monsieur*."

"Seduction! Hell, is that why Wil has more self-control than me? Because he got laid by that woman and I didn't?"

Sade leaned his head back and inhaled the San Francisco breezes before looking back at Keith.

"Touching of the genitals is not the important aspect," Sade said, "although it does add to the vibrancy and strength of the kill. First you must learn to accept with an open heart."

"You don't have an open heart."

"True, but I can at least feign an open heart. Did you not trust me, *monsieur*, and are you not currently trusting in my guidance?"

"I'm beginning to think I'm a jerk."

"*Précisément!* That is your first lesson in survival. Don't be a jerk. Be aware of all that surrounds you. Watch the mortals closely and use their weaknesses against them. Sense what their needs are. Win their trust."

"I'm sitting in this wheelchair. A guy trusts me. Figures I can't make any fast moves. Even pities me. But they always fight me."

"You are too needy without the appropriate spirit to try. You sit and expect people to do for you. You are like a starving vulture that sits and waits. Even to the way you sit, *monsieur*. Your shoulders hunched." Sade hunched his own shoulders. "Your beak nose extended and your cruel eyes waiting for the death that will come to your victim.

Quenched

"Win me over, *monsieur*. Give me a reason to help you beyond arresting my own boredom."
Sade turned his back on Keith and muttered:

Flattez-les, payez-les d'agréables mensonges,
Quelque indignation don't leur coeur soit
* rempli,*
Ils goberont l'appât, vous serez leur ami."

Chapter Twenty-seven

Wil lay on the bed, watching his father, who stared into the scratched, distorted mirror. He had noticed that his father had begun spending hours sitting in front of the mirror seemingly staring into his own eyes.

"Are you all right, Dad? The police haven't been around in several days, if that worries you."

"They believed me," Keith said, amazed at the reminder. He wheeled himself around to face his son. "Do you like me?"

"I love you, Dad, or I wouldn't bother taking all the hell you give me."

"No. You love me because I'm your father, but do you like me?"

Wil sighed. He didn't remember his father ever caring whether anyone liked him.

"You're a difficult guy to like."

Keith wheeled himself up to the side of the bed. "Look into my eyes, son. What do you see?"

"Have you taken up hypnotism?"

"That's what Mr. Sade does. He hypnotizes his victims. He weaves some sort of spell around them where they believe his eyes reflect warmth. There is no real warmth in the man's eyes, is there?"

"Oh, all this is about Sade." Disappointed, Wil scooted himself off the bed. "You do what you want with Sade. I hate the man and don't even want to hear his name mentioned."

A knock at the door prevented Keith from responding.

Wil opened the door and saw a sheepish Tim standing in the hallway.

"Your dad said it would be all right."

"All right to do what?"

"To stay the night here. That guy's back with my mother and wants to stay the night as long as I don't show up."

"Excuse me. I'm missing something here."

"My mother's client. I need a place to sleep."

"Tim, my son." Keith spoke with a minister's warmth. "Of course we would be most happy to invite you in. What time will you be showing up?"

Tim shrugged. "Actually I'm not sure I'll show up at all. I was thinking about going down to the club tonight, and maybe . . ."

"The charming girl Cecelia," said Keith. "What a good eye you have. If you alone need a place to stay, you can stay here, but I can't condone hanky-panky behind your mother's back. Give Tim the extra key to the room, Wil."

"We don't have one."

"Give him your key."

"I have a better idea. Why don't you and Tim look for some other place to stay tonight?"

"You'll be getting home late, I'm sure, Tim. Why don't you just knock on the door, and one of us will let you in," Keith said.

"Unless neither of us is here, Dad."

"I can make a point of being here. What time do you think you'll be getting home?"

Tim shrugged.

Wil was sure this was not the answer his father wanted. He could tell by the way his father dug his nails into the already ratty arms of the wheelchair.

"Tim, let's just say I'll be home by three," Keith said. "Does that sound okay to you?"

"Sure. I never know when my mother's getting home, but then I have a key to the apartment."

"I don't think it's a good idea for you to stay with us, Tim," Wil declared.

"Be generous, Wil," Keith said through clenched teeth. "I promise the boy will be safer here than on the street."

"Then I'll be here, too," Wil said. He saw his father's lips spread into a smile, and didn't see the tension that was usually there.

"Oh, if you want, I can take you to the club again for another fifty," Tim told Keith. "Sorry about last time. Hey, when I think about it, you were the one who completely disappeared."

"See how generous the boy is?" Keith asked Wil. "I met a friend last time, and we got carried away talking about old times and the changes some of us need to make. But you needn't worry about me tonight, Tim. My friend and I have another spot to meet."

"You think you'll forget to come home?" Tim asked.

"My son certainly won't."

Wil knew he had been had as he closed the door on Tim.

"You're copying Sade, aren't you?" Wil said.

Keith wheeled away from the door. "Do you think Tim trusts me?"

"He's a scatterbrained kid who doesn't know any better."

"You know all the violence that's involved in our killings? Granted, you're a bit more sensitive than me and don't overindulge. But the violence isn't necessary. We can have people offer themselves to us."

"Oh, please, old man, bite me on the neck and rip open my throat."

"Just a nip. That's all one needs to take, and sometimes you can allow the mortal to survive."

"Sade takes more than a nip from his victims, believe me."

"That's only when he feels . . . tense. Otherwise, he's a gentleman. Mortals at the club offer themselves to him. They compete for his attentions."

"They're freaks."

"Were you a freak when you were mortal? Did you feel like a freak when you indulged in pleasures that satisfied your lust?"

Wil remained quiet.

"They just need the warmth and contact of

another person. You can do almost anything to some one who loves you."

Amazed that his father would speak these words, Wil turned away from his father's eyes. Eyes that had always sought to find the nub of his pain.

Chapter Twenty-eight

"I warned you, Cecelia, not to give yourself to my uncle, but you refused to heed. Now you ache for something other than this bond you share with Uncle. He will never be totally yours, and you will never find the prestige you thought he would bring you. Yes, children your own age adore you for the secret bond you have with Uncle, but it is not adoration for you, my dear Cecelia, it is envy. They too believe that to be within the circle of his glory is all that one needs for complete satisfaction. Tell them how you feel, Cecelia. Tell them of how he demeans the gift of self that you gave him. Tell them about the fear that too often fills your breast when he is near. Tell them and they will not listen."

Go away, Liliana. Cecelia closed her eyes and tried to sleep. The casket, however, seemed too confining, her mind too jumbled with words. Liliana's words, warning her, begging Cecelia to bring her back.

"Give me material existence, Cecelia, and I can take my uncle away, far away, so that he may never make demands again on you. You have learned all you can from him. Yet he will never let you go without one to replace you. It is I, Cecelia, who can charm back the love in my uncle's heart."

Cecelia braced her hands against the soft satin that lined the sides of her casket. She pushed against the sides, and only stopped when she heard the wood squeak from the pressure.

"Invite Tim back, and he will save us both. Feed your hunger, if you must, after he has impregnated you with my soul. Cecelia, do not sleep when he awaits you."

But I need to rest at least a few hours, she answered Liliana in her mind. She would make no audible sound inside the casket. She would lie as one truly dead and free from the wayward ways of the mortals. *I will do what you want, Liliana, only let me rest for a while.*

Her breath halted. Her muscles went flaccid. Her flesh began to take on the odor of decay. Her bones slipped from sockets to gift Cecelia with the weariness necessary for sleep. Some fingernails slipped from beds and fell into the earth on which she rested. Those nails would

170

break down into rotted minerals feeding the earth on which she lay. New nails would emerge when she awoke, so that she could once again see herself whole and not as what she was.

Chapter Twenty-nine

Tim brushed his hand against Cecelia's glittering backside as she passed. The gold-sequined dress she wore touched each curve of her flesh. Her bare feet inched out from beneath the folds of her dress with each step she took. Her fat round nipples heightened the sensuality of the glitter.

Had so many hands touched her that now she did not acknowledge each caress? he wondered.

Her arms stretched out to hold a man, his flesh painted whiter than it really was. Eyeliner enhanced the sunken eyes. His lips were painted a deep purple with red drops tattooed from the right side of his bottom lip to the tip of his chin. Safety pins drooped from each of his earlobes; at the bottom of each a tiny skull hung. Tim could barely make out the skulls' features, but under the glow of a passing strobe light he could make out the shape of the skulls. The excessively tall man shrunk his body to fit within Cecelia's embrace. The dark velvet of his suit served as backdrop for the outline of her body.

Slowly the man lowered his knees to the floor and knelt before her. She swept his straight, long blond hair off to one side and bent to nip his neck.

Tim felt sweat break on his skin. His pulse raced. There was not enough air to feed his lungs nor light enough to ease his vision. He felt jostled by the crowd around him, but he couldn't move, couldn't lose sight of Cecelia, even after the kneeling man wrapped his hands around her thighs.

Felipe, the bartender, pulled the tall man to his feet, forcing Cecelia to give up her prey. Felipe shook his head no and his lips moved, but Tim was out of earshot.

Please don't take him to the back room, Cecelia.

The man in velvet turned and hugged Felipe as a lover would. Felipe kissed the man's cheek and licked a spot of blood from his neck.

Tim sensed Cecelia's awareness of him. She had turned toward him and was smiling, waiting for Tim to acknowledge her. When he nodded to her, she walked slowly to him.

"Take me home," she whispered, standing immediately in front of him.

"Where do you live?" he asked.

"Take me far from where I rest. Take me home with you."

"I . . ." He couldn't. Couldn't refuse her.

He took her cold hand and attempted to warm it between his own hands.

"Now," she whispered.

A command that sent the blood rushing through his body. His mother, her john, Wil, and Keith . . . *Now, she had said*.

The scent of sweat filled the air surrounding him. Arms reached out to touch Cecelia, but never got to feel her flesh. They reached out, but could never make contact with their princess.

"The exit is right behind you, Tim." Her voice was soft but strong.

Holding her hand, Tim turned and headed for the exit. Patrons of the club parted for them, leaving enough room for Tim and Cecelia to walk side by side.

Tim shivered in the San Francisco dampness. He wanted to put an arm around her shoulders to keep them both warm, but she refused to let go of his hand. Aware of the stares from those who passed by, Tim gripped her hand tighter. She did not cry out, but he heard a cracking noise. Had he held her hand too tightly? Fearfully he looked at her face for an answer.

"I'm sorry if I hurt your hand," he said.

"You couldn't," she replied.

She squeezed his hand and it ached. Her strength seemed equal to his own.

They were blocks from his building.

Damn, Mom's going to be real pissed.

They were about to step off a curb when he realized broken glass littered the street. Remembering her bare feet, Tim drew her attention to the glass. Now she allowed his hand to slip from hers, and he lifted her into his arms to carry her across the street. Catcalls and whistles teased his ears; yet when she rested her palm on his right cheek, the noises were silenced. He turned his head slightly to kiss her wrist, and she responded by rubbing her cheek against his stubble. Lightly her cheek made contact with his. No pressure, just the invigoration of her chill that sparked his need. He felt himself grow hard, and almost refused to set her back on her feet as he stepped up on the opposite curb, except that he felt her chill pull away. Her cheek left his. Her palm moved down and settled on his chest. Immediately he put her down, and she once again took his hand as they walked.

Jones, huddled in the vestibule of the hotel, looked as if he were dozing. Instantly he awoke when Tim and Cecelia stepped into the small space. Seeing who it was, Jones put a finger to his pursed lips. Tim thought Jones looked cleaner than normal, and remembered the old man had been allowed to sleep in his room just the other night. He caught Cecelia staring at Jones. Her eyes fixed on his layered shabby clothes. Her nose twitched, and Tim felt his cheeks flush. Even if the old man had bathed, his clothes still smelled. Tim's mother was humping a john in her bedroom. The tile floors of the halls were stained and yellowed. Bedbugs, water bugs, and roaches swarmed throughout the building. Tim paused for a mere second when suddenly a chill entered his body.

"Take me to your room, Tim," she whispered.

His legs ached with each step. The flush of embarrassment became a chill.

Pete sat behind his desk, listening to police radio calls. He didn't even bother to acknowledge Tim.

"We should use the stairs," Tim said, guiding Cecelia to the stairway door.

"Why not use the elevator?" Cecelia pointed toward the elevator doors just opening.

No one was on the elevator, and no one was waiting, giving him an eerie premonition. Tim had avoided using the elevator since the deaths.

Tim felt Cecelia let loose his hand and walk toward the elevator as if beckoned by it. He followed.

Chapter Thirty

Cecelia scented the blood. The walls and the floor had been showered with blood. She touched the walls of the elevator, running her fingertips along the surface, cursing the pine odor that had been used to bury the sweetness of blood. Cecelia muttered to herself.

"Are you all right?" Tim asked.

He stood partly in and partly outside the elevator, his clever eyes looking so full of fear.

"What floor do I push?" she asked.

Tim's long legs moved onto the elevator and he punched a button. She did not notice what floor and didn't care, for when the doors shut and the elevator began to rise, she felt faint and rested herself against the back wall. Her toes wiggled against the darkly stained floor.

"People died here, Tim."

She noticed the surprise on his face.

"I can smell it." She smiled and looked at Tim, still full of blood.

"Maybe we should go someplace else," he said, and the doors opened.

He reached for the lobby button, but Cecelia walked off the elevator before he could push. He followed.

She found herself in a beige hall pitted with dark brown doors. She didn't like the odors here. The odor of mortal food mingled with rubbish, vomit, paint, urine, and sex. Funny, she thought, they would try so hard to cover the blood, and now there was barely a hint of cleanser.

"We have to be real quiet," he said.

"Why?" she asked, passing a room from which heavy metal blasted.

He looked shy and then said, "My mom's home."

"Oh," she said. "You're taking me home to Mother."

He winced.

"We're both young, Tim, and need to live with an older, wiser person, or we would make fatal mistakes. I live with Sade."

"Who the hell is Sade?"

"A man you met, but cannot remember."

"Is that the guy whose bill we kept putting our drinks on that night? You called him something else."

"Louis."

"Yeah. Hey, is this going to cause a problem? I

mean, I like you and everything, but I don't want no shit from your old man."

"My ancient old man likes you, Tim. You have young blood. Why are we standing in the hall? Is this where you live?" Her hand touched the brown door at which they had stopped.

"Shit! Don't knock or anything. Listen . . ." he said.

"Let me in." With one hand on the door and the other on Tim's chest, she stepped back slightly to allow him to unlock the door.

Tim did as she had commanded.

Chapter Thirty-one

Wil gave up on feeding his hunger and started for home. Too many distractions kept him from trusting his timing. If he grabbed someone and they were able to scream, he might be caught.

At the end of the corner a family, consisting of a mother, father, and two siblings, stood around an old car. He guessed the car to be a '60s Buick. As he got closer, he could see the pile of bedding on the backseat. The children were no more than a year apart in age, and he guessed them to be four and five. However, which was four and which was five he couldn't tell. He couldn't even make out their sexes. Both had shoulder-length dirty-blond hair, but so did Dad. Both wore green pajama leggings and bright yellow sweatshirts that were more than a size too large. As soon as he noticed Wil, the whiny child stuck out his or her tongue, and Wil stuck his tongue out in return. The mother, a thin nervous woman, smacked the child across the cheek, causing hysterical tears.

As Wil got closer, he could smell alcohol and noticed an empty whiskey bottle standing on the curb. The father lifted the quiet child and placed him or her onto the front seat of the car. Snot rolled over the quivering lips of the crying child, and the child lapped at it. Wil pulled a clean tissue out of his pocket and knelt to offer it to the child. The child quieted into a sniffle.

"He don't take nothin' from strangers," said the mother.

"I'm sorry, but it's only a tissue. I think the little man needs one." Will smiled at the boy, who quickly stuck out his tongue and retrieved it before his mother could notice. This caused Wil to break out into laughter.

"You think it's funny we gotta live this way?" asked the woman.

"No. It's just that . . ." Wil couldn't squeal on the kid. "Maybe I could help in some way." Still on his knees, Wil could see the boy's eyes shimmer in the dim light of the lamppost.

"Move on, buddy." The father had stepped in front of his son.

With those exhaled words, Wil knew who had been drinking. Wil stood. He thought about offering some money for food for the children, but knew they'd never get the benefit.

"He was offering Pete somethin'," the woman said.

"Just a tissue," said Wil, holding it up so the man could see.

"What the fuck you think we need with snot-rags? Give us a few bucks and we can buy our own. Hell, if you have enough money, might even sell Pete to you."

The mother grabbed the child's hand and pulled him closer to her.

"Fuckin' bitch wanted to keep the kids. I tell her sell them. Can get a pretty penny for white babies. They're getting kind of old now, dammit. Put the boys out to work soon, washing cars, whatever." He leered at his wife.

"They're too young to do anything but go to school," Wil said.

"The boys are getting their schooling right here from us, don't you worry about that. So are you gonna throw us a few bucks or move on?"

The child that had been in the car was back on the curbside. His eyes were dark and small, similar to his mother's. A fading bruise marred his chin.

"The boy fall?" asked Wil.

Surprised, the father turned to look at his son.

"Yeah, fell right into my hand, didn't you, boy?"

"I don't think we should be tellin' no strangers about what goes on in the family, Barry." The woman eyed Wil suspiciously.

No doubt this family had already tussled with Social Services, thought Wil.

"Why do you keep the boys?" Wil asked. "Look at the way you have them living. Give them up to a good family, and let them live normal lives."

"We're as normal as they come," responded Barry. "Just we don't have the cash to give them every fiddle and fart they want. Someone give us enough money, though, and I might be able to talk the bitch into giving one up. That's an idea. I can hang a sign on the car, 'Kids for sale to the highest bidder.' Auction them off, that's what we can do."

The woman pulled the boy closer into her bowed legs. The other child had wandered into the street.

When the father noticed, he ran over and picked up the child, yelling, "My little gold mine's running off on me." He lifted the child onto his shoulders and roared, "Kid for sale. Slightly damaged." He reached up to chuck the child under the chin. Frightened, the boy hunched over and grasped tightly onto his father's bull neck. "Whadda you say, Rose, we set them up on the roof of the car and hang signs from their necks. Think we'll get some takers? Sure we will."

The boy's pajama bottom had risen up his legs, revealing a broad welt on the lower portion of his thin right leg.

"You beat your boy?" Wil asked.

"Pete, I ever lay a hand on you?"

"No, I'm talking about the child sitting on your shoulders."

The father swung the boy off his shoulders and threw the child onto the front seat of the car.

"You bastard. You think you gonna make trouble for us?"

"Barry, let's get out of here. We don't have to stay here. We can find someplace else to sleep."

"What if I like it here?" he yelled at the woman.

"Maybe we can talk this out," said Wil. "There's an all-night liquor store two blocks from here. Why don't we wander down there and pick up something for our parched throats before making a deal?"

"Don't, Barry."

"You want one or both the boys?" Barry asked Wil.

"Maybe both. But I don't think we should discuss this in front of the children."

"You some perv?" Barry raised his hands. "I don't want to know about it if you are. Don't know if the bitch would go for givin' up the both of them. But as easy as she did with these two, she could get herself a new pair in no time. Ain't I right, baby?" He reached out for her cheek, but she drew her head back before he could make contact.

"We'll be back, ma'am. Take care of the boys," Wil said. If she were smart she wouldn't wait here for her man to return. She would wait, though; frightened and without money, she'd feel she had no other choice.

Barry staggered and Wil walked down the block.

"Where the hell is this store? I don't remember any all-night liquor store around here."

Wil didn't answer; he kept walking, leading Barry around a corner and out of sight of his children.

"Freakin' dark down here," Barry said.

"The kids throw rocks at the streetlights. Don't worry, though, the store's just up ahead."

"You serious about taking those kids off my hands? I can't stand the little bastards. The bitch is the one who wanted them. Me, I would've flushed them down the toilet."

In a flash, Wil managed to squeeze the father's vocal chords and drag him into a familiar alley. He and Keith had killed many times in this vicinity and liked the seclusion and darkness here.

Whiskey and salami, thought Wil after he had sated himself on Barry's blood. Not a combination he would have chosen, but hell, he felt he had accomplished two objectives.

Would the mother go to the police and give a description of him? If she did, would they believe her or assume the asshole had run off? And what would the woman do with the two boys? Was she smart enough to get her life in order? He could stuff both adults' bodies in the trunk of the Buick and drive them out of town to a deserted waterway. The boys would need care. He could drop them at a police station or church.

Wil started back for the woman. When he turned the corner he was amazed to see that the car was gone. Either she had decided to leave Barry behind, or was driving around looking for him. He'd have to dispose of Barry's body in the local bay. But he still felt bothered by the fact that this woman had the boys. What if she met another Barry? Stupid bitch. He smiled. Maybe he didn't give her enough credit. After all, she didn't wait around to have her blood sucked away. He'd keep an eye out for her, though, just in case.

Wil waited another half hour, watching the streets for the Buick. When she hadn't come back by then, he turned in the direction of the alley to dispose of the remains of his meal.

Chapter Thirty-two

Tim knew his way around the dark living room. He hoped Cecelia wouldn't need to use the bathroom. That would be way too close to his mother's bedroom. Shit, he hoped Cecelia could be quiet while making love. He couldn't clearly remember the details of the last time they had been together. The last thing he needed was a screaming lover. He held her hand tightly, not wanting her to roam free through the apartment. She seemed content to hold his hand and be led.

"I have to make the bed," he said, pointing at the couch. "Mom's got someone in the bedroom. If you're uncomfortable with the idea someone's liable to interrupt us, I can understand. The john's kind of a weirdo." He hesitated. "You sure you don't want to go back to your place? I mean, if you think that guy you live with don't mind."

"Sade mind? You're so naïve."

Tim prickled at the comment. Letting go of her hand, he began to remove the cushions from the sofa.

"You always sleep here?" she asked.

"Better than the street."

Gently he opened out the bed. A stale yellowed sheet covered the mattress. He hoped she'd be unable to tell in the dark.

"Want a blanket or sheet?"

Her head was silhouetted by the backdrop of the moon's light. He could see her shake her head.

Damn, she and he were the same age. Why should he feel so nervous?

She started to shed her long gold dress, lifting it up over her legs and trunk as if she were removing her skin. Tim stood fixated on the white, shapely body she revealed to him. She paused before pulling the dress over her head. Nothing but body. Faceless. Her breasts thrust forward. Her midriff stretched over ribs barely visible. Her rounded belly leading to blond curls covering her pubis. The legs long, satiny, white. Fear now replaced with lust drove Tim to undo his jeans, slipping them down and letting them fall on the floor. Without untying his laces, he pulled his feet free from the sneakers. In unison both pulled off the last of their clothes, he dropping his T-shirt to the floor, she neatly draping the golden dress over a nearby chair.

She beckoned him to her, and he went, his

feet feeling the brittleness of the dirty stiff carpet, his hands sweating in anticipation, his
breath measured, his penis painfully hard. He
stopped when she lifted her right hand.

Cecelia slowly lowered herself to her knees.
Her blond hair glinted in the moonlight as she
lowered her head.

Chapter Thirty-three

Later, with Tim lying on top of her, Cecelia heard him groan as he came and she contracted her muscles to drain his semen from him. The warm flow shot deep inside her, relieving her fears about becoming pregnant. Yes, he is the one to father Liliana. Hungry, she sunk her fangs into his shoulder, drawing out fresh blood. He moaned in a trance that caused him to lie limply atop Cecelia, allowing her to feast.

His blood tasted rich and coppery and spiced by the salt of his skin.

The edge of a doubt intruded upon her feast. What if she were not pregnant? What if she needed him to fuck her again?

Cecelia pulled back her head, capturing a drop or two of blood with her tongue.

Freed from her embrace, Tim rolled off Cecelia and seemed to sink into a pleasant dream. His smile indicated satisfaction. The flutter of his eyelids let her know he was in deep sleep, his breathing peaceful and lips ever so slightly parted.

She chuckled to herself, thinking how she had outwitted Sade. He couldn't stop Liliana from being born. Cecelia knew that when her womb was full, he would never dare destroy the only person he had truly loved. He'll have to accept the baby, she thought. He'll have to agree to be a father to the child, and as the child grew, he would become more fond of the baby. How Cecelia would then run amock! No one to control her whims and wishes. She was glad now that she had not drained Tim dry. She hungered, but knew she could have him again whenever she wanted.

Cecelia glanced over at Tim's rising and falling chest and saw a tiny spot move in the stillness of the moonlight. Her right hand touched his barren chest, allowing her index fingernail to nudge the tiny object closer for a better view.

A small wingless insect with a flattened oval body. As she peered closer, she counted the segments. Six stout legs carried the insect quickly away from her fingernail. Pale brown in color, the insect rested at the curve of Tim's hip. All three were quiet for several minutes, then she saw the pale brown change into a red brown.

"Competition," she said.

Tim turned his head to her.

"What'd you say?"

"Can you smell it? Their glands give off a sweet sickly smell. That's how they communicate."

Tim's lids opened wider. A puzzled expression wrinkled his brow.

"They depend on blood for their complete nutrition and they only come out in darkened rooms. It lowers its beak and pierces the flesh to suck up blood. A male will eat his own weight, but a female eats twice her weight. She needs the extra blood for spawning her young." Cecelia thought a moment and realized she too should be taking in more food.

"Oh, shit, you've seen a bedbug. Where the hell is it?" Tim jerked his trunk up off the sheet, searching for the bug.

Cecelia lowered two fingernails onto Tim's hip and picked up the insect.

"He's mine," she whispered, bringing the insect close to her lips. "I don't share." She placed the anthropod between her front teeth and bit down. A slight pinkish color stained her front tooth.

"Oh, my God, that's disgusting. What'd you do that for?" Repulsed, Tim hopped out of bed.

"I'm hungry, Tim. Famished." She stared into his eyes. "Please come back and feed me."

"Hey, there's a couple bagels in the fridge. Maybe some fruit."

"No, no. I'm not hungry for food. No, I'm hungry for you. Come back and lie next to me."

He knelt on the mattress. "I wish you wouldn't

192

do things like that. Not sexy to see a woman eating bugs."

"What should I be eating, Tim? Suggest something."

And you drink this burning liquor like
   your life
Your life which you drink like an eau-de-
   vie . . .

          Zone
          Guillaume Apollinaire

Chapter Thirty-four

"First of all, *monsieur*, you must learn to be social," said Sade.

"I have to entertain people before I kill them?"

"Monsieur Bridgewater, you must win the victim over, and it is not always *nécessaire* to kill. Although I would admit that there is an *extraordinaire* rush to overeating occasionally, but *monsieur*, at the rate you feed, you would eventually empty the world of our prey. We shouldn't do that."

Sade pushed Keith's wheelchair down Embarcadero. Not many people roamed the street at that late hour, but both men kept their conversation to hushed tones.

"By now you should know the orgasmic thrill of mixing feeding with sex," Sade went on.

Keith twisted around in his chair to look up at Sade.

"Ah, *non*! I cannot believe that you have not taken advantage of the charms you now possess as a vampire."

"What the hell are you talking about?"

"Sit back, *monsieur*. You look so uncomfortable twisted around like a *bretzel*. We vampires are sought after, dreamed about, and glorified in dark tales. Non-vampires bleed each other, seeking the special high that only we can truly attain. *Oui*, we are lucky creatures."

"Dammit, Mr. Sade, remember I can't walk. I don't feel lucky."

"We will work on the mishap that occurred at your birth. I mean, of course, at the time of your crossing over into becoming a vampire." Sade certainly believed that Keith's birth as an infant was truly a mishap, but avoided confrontation with the man.

"What went wrong?"

"I don't know, *monsieur*. Certainly my mother-in-law had no intention of making you a vampire. You would not have been worth the risk."

"But my son was. Wasn't he?"

"*Oui*, although even he might have been passed over, except for the misunderstanding she and I had. She always challenged me. I do not miss the wicked woman."

They moved on in silence, Sade ruing the fact that he had agreed to turn his mother-in-law into a vampire and knowing that Keith had no fond memories of the woman. A bond seemed to be growing between the two men. How distraught Marie would be to find out that Keith still existed. And how much more pain it would cause her to know that Sade intended to seek to make Keith whole. The fantasy bubbled into a smile upon Sade's lips.

Two male youths clinked bottles as their drunken feet struggled down the street.

"Now there's easy prey," Keith mumbled.

"Ack, *monsieur,* they are drinking cheap beer, and who knows what other rotgut is flowing through their veins. If I offered you a choice between the finest champagne or a cheap sparkling wine, which would you chose?"

"I drink beer, nothing stronger. Maybe wine if my son wants us both to look classy. I kind of like the beer they're drinking, matter of fact."

"Et tu bois cet alcool brûlant comme ta vie
Ta vie que tu bois comme une eau-de-vie . . ."

"What does blood taste like to you, *monsieur?*"

"Like blood. Doesn't remind me of anything else."

"Does not each victim have his or her own essence? A tingle on the tongue, a spicy burn passing down the throat. A shimmer of herbs pressing against the palate. A bitter rush sparking an involuntary wince. *Ou* a sublime sweetness that the taste buds savor."

"You get all that when you feed?"

"Ah, Monsieur Bridgewater, when you were

mortal you probably feasted on fast food and TV dinners. *Alors* it is time to expand your appetite so that you are not just feeding, but savoring."

The two youths were laughing. After each swig of beer some liquid slid down their chins, causing more laughter.

Sade sensed Keith's body stiffening as the two passed.

"*Sang-froid.* Self-control, *monsieur.*"

Sade heard Keith take in a deep breath. The man's nose sounded clogged. No wonder the poor soul couldn't think clearly, Sade thought.

"But I need blood to regain the use of my legs."

"No, *monsieur,* you need to gain control over yourself. You need to feed slowly, taste what is passing through your lips."

"It's blood. I mean, if I were still mortal, I'd think it was disgusting."

"You are no longer mortal, *monsieur,* and must learn to take joy in the variety of blood that exists."

"All I know is I get this need to drink. It's like being lost in the desert without any water supply."

"So, *monsieur,* you drink too much too fast to quiet the thirst. *Non.* Have you ever tasted one for whom you felt strongly?"

"What do you mean?"

"A woman perhaps. A stunning woman for whom you lust and possibly love."

"There was this hooker who lived next door. Man, she had a bod. Almost thought I'd like to fuck her, except by the time I was finished imbibing, she didn't look so good."

"That is what I mean, *monsieur*. If you had taken the time to win her over, taken the time to sip her blood, not gulp it down, then you would have noticed her flavor."

"Each has a different flavor?"

"*Oui*. A blend of the body chemistry and the foods mortals ingest make for a *délicieuse variété*."

"Is this like wine? Do the years count? Say an old broad versus a young one?"

"That is body chemistry. An older *anneé* does not have to taste like vinegar. Some mellow and become richer."

"Hard to believe. I notice you go for the younger ones. Don't see you hanging out with any retirees."

"*Vrai. Mais* I have finally learned my lesson. No longer will I be blindly seduced by youth."

"You're going to start hitting geriatric centers?" Keith twisted around to smirk up at Sade.

"Someone who needs my help as you do, *monsieur*, should not exhibit such a rowdy sense of humor."

For a few minutes they walked in silence.

"Sorry, Mr. Sade, but when do we get to eat?"

"Tonight, not at all. We merely enjoy the crispness of the salty air and the *plaisir* of each other's company."

Sade patted Keith on top of the head. Keith responded with a drawn-out groan.

Chapter Thirty-five

Jerry awakened to the sound of the squeaky floor just outside the bedroom door. Shit, that kid's back again, he thought. Just as he was about to turn toward Sondra to complain, he saw the bedroom door open.

An apparition walked in under the glow of the burning candles Sondra had set around the room. She had never mentioned a daughter. On the other hand, Sondra hadn't bothered to mention the son.

The girl bloomed with youth. The blond curls fell into her eyes so that she looked as if she were peeking at him. Blue, he recognized. The shine in her eyes almost prevented him from studying the rest of her body. But as she came closer, the smell of blood grew stronger. Her lips seemed tinged with a bloody crust. She used her tongue to wet down the dry, scaly tissue. And there was another odor. One almost rancid, but it wavered in the air, almost present, but not quite.

She had the whitest skin he had ever seen. The light in the room caught her body in elaborate shades, making the girl look unreal.

Hell, it could be a dream, Jerry thought. A damn good one if it was.

No smile curved her lips. No blemish mocked her flesh. A waxen image with folds and crevices and a bush of blond locks jumbled together covering her pubis. The hair looked matted and sweaty, but her touch told him that she was not hot. Instead, she chilled his belly with her touch. In incredible response, his flaccid penis rose into an erection. Her hand moved down to hold him. Her fingers wrapped around his aching member caused him to quickly suck in air through his mouth. He thought for a brief moment he had tasted the remains of blood and waste. He shook his head. He didn't know whether a dream had overtaken his senses or whether the real thing was climbing on top of him.

Her skin felt smooth to his touch, her legs long. He wondered how she tasted. His hand drifted to her bush, and he forced his fingers through the encrusted hairs. Not long ago she had been with someone else.

Jerry reached over to the night table and picked up a sealed packet. He tore the top off and dug out the condom. The girl laughed quietly when she saw what he was about to do, but did not stop him from placing the sheath over his erection. If he were dreaming this up, she would have been a virgin. Nah, he thought, one of Sondra's whelps.

The girl's fingers teased the exposed skin on his balls and rubbed each against her crotch.

He stifled a moan and checked briefly to make sure Sondra still slept. When he turned back to the girl, he could have sworn that a twisted malice had lit up her eyes behind the ribbons of curls. But her eyes were so clouded by her fine hair that he could not be sure of what he saw.

She scooted down and nipped lightly at his balls, her teeth feeling like sharp, prickly needles. Jerry reached down, placing his hands on her cheeks, resting his thumbs on each side of her nose and drawing her back up to a seated position.

He tried to recall whether he had enough cash to pay for this bit of extra ass. No matter, he'd leave an IOU if necessary. Steady customers should get extra privileges once in a while. He flicked his hips up toward the girl, wanting her to get on with the scene.

She wetted both her hands and rubbed them on the latex condom; then she inserted his erection inside her.

Tight, he thought, remembering the loose fit of Sondra.

The girl's hips traveled up and down. Eventually she leaned forward and presented her nipples to Jerry. He reached out his tongue, but she kept her nipples just out of reach, teasing and inflaming his cock. Gradually she settled her breasts against his, rubbing flesh on flesh slowly in a circular motion.

On the verge of orgasm Jerry attempted to slow the girl down. He wanted to take his time. Her tongue lapped at his shoulder, his neck; pausing, she sighed. He knew that the nip she had taken in his neck had to have drawn blood, but he didn't care as long as she kept pumping.

Orgasm came in a shiver of pleasure, and the room drifted far away from him. Sucking and lapping noises resounded in his ears. A coldness chilled his spine. A malaise swept his body. The smell of blood rendered his senses into a state of euphoria. And it all felt right. Perfect. Sublime.

Chapter Thirty-six

Tim woke up to female screams. He shook his head to relieve the groggy feeling. As he stumbled from the bed, the screams became more hysterical. He found his way to his mother's bedroom door and swung it open. His naked mother knelt on the bed, growing hoarse with each scream.

"What the hell's wrong, Mom?" He moved closer to the bed. The john lay still, his eyes staring up at the ceiling. Blood tinged the side of the man's neck a jagged red. "What happened to him? What did you do?"

He grabbed his mother's arms and shook her until she quieted into soft sobs.

"What happened? Did he try to hurt you? Mom, you have to tell me what happened, please." He climbed over the john's body to embrace his mother. She sobbed into his shoulder. When she pulled away, a faint pinkish tinge colored the tip of her nose. He hadn't noticed it earlier, but in all the confusion the stain was so faint that he could have missed it.

"He's dead, Tim. He's dead. I thought he was lying there thinking, and I shook him, and he's so cold."

Tim rested fingertips on a presumed pulse point and felt nothing.

"His eyes, Tim. I couldn't see them until I sat up. Look at them. He's dead, Tim. What are we going to do? There's some blood on his pillowcase. How could it have happened?"

He saw his mother's eyes finally focus on him.

"My God!" She pulled away from Tim. "You have blood on your shoulder."

A heavy pounding sounded on their front door. Zombielike, Tim stepped down on the carpet and headed for the sound. Without dressing or checking who was at the door, Tim opened it.

"Your neighbors next door called down to complain about a racket you and your mother were making. At eight in the morning, what are you doing, having a party? Where the hell is your mother?" Pete pushed the door farther back so that he could enter. "Go put some clothes on, kid."

Sondra stood in the bedroom doorway in a peach dressing robe that shimmered in the morning light like true polyester satin. She shivered and wrapped her arms around herself.

"What the hell are you and your son doing?" Pete asked.

Sondra shook her head.

"You got a man in there? Having some kind of wild party, is that it? Got news for you, the asshole's gotta go. I don't have the time to coddle irate neighbors."

Pete walked across the room and pushed past Sondra to enter the bedroom.

"Holy shit! What the hell . . . ?"

Tim had followed Pete to the bedroom doorway. Sondra pulled away from her son and rushed into the bathroom, closing the door behind her.

Pete swung around.

"You do this, kid? He try to hurt your mom?"

Tim turned and went back into the living room. He looked at the bed. Two people had been sleeping on that yellowed sheet. It was easy for him to tell by the rumples and folds. Where had she gone? What had she done? And why do this to him and his family?

"I'm going downstairs to call the cops," said Pete. "I'd be thinking fast if I were you, kid. Between this and the elevator murders, this shithole is going to be buzzing with the law." He slapped Tim on the back. "Hey, kid, get some clothes on before the apartment becomes a three-ring circus. Not that it hasn't always been a circus here—just used to be able to contain it better."

Pete walked to the front door and stopped.

"Sondra, get out here and see to your kid for a change. You hear me!"

No response. Pete shook his head and crossed the apartment's threshold.

Part Two

It seems to me, lulled by the monotonous
  thuds,
That somewhere a casket is being nailed in
  great haste.
For whom? Yesterday it was summer; here
  is autumn!
This mysterious noise sounds like a depar-
  ture.

Song of Autumn
Charles Baudelaire

Chapter Thirty-seven

Cecelia stood at a newsstand in Union Square, reading a front-page article.

"Tim Lambert's trial is scheduled to begin this morning. He is charged with one count of murder, but is suspected of killing two others in his residential hotel six months ago. His mother swears she heard nothing during the night of Jerry Eagle's murder, even though the victim had been sleeping next to her in the same bed when he was killed. Sondra Lambert acknowledges that her son and Mr. Eagle were not on good terms at the time of the murder.

"Tim Lambert claims he brought home a young female the night of the murder and swears that she must have had something to do with it. However, the woman has not come forward and . . ."

And she's not going to, honey.

"Hey, punkette, you with the Yul Brynner and the safety pin holding your earlobe on."

Cecelia looked up from the newspaper to see a thin ghoulish man with sunken eyes and missing teeth staring at her.

"You buying that paper or just trying to learn how to read?"

The newsstand man's greasy hair was cut unevenly, as if he had taken the time to do it himself after having several beers. She couldn't tell what color his eyes were, but noticed the yellowish tinge to his skin.

"Come on, give it over." The man extended a limp hand to her and she flung the paper in his face.

"Little bitch, I outta . . ."

"You okay, Sardi?"

A chubby man in a business suit had approached the stand and was now attempting to calm the owner.

Cecelia turned away and continued down the block.

She had shaved her head the day after she had been impregnated by Tim. He had rattled on about her beautiful golden hair and blue eyes and had given an excellent description of her. Excellent enough that a few days later, when a drawing of her appeared in the newspaper, she had decided to change the color of her eyes to brown by wearing contact lenses. She'd added a tattoo of a fire-breathing skeleton, now spread across her back, and also tiny rose tattoos drifting down from her shoulders onto her upper arms. But over the months, the child she bore took its own toll on her beauty. Even though she still fed heartily on mortals, her arms and legs seemed to have withered. Her stomach had blown up suddenly when she was in her fifth month; prior to that, the only noticeable change she had exhibited was a paler complexion.

No longer did she sleep inside her casket. Afraid that if she allowed death to take her over completely the baby would die, she now got through her days on meditative trances that gave some peace, but did not replenish like the deepness of death.

She and Sade had both stopped going to the club, she because she feared identification and he because of his special interest in his newest protegé, Keith. Somehow, Keith did not seem to blend in with the youthful crowd at the club.

She had managed to easily avoid Sade over the past month, perhaps because he wanted to avoid her. He hadn't seen her blossoming stomach as yet, and she dreaded what would happen when he did. However, she'd be able to weather his tirade, and she guessed he might hold her in awe if he believed she carried the beloved Liliana. Liliana's voice had stopped haunting Cecelia, for which Cecelia was glad. Three more months and she would be completely free of Liliana. Sade would take care of the baby and make sure the infant Liliana had everything she needed.

As she walked by a store window, she caught a glimpse of herself. The sight did not make her happy. This was not how she had planned on living her vampire life when she first agreed to join Sade. Although she hardly ever thought about her family, her pregnancy made her wish her mother were around. She had even been tempted to return home to give birth, but what a lot of explaining she'd have to do! Her mother would get all soft and want to take care of the newborn, even try to turn Cecelia into a mother.

No, Sade would see to it that they hired the best nanny from England. Cecelia would be allowed to decorate one small room at their Victorian house into a nursery. She knew which room that would be: the one closest to her own. The nanny would have to sleep in one of the bedrooms down the hall with a little monitor on her night table, since Cecelia planned on taking long rests once the pregnancy had ended.

This wasn't quite the life she had initially planned with Sade. No matter, he would eventually cater to both her and the baby. He wouldn't be able to help himself.

Chapter Thirty-eight

"I got to put up with dumb-ass kids ruining the walls in the hallways. Not to mention the one who decided to kill his mother's client," Pete shouted at Sondra. "I should throw you out."

"I'm one of the only people you have that pays the rent on time. You can't get rid of me, and if you try, I'll sic a lawyer on you."

Wil had just entered the lobby.

"How you doing, Sondra?"

"Oh, Wil, I just complained to Pete about the graffiti on the wall outside my apartment."

"I'll give you a rag and some cleaner, and you can try erasing that shit they use," Pete shouted.

"Personally, I think the place could do with a new paint job," Wil said, and looked at Sondra for agreement.

"When there's a new paint job, then you'll be

paying a new higher rent, smart-aleck," said Pete.

"Least you could do is whitewash the wall," said Sondra.

"Least you could have done is properly potty-trained the kid so he wouldn't have grown up to be a killer," retorted Pete.

Sondra swept her arm across the front desk, knocking papers, books, and ashtrays onto the floor. Pete barely rescued his coffee cup with an astonished-looking Tweety Bird character painted on it.

"I want that wall cleaned up now," she raged. "I don't want to hear another fucking excuse, or there'll be another murder in this building."

"Take it easy, Sondra." Wil placed his right arm around her shoulders.

"You threatening me now?" said Pete. "You hear her, Wil? She says she's going to kill me. You're a witness."

"I don't think she meant it, Pete. Let's go upstairs, Sondra, and you can show me the damage the kids did outside your door."

Tears streamed down her face.

"Tim didn't kill anyone," she cried. "Jerry must've died in his sleep. Maybe he was dead already after we'd fucked. Hell, he couldn't get enough that night. Maybe it was a heart condition from overexertion."

"That why two thirds of his blood had seeped out of him?" asked Pete. "He bled to death. That freakin' son of yours was playing vampire, that's what. That's why the john and Tim were smeared with blood."

"That wasn't Jerry's blood on Tim. It was Tim's own blood. My son fell victim to whatever attacked Jerry."

"Sondra, you know Pete won't do anything for you," said Wil. "I'll come up with you and maybe paint the wall myself. Okay?"

Sondra allowed Will to usher her onto the elevator on which Wil's father had killed two people.

When Wil first heard about the john's death, he had immediately thought the killer to be his father and had therefore kept quiet. But when he saw the sketch of the woman Tim had claimed to have brought home, he knew Cecelia had to be the killer.

"Tim's not holding up too well in prison. I went to see him today." Sondra paused a moment and took a giant gulp. She had been trying to keep herself under control, but was starting to fall apart. "He's like a little boy again. Tears come to his eyes when I have to leave. I want to wrap him in my arms and take him home with me. Instead, I tell him they'll find the real murderer before he comes to trial. But I know they're not looking for anyone else. They've stopped looking for the girl he brought home. They think he's lying. He's not lying, is he, Wil? My baby boy couldn't kill anybody. There has to be an answer for all that missing blood; after all, there would have been huge stains on the sheet and pillowcase if he had tried to bleed Jerry. And all they found was a small stain on the pillowcase. Maybe Jerry was anemic or something."

The doors of the elevator opened, and both

she and Wil got off. When they arrived at her door, Wil saw a stick man with a noose around his neck painted on the wall. The same kind of stick figure one would make when playing the child's game "hangman." Under the figure were written two filthy limericks.

"Can't clean this stuff off, I'm afraid," he said. "Tell you what, I'll pick up some white paint when I'm out and cover over all this garbage."

"I can't sleep, Wil. Suppose whoever killed Jerry comes back?"

"I think your son brought the killer home with him, and she won't be coming back."

"How do you know?"

He ignored the question. "I'd offer to change apartments, but my dad and I are only living in one room. We can't afford anything else."

"Live with me."

"Excuse me, Sondra?" Wil stepped back several paces from the woman.

"I'm not used to living alone. Matter of fact, I don't ever remembering living alone. Always had my family or a good friend to live with. You're a good friend, Wil. You could always go up and see your father and I'd continue paying the rent here."

"And what happens when one of your johns stays over?"

"Never again. No client of mine will get more than a couple of hours from me."

"Listen, I have to go upstairs and see my father." Wil turned away.

"Wait. Will you think about living with me?"

Wil shook his head and turned to look back at

her. "No. And it isn't just my father that prevents me from living with you."

Sondra's eyes hardened and her face grimaced unattractively under the fluorescent hallway lighting. She spat at his shoes, unlocked the door, and left Wil alone in the hallway.

Chapter Thirty-nine

Wil found his father whistling while smoothing out the tight jeans that he'd need help putting on.

"Great, you're back. Would you mind helping me pick out a shirt for tonight?"

"Where the hell do you and Sade go?"

"You said you never wanted to discuss Mr. Sade or know what we do, and I've always honored that. Think red's a bit too loud for a man my age?"

"That's not even your shirt. It's mine. What have you been doing? Going through my clothes?"

"Ran out of clean clothes and . . . my friend hates fringes of dirt around a cuff or yellow stains under the arms or . . ."

"Send him down to the corner laundry, then, instead of stealing my things."

"It's not stealing, Wil. It's sharing. By the way, I'm going to pick out a coffin for myself tomorrow. If I see anything for you, do you want me to pick one up?"

"Coffin! Where the hell are you going to put a coffin?"

"We could get rid of the bed and replace it with two coffins."

"Dad, you think sleeping in a coffin is going to bring back the use of your legs?"

"Nah, I wish it were true. I'm just becoming comfortable with myself and who I am."

Wil sat down on the bed. "I don't believe this. You and Sade are practicing New Age self-help."

"Nothing New Age about having confidence in yourself. I was thinking about having the coffin lined with something other than satin. Something more manly. What do you suggest?"

"Try denim."

Keith shook his head. "Not very comfortable against my cheek."

"You sleep on your back, Dad."

"What if I should . . ."

"Roll over? That would be difficult with you dead and all."

"Don't want denim. Maybe I could get a denim satin color. Dead bodies always look so vulnerable surrounded by all that satin."

"What makes them vulnerable is the fact that they're dead. By the way, how do you plan on getting this coffin home? They make deliveries, or is Sade going to carry it here on his back?"

"Mr. Sade has minions that do his bidding."

"And I bet some of that's rubbed off on you."

His father sniffed the air. He wheeled his chair over to the front door.

"Menstrual blood," Keith said. "But we're surrounded by old men. Think someone has a daughter visiting. Prostitute would make sure she didn't bleed while working. Unless someone other than us is into blood."

Keith pulled open the door. A girl of about thirteen or fourteen stood in the hall, a backpack at her feet. She squinted in Keith's direction, obviously needing the aid of eyeglasses. Her black tank top and jeans seemed to be covered with white cat hair.

Wil walked closer to the door to have a better view. She wore no makeup, and her orange hair clashed with the paleness of her complexion. She carried a zipped-up canvas sack that seemed to have something living inside, judging by the undulations of the material and the meowing coming from the bag.

"Hello, young lady," Keith said.

Wil could already sense his father tensing. He knew the hunger his father felt.

"Hi." She answered with a single word that sounded flat and unfriendly.

"You looking for someone?" Wil asked.

"Waiting."

"Why wait in the hall when you can come in here and sit down?" Keith offered.

Wil hadn't realized how hungry he was until he found himself silently urging the girl to come in. He knew it was wrong. This place was hardly the right one for murder. Too many had already been committed. Another murder, and either the place would be closed down or everyone in it would be put under arrest.

"Because I want to," the girl said.

Dad was making progress with the kid, thought Wil; she had actually responded with four words.

She delicately put down the canvas bag and unzipped it to allow the head of a white furry cat to stick out.

"Pete doesn't allow pets," Keith said. "If he sees you with that cat, he'll throw you out."

The girl sucked on her bottom lip and leaned against the door opposite Keith's and Wil's.

"You're waiting for Sammy," Keith went on. "He sometimes stays away for days at a time. We think he gets arrested once in a while or thrown into the hospital for a couple of days. Have you seen him around lately, Wil?"

"Dad, close the door."

"If you should change your mind, little one, knock on our door. We'll be glad to take care of you." Keith slowly closed the door, leaving the girl outside.

Wil's thirst pained his insides.

"Why don't we take a walk, Dad?"

"We haven't gone for a father-son stroll in a long time. But we really don't have far to go. Don't think anyone would miss her. Sammy probably doesn't even know she's here. And what's he going to complain about? He tries to keep a lower profile than we do."

Wil's mouth was watering so badly he could barely speak.

"What do we do with the body, Dad?"

"Shove it out the window."

His father's retort came as a cold slap.

"You crazy old man. We couldn't allow her body to be found anywhere near here. We'd have to find a way to smuggle her body out."

"Cut her up and stick her in the cat bag and set the cat free."

"Your answers are so simplistic."

"Mr. Sade wouldn't kill the child. He'd take enough to slake his hunger. He'd have her knocking on the door pleading to come in."

A knock came at the door, and the scent had remained constant.

Wil opened the door this time.

"Either of you know this girl?" Pete stood with both his hands spread on the sides of his waist.

The girl had zipped up the cat bag, but the cat wasn't being cooperative, for the mewling noise had become louder.

"There's no damn pets allowed here, you two know that." Pete hadn't needed an answer to his question. He obviously assumed the two troublemakers were bringing in reinforcements. "The cat has to go. The girl can stay long as the cat goes."

"I'll take her around to the pound tomorrow," the girl said, moving past Wil with the canvas bag in hand and wearing the backpack. She entered Keith's and Wil's room, thereby accepting Keith's earlier invitation.

"It'd better be gone tomorrow," said Pete. "Don't allow no pets here."

"Just murders," mumbled Keith.

"You tell your old man to watch what he says, Wil, or none of you will be here after tomorrow."

Wil closed the door.

"How long have you been waiting for Sammy, dear?" asked Keith.

The girl shrugged her shoulders.

"Does he expect you?"

Wil saw a strange warmth grow in his father's eyes. His father was turning to mush in front of this girl.

"Kinda."

"Did you actually tell him you were coming or did someone else?"

"He's my godfather."

"Godfather. Have you ever met Sammy?"

The girl shook her head.

"How do you know Sammy wants you to visit?"

"Don't. He's the only person I know here in San Francisco."

"Bet you didn't expect his place to look like this." Keith smiled warmly.

The girl shook her head.

"Wil, do we have any food or drink to offer the young lady?"

"No, and I'm not leaving to get any."

Keith turned his head to Wil and tsked. Wil folded his arms and stood his ground.

"My son here ran away from home when he was younger. Know what? I wasn't angry when I finally found him. Instead, I was so happy I could barely stop hugging him."

Bullshit, thought Wil. When he was brought

home, he got his ass whipped. He couldn't remember any hug.

"Bet your parents are missing you. And maybe you're just a bit sorry you ran away. It doesn't look so nice when you see parts of San Francisco up close. Where are you from?"

"Oklahoma."

"Small town?"

She nodded.

Wil felt the hunger pains grow. His hands shook, and his skin prickled with excitement. How could his father contain the thirst? Since when had he taken up counseling runaways?

"I bet your kitty ain't too happy about the trip." Keith pointed toward the canvas bag, which was one continuous movement.

"Claire. She's a house cat. Never goes outdoors." She unzipped the bag far enough so that the cat could pop out her head.

Keith reached out to pat the cat, but pulled away when the cat let out a loud screech. His father's newfound talent was limited.

"Dad, we can't keep her in the room." Wil felt that he would be the one to lose control if she didn't leave.

"I doubt she wants to stay. I'm Keith, and this is my son Wil. Your name?"

"Florence."

"How pretty. You don't want to stay in this place, do you, Florence?"

She shook her head.

"How did you get here?"

"Amtrak."

"We'd be happy to take you back to the station."

"Don't have enough money for the ticket back home."

"We do, don't we, Wil?"

"Hell, I don't even know how much it would cost," Wil said.

"We have enough, don't worry. We could go now, unless you'd like to stop for a bite to eat first."

"I am hungry."

"Wil and I know the perfect place. Lots of young people hang out there."

"Where?" asked Wil.

"My son has such a poor memory. Why don't you rest the backpack on my lap, and you can carry your precious Claire."

"We're walking farther away from the station, aren't we? I remember coming from the opposite direction, and there were lots of places to eat on the way."

"Nothing like this restaurant. And the weather is so nice for a walk."

Wil pushed his father.

"I have to get myself one of those automatic wheelchairs that I can handle instead of being such a burden on my son." He smiled at Florence, and she gave him a half smile.

"Sure there's restaurant down this way?" she asked, looking around.

"My son and I used to eat down here often."

Wil recognized the deserted streets and the empty warehouses. A dark alley was just ahead: the very same alley in which he had disposed of

Barry many months earlier. For a fleeting
moment he wondered whatever happened to the
kids. If he walked to the end of the block and
turned a corner, would he see the Buick parked
at the curb? He didn't have long to ponder the
fates of Barry's brood, for his father had already
reached out a hand to touch Florence's arm,
guiding her in the midst of conversation toward
the alley.

Beauty of women, their weakness, and
    those pale hands
Which often do good and can do ill.

Sagesse
Paul Verlaine

Chapter Forty

"I'm proud of what I did today." Keith found that his arm muscles were stronger than they had been several months before. Now he could gain a good momentum in the wheelchair, and had learned how to direct the chair himself.

"*Oui?* What is it that you have done, *monsieur?*"

"I quietly took a life. Sort of quietly. It wasn't until the very last moment that she put up a fight. She trusted me, Mr. Sade."

"Ah! And how old was this woman you speak of?"

"Thirteen, fourteen. Although she could have looked younger than her real age."

"Or she may have been younger than she looked."

"Why can't you give me encouragement

instead of putting what I do down in some way?"

"*Moi?* I do my best to train you, *monsieur*. It would not be good to give a pat on the back without correcting *une erreur. En plus*, you are good at complimenting yourself. I'm sure your own arm reaches far enough behind your back."

Sade patted Keith on the head while Keith silently cringed.

"That boy who lives in your building, *monsieur*. Tim, I believe."

"Isn't my building and he's not living there anymore."

"*Il est accusé de meutre, n'est-ce pas?* Oh, I am sorry, *monsieur*. I forgot that your ear for languages is abominable. He is . . . How do you say it in English?"

"He's in jail, accused of murder. And I can't help it if I don't have an ear for languages. Just because your last precious protégée did is no reason to make fun of me. You can sure remember the correct English word when you want to." Keith had started the evening in an up mood, but Sade had quickly canceled out the joy of the day.

"How is he taking to prison life, *monsieur*?"

"Who the hell would enjoy it?" Keith said. He heard Sade sigh. "His mother visits, I guess. I don't go near the police. Although I must say that sketch of Tim's alibi looked a lot like Cecelia. Is that what worries you?"

"*Une jeune fille* sometimes does things that she and the rest of us will regret later."

"Think she turned him into a vampire?" Keith asked.

"*L'enfant* is *très* unpredictable."

"Then why the hell don't you get rid of her? What is it you have to do? Chop her head off? Stake her through the heart? Burn her to a crisp?"

"*Monsieur,* you are an unforgiving man. Cecelia still bruises your ego, even though it has been long since you have seen her, *n'est-ce pas*?"

"Don't ever want to see her again. She took my Tim. I had plans for the boy. You know, like you have all those admirers who follow you around and let you suck from their necks? That's what Tim was going to be for me."

"*Oui, et vraiment* you would have been a superior master for the boy. Do you believe Cecelia has turned him?"

Keith shrugged his shoulders. "What's he going to start doing? Biting the guards on the neck?"

"He will not understand his hunger and will bloat from the internal decay that will grow inside him day by day. Just as happened to *moi.* I fear *une tragédie* may be repeating itself, *monsieur,* and I have been the force to set it into motion.

"Another lesson for you, Monsieur Bridgewater. Never trust the sweetness of a woman's breath or the softness of her touch. Her adoring eyes will always lie. Acquaint yourself not with her soft side. Women are capable of ripping our souls apart.

*"Beauté des femmes, leur faiblesse, et ces
  mains pâles
Qui font souvent le bien et peuvent tout le
  mal."*

"Whatever you said, I probably agree with it."
Keith wrinkled his brow wisely.

Sade burst into laughter.

I am the wound and the blade!
I am the slap and the cheek,
I am the limbs and the wheel,
The victim and the executioner!

Heautontimouroumenos
Charles Baudelaire

Chapter Forty-one

Keith sat, awed by the number of whips and crops hanging on the wall. Sade stood next to him and ticked away the names of each. They all seemed to jumble up inside Keith's brain. The fringe whip, the rubber whip, the signal whip, and what was each used for?

"And the braided cat, *monsieur*." Sade reached over to the wall and pulled away a whip with braided thongs. "This gives more of a thud." Sade illustrated by hitting the vacant armrest on Keith's chair. "Than, say, the flat-tressed whip. Are you following, *monsieur*?"

"Avidly." Keith sat taller in his chair. What the hell was he doing in this room? Mr. Sade had suggested visiting this brothel. Initially Keith, feeling rather at a loss, had hesitated, but Sade had promised to see that the invalid would be satisfied. At this point, Keith wasn't sure what Sade had in mind.

"*Peut-être* you are a paddle man, Monsieur Bridgewater."

Keith winced at the sound of his name. Certainly he was interested in learning the gentlemanly sport, but didn't want everyone to know. Two women waited by the door. He didn't know whether they were ready to flee or were there to prevent his escape. However, each wore leather swatches to cover their privates and nothing but chains circling their breasts.

Sade threw the whip to the floor and walked two paces to stand in front of a row of paddles. He selected one and turned toward Keith.

"This is the studded paddle. Do not fear the studs, *monsieur,* for you cannot cut anyone with these rounded studs." Sade glanced at the wall once more. "Ah! An historic piece. New to the collection, mistress?"

The black-haired woman nodded.

Sade hung the studded paddle back on the wall and pulled down the newest acqusition.

"By the feel and the heft, mistress, would I be correct to guess that it is an original?"

Another nod.

"*Vraiment* priceless. This, *monsieur,* was used on the backside of disobedient Scot schoolboys. It is called a tawse. Would you like to feel it?" Sade extended the slitted strap to Keith.

"Should have had this when Wil was little." Keith chuckled and accepted Sade's offering.

"There are riding crops, canes, both rattan and synthetic. *Paradis, n'est ce pas?*"

"I guess so. I've never tried playing around with this stuff." Keith held the tawse in the palm of his right hand.

Sade beckoned the women to come closer. As they moved, Keith could hear the clinking of the light chains they wore. The redhead, Keith thought. That would be the one he would select. The innocence in her brown eyes belied the punishment she deserved. Keith slapped the leather against the side of his chair. Was it his imagination, or did the sound of the smack cause a shiver to shake the redhead's body? A single tattoo blemished her midriff; otherwise her skin seemed flawless. For now, he thought. The redhead's body curved full around the hips, with a tiny waist leading to two luscious, full breasts. Keith had been hard before, but not like this. Hell, Sade kept talking about heightened sexual pleasure as a vampire, and Keith hadn't tried it out yet. Damn, he hadn't tried it out for years before he became a vampire.

"Now, *monsieur*, you may think that you will be forced to choose between these capable young *femmes*. *Mais non*, you shall be gifted with both. It will be my *plaisir*, Monsieur Bridgewater, for all that we have been through together. I must ask you, though, to choose the instrument you wish to be used."

Keith liked the feel of the tawse, but had heard many stories about caning.

"Can I choose two?"

"*Oui*, one for each of your partners."

Keith pointed at the rattan cane, and Sade immediately removed it from the wall. Keith noted the excitement that seemed to be building not only in himself but also in Sade. The man seemed hurried, anxious to start the entertainment. Keith figured it was about time he try this S and M business. He had always been a gentleman before, but now he would rip.

"Mesdames."

At Sade's command the women started to undress Keith. He guessed he would need some swinging room. The areas they touched tingled in ways he could barely remember. The redhead allowed her breasts to sway at Keith's eye level. Occasionally one breast would skim the side of his cheek or the tip of his nose. She smelled clean, fresh, and full of blood. Blood that he would be releasing within a matter of minutes.

Naked, Keith looked down to see that he had an ample erection. Sade lifted Keith out of the wheelchair and carried him to a strange-looking table. The top was covered in black leather. Real leather, he thought, after being laid nose-down upon it. A hump in the center raised the lower half of his body, bringing his bottom high. But wait; lying down would certainly hinder his swing. The women's hands made him forget momentarily until he felt straps tighten around his wrists.

"How the hell can I beat these two if I'm bound?"

"Ah, Monsieur Bridgewater, you are mistaken. *Mesdames* will be using the selection you made to transform your flesh into a palette of pain and pleasure."

"I didn't agree to any of this."

"*Mais* you complained to me about your impotency *et* we seemed to have made a good start in the cure." Sade lightly touched the tip of Keith's erection, which pressed against the slope of the leather hump. "In France in the eighteenth century the cure most used by gentlemen was flagellation. Men who could not make love to their wives chose to be beaten in bordellos to achieve release. Even Rousseau, poor man, wrote of his fantasies involving flagellation, although he never actually had the courage to satisfy his desires.

"You, *monsieur,* are no coward. A few marks on your toughened skin will not deter you from obtaining the pleasure you deserve."

Keith turned his head from left to right and saw that there was a woman on each side of him. The redhead held the rattan cane. The dark-haired woman held the tawse. And Sade. He had taken a seat and was now masturbating.

And as the tawse and cane struck, Keith heard Sade gleefully cry out:

"Je suis la plaie et le couteau!
Je suis le soufflet et la joue!
Je suis les membres et la roue,
Et la victime et le bourreau!"

The dead, the poor dead, know deep grief. . . .

The Warm-Hearted Servant
Charles Baudelaire

Chapter Forty-two

Cecelia sat vigil on the floor of Sade's room. His coffin stood proud on the altar table. The fine linens, silks, and leathers of Sade's wardrobe hung from a bar that connected two walls. The old Victorian closet had been too small for such a fine and varied wardrobe.

When Sade had returned earlier, he had been in a riotous mood. Instead of skulking up the stairs, he stomped and sang old bawdy songs. Cecelia could hear the melodies clearly, even if the words were muffled and slurred. A drunken Sade. Drunk on blood, she thought, remembering how he would react when he overfed. Not the right time, she decided, to tell him about Liliana's return. Instead she fell into a meditative trance and feared, when she awoke, that Sade had already left the house. But a quick peek beneath the lid of his casket relieved her anxiety.

How would she tell him? A quick look at her middle reminded her that words wouldn't be necessary. Her fingers fumbled with a ribbon Liliana had long ago put in Cecelia's hair. Pink velvet that shined from age. She wondered whether she should tie the ribbon into a pretty bow around her neck or simply hand it to Louis. She knew the material still smelled of Liliana. Liliana had taken it out of her own hair to smarten up Cecelia's coiffure for a school dance. How old was the ribbon? Could Louis have given it to his favorite niece long before Cecelia existed?

Cecelia dared not approach him without some powerful talisman to quiet his spirit. She kissed the velvet and tied the ribbon around her neck in the back, so that at first glance the velvet was a simple band against her pale flesh. Cecelia wore the dress in which she had been buried, a silly, frilly garment spotted with a stranger's blood. She had left the dress unfastened so that she could fit comfortably inside it. With her legs crossed in front of her, she waited.

Hadn't he been sleeping too long? There were no clocks in the house. Louis and she sensed the passing of time. The time to sleep, when lethargy replaced the energy of the predator. And the time to forage. Dusk darkened the room. She would wait for moonlight to brighten once again the marble table before her. She marveled at how Louis could place things to show them at their best. Whether inanimate or living, he could shine a brilliance on an inner . . . not beauty, she thought, but an inner whisper of transparency. The object or person was more than itself. He gave history to everything and everyone.

Yet the question remained whether she had read Louis's history correctly. Did his love for Liliana overcome his ego to the point where he would accept Cecelia's disobedience?

The lid of the casket flew open, giving Cecelia a start. The baby inside her seemed to tumble for a moment, frightened, seeking retreat. Cecelia did not bother to place a hand on her stomach. The baby would have to learn to deal with its own cowardice.

Louis did not rise. Cecelia refused to budge. The baby kicked so hard that she could see the thin material covering her belly rise and fall.

"Leave the room, Cecelia. I cannot deal with you now." Sade's voice sounded weary.

How strange, she thought, after such a long rest.

"I am not alone, Louis."

"Ah, I know, *ma petite*."

"The other person will not permit me to retreat."

"The other is only a phantom of your mind."

"My distended belly is real. Come see it. But you sense the child. You know of whom I am talking."

"Laissez-moi tranquille!"

His shout seemed to freeze the baby in place,

for suddenly the movements inside her womb stopped.

"No, Louis." Awkwardly, she began to bring herself to her feet. The baby seemed heavier than she had remembered. "We must face each other now. You have sensed the baby for months. That's why you've avoided me." Cecelia realized finally that he feared her and the baby more than she could ever fear Sade.

"What will you do for the pretty baby when she is born?" Cecelia asked. "Do you think she'll look just like you remember her? Did you get to hold her often when she was a baby? Now you'll be able to, because she'll be yours."

"The babe belongs to you and that foolish boy." Sade sat up in the coffin and sprang out of it in a swift movement. "What did you do to the boy, *ma petite*?"

"His fate is not my fault. I merely fed my hunger the way you taught me."

"Is he a vampire?"

"Would I disobey you?"

"Answer truthfully, Cecelia. The boy could be suffering great torment."

"The only torment or grief he feels is that of being human instead of being one of us."

"*Les morts, les pauvres morts, ont de grandes douleurs. . . .*"

"Not me. Not anymore. I have what I want."

"A hold over *moi*? *Détrompe-toi!* No one can do that anymore. And Liliana would never assist you in trying."

She watched Sade take several steps toward

her, his clothes still soiled and wrinkled from the debauchery of the previous night.

"You look disgusting and weak." Cecelia stood her ground even when she saw the hardness fill his eyes. She wasn't alone. She stood with Liliana, no matter how much he would deny it. "She moves! Feel her, Louis. She wants your acknowledgment."

Cecelia reached out for his hand, and he stepped back.

"Retreating?" She could crush his bravado beneath the weight of her fruitful body.

"The babe is only a bastard child produced by you and that boy. A bastard that will suffer for your eagerness to flex your pitiful strength."

"Pitiful? No, awesome. I see it on your face. I hear it in your voice. This child you already love, or you would have physically lashed out at me, not wasted your time with words. Louis, give in to desire and touch my belly. Fill the baby with joy."

Again Cecelia attempted to reach out for Sade's hand. This time he allowed her hand to intertwine with his.

"*Ma petite fille*, why must you taunt me? I have given you whatever you desire, except for freedom. Only one may rule, *fille*. Expel the babe before you cause it and myself great pain."

"No, Louis." She brought her belly close to his hand, but he refused to touch the mound. "She's here, close to you. Why can't you be happy?"

"Happy for a life that doesn't wish to exist?"

"If she didn't want to come back, why is she here in my womb?"

"Oblivion is frightening. When you cannot see in the dark, when you cannot make out your own hand, fear replaces sane thoughts. Liliana needed time to adjust."

Cecelia gave a broad grin.

" 'Needed.' Then you acknowledge the baby inside me."

"This can only cause *ma* Liliana greater terror. She will be lost again and you, *ma petite fille,* will be the cause of it. I will always remember that." He pulled his hand from her.

Chapter Forty-three

Edwina winked at Keith as he passed through the lobby. Her skinny body posed seductively for him. He might throw up, he thought. After the redhead and the black-haired mistress, his libido was exhausted. And eighty-year-old Edwina did nothing to bring back any sexual urge.

After his sleep, his bruised body had returned to normal. Not his legs, though. He had had a hell of an orgasm. Three, to be exact. Feeling especially macho, Keith winked back at Edwina. Not that she had any chance in the world of experiencing his prowess, but he did feel generous.

Sondra walked through the front entrance, her makeup tear-stained, her walk wobbly, her clothes cheap and lurid.

"You okay, honey?" asked Edwina.

"They're trying to say that Tim committed all three murders. They don't even have solid proof that he killed Jerry."

"Makes the cops' job easier," Edwina said.

"Even if my son didn't kill anyone?"

"Who the hell else would have had the strength to overcome them?" asked Keith.

"You're just sour because you can't walk," chastised Edwina.

"My boy was nice to you, Mr. Bridgewater. I happen to know he took you places."

"For money," he shouted back.

"Why are you lying, Mr. Bridgewater? You do know the girl my son took home with him, don't you? You told the police you didn't recognize the sketch, but you do know who she is. Whatever I may have done to you, please don't take it out on my son."

"Your son murdered at least one person, Sondra. I can't change that. How could a little girl like he described overcome that bear you took to bed with you? Nope, you fucked up with that kid, Sondra, and I feel sorry for both of you, but don't try to drag me into something that doesn't concern me."

"You introduced him to that club."

"It was a lark. I took him there once. Personally, I thought it was a bore. He went back, though. He asked to go."

"No, he said you asked him to take you."

"Killers lie, Sondra."

"Shut up, you old asshole!" Edwina said, hurrying over to Sondra, who had broken into a loud sob.

"You're a wicked man, Bridgewater. Crueler than me," said Pete from behind the desk.

Keith wondered what had happened to his feel-good mood. Seeing Sondra seated on the old "Danish modern" couch, sobbing on Edwina's shoulder, certainly made him feel lousy. He had been on the defensive, scared someone would find him out. He reminded himself that they weren't smart enough or gullible enough to believe in vampires.

"Can't you take her upstairs or something? Nobody wants to watch her bawling in the lobby," Pete whined.

"I'll go with her upstairs. See that she gets back into her apartment all right," said Keith.

"You!" shouted Edwina.

She was a tiny old lady, and Keith was amazed by her lung capacity.

"Yeah, me. I owe her an apology anyway."

"And I had such a high opinion of you, Bridgewater." Pete shook his head.

Sondra could make his life miserable by constantly bringing his name up to the police and the lawyer assigned to her son's case. She had the ability to cast serious suspicion on him. Whether they chose to believe her or not, it would be better to have her thinking he was sympathetic. Killing her would only attract more attention, and might even help to get Tim released. He had already gone over that scenario. He was beginning to understand the prudence Wil and Sade preached.

"I'm taking her upstairs," Edwina declared.

"No," Sondra said. "Keith is right. We need to talk. Let him take me upstairs."

Sondra dried her eyes on the tissue Edwina had supplied and took a deep breath.

"If you press the elevator button, Keith, I'll join you."

Keith pressed the button and felt the heat of Sondra's body come closer. She smelled of cigarettes even though she didn't smoke. Could it possibly be from the visiting room of the prison, or did the officials there enforce the no-smoking rules? The smell of her body was strong today. Sweat, salty tears, and a hint of some cortisone cream.

The doors opened, and he waited for her to step in. She did so quickly, and pressed the floor button only when he was safely inside. The doors closed.

"I mean it, Sondra, I'm sorry for what I said. Tim's a decent kid. I don't know why I suddenly lashed out like that. Maybe because I'm so vulnerable myself. Sometimes scares me to get on the elevator, especially with someone I don't know or recognize."

"Tim never harmed you, did he?"

"No. He helped me on occasion."

The doors opened, and again he waited while she stepped off. She kept hold of the elevator door until he cleared the threshold. As they moved down the hall, Keith could see the stick figure drawn on the wall next to the door to her apartment.

"Pete should take care of that, and if he doesn't then I'll have Wil clean it off."

"No. I'm afraid that like you, I wasn't thinking clearly the other day. I'm sure Wil would rather not have anything to do with me."

Sondra unlocked the door, opened it, and invited Keith in.

Inside the apartment Keith tried to maneuver around the multitude of objects on the floor, mostly clothes and candy wrappers. The smell of stale air almost made Keith feel at home.

"Can I get you something, Keith? Water? I'm afraid I don't keep much food in the house anymore. Tim was the big eater."

"Water would be good." Keith had learned this to be the answer mortals expected: *See, I'm like you. I drink.* He forgot which number this was in Sade's lessons manual.

Sondra let the tap water run for several seconds before filling up a questionably clean glass. Keith felt lucky that he wasn't thirsty for water. She carried the glass to him. Kneeling in front of him, she handed over the glass.

"Tim needs to find that girl, Keith. I'd do anything if you would help." Sondra began to open the buttons on her blouse.

Keith wondered whether last night's performance was only luck.

Sondra slipped the blouse off her shoulders. He noticed that the black lace of the bra barely covered her nipples. Couldn't hurt to give it a try, he thought.

Chapter Forty-four

"I need your help, Wil."

"Listen, Dad, lately you've been getting all your help from the master, remember? Why don't you call up the Marquis de Sade for some assistance?"

"I can't. First of all, he doesn't have a telephone, and secondly, I don't think he'd approve."

"Approve of what?"

"I had sex with Sondra."

Wil sat down on the bed. "Where?"

"Her apartment."

"Is she alive?" Wil closed his eyes.

"I got overzealous. She was on my lap, facing me, her legs resting on each of the arms of the wheelchair. She slipped me inside her and started moving up and down. She thought . . ." Keith looked down at his lap. "She made the moves. She undid my pants. She put her lips next to my right ear. I could feel her cheek rubbing against mine. I could smell her. She babbled on about helping Tim. I knew she was trying to use me to get her son off. I tried to listen, thinking that would take my mind off the blood racing through her body. But after a while I couldn't hear her anymore. There was only the smell of her body." Keith shrugged.

"What did you do with the body?"

"Son, that's why I'm here. I need your help."

"Not anymore, Dad. You have someone else who can help you." Wil lay back on the bed, trying not to envision the limp body his father had left behind.

"There's an additional problem, son."

"Son? Do I know you?"

"No time for games. Pete and Edwina saw me take Sondra up on the elevator."

"Another body on the elevator." Wil smirked.

"No! I wouldn't have had sex on the elevator." Wil laughed.

"Listen," Keith said, "after a few days she'll start to smell, and they'll check out her apartment."

"Don't think her son will be missing her before that?"

"Nobody'll care when he starts whining for Mommy. But the odor . . . Either we have to get her out of this place or find some way to eliminate the body. Maybe acid or something." Keith pulled closer to the bed. "I'm your father, son."

"I think this may be a good time to give you your freedom. You never wanted to be my father, so let's disown one another. Matter of fact, you can have this damn room." Wil rolled away from where his father sat and got to his feet on the other side of the bed. "Think I'll start packing." Wil pulled a large duffel bag out of the closet.

"You disappear, and they'll think you did it."

"No one saw me ride up on the elevator with Sondra," Wil said. He opened drawers on the old maple dresser, shoving whatever he could easily grab into his bag.

"I won't cover for you, son."

"Meaning you'll try your damnedest to make people believe I did it. Right, Daddy?"

"Don't waste your time being sarcastic. We should be planning how to get rid of the body."

"I don't do shit for you anymore." Wil went back to the closet and pulled out a suitcase filled with soil.

"Can't take that with you. I need it."

"We both need it. I'm taking some for myself."

"Splitting up like this will only cause problems. We won't be able to work together like we did."

"We haven't hunted together in ages." Wil searched the bottom drawer of the dresser for something to put his share of the soil in.

"I can't take care of that body by myself," Keith said. "I'm disabled. Disabled because I tried to protect you from that wicked woman. I tried to enlist Liliana's and Mr. Sade's help in protecting you."

Mary Ann Mitchell

Wil pulled a large paper bag and several paper clips from the bottom drawer. He spread open the bag and with his right hand shoveled dirt inside.

"Pathetic," Keith went on. "Where the hell you think you're going? I shouldn't even allow you to take any of that dirt with you." He rolled over to where Will knelt and grabbed the paper bag, ripping it, allowing the dirt to pour out onto the floor. "You leave empty-handed. Take nothing with you."

"How do you expect me to survive?"

"The same way you expect me to. Think I'm going to continue sitting around worrying about you?"

"You never have."

"Then let's start out even." Keith took hold of the suitcase and overturned it. "Let's both leave and see what happens without each other and the soil. Think, you idiot! Neither of us wants to go to Hell, and that's where we're headed, unless we stay together and support each other."

"Living with you is Hell." Wil began scooping up fistfuls of dirt and putting them in the bag on top of his clothes.

A loud knock on the door made both men face each other.

"Keith, you in there?"

"That biddy Edwina has the strength of a truck driver," Keith mumbled.

"Keith? Wil? Somebody's got to be in there, I can hear noises. Eyesight's getting bad, but not these ears."

"Answer the door, Wil."

Astonished at his father's request, Wil paused for a moment, then zipped up the duffel.

Edwina persisted in banging on the door.

"Come on, you sour old reprobate, open the door," she called.

"Sour." Keith sneered and opened the door.

" 'Bout time you opened up. Think I was going to slip away like a dainty old lady? You know me better than that, Keith Bridgewater."

"What do you want?" Keith spoke softly, obviously trying to regain his self-control.

"I want to know what happened to Sondra."

"What do you mean?"

"I've been banging on her door, and you know I can really bang, and she hasn't answered."

"She said she was going to sleep."

"Come on, she had to hear me." Edwina poked her head around the door.

"She ain't here. I left her at her door."

"Did you apologize like you said you were going to?"

"None of this is any of your business."

"Somebody's in there with you."

Wil came into Edwina's sight.

"Oh, hi, Wil. How are you doing?"

"Not so good, Edwina."

"I was just having a chat with my son," Keith said, "when you started making that racket. Mind if we go back to our conversation?"

"I think we should check on Sondra," she said.

"You already did, and she's made it clear she doesn't want to be bothered with you," Keith said.

"I'm getting Pete to open her door. She's in a

bad state; shouldn't leave her alone like you did."

"She wanted to be alone, Edwina. Besides, Pete's not going to open the door for you."

"He sure as hell will after I get finished nagging the dude."

"Come in, and I'll tell you what Sondra told me." Keith opened the door wider.

"No! I don't want any part of this," Wil said.

"Then leave." Keith's voice was raspy, hungry.

"What you got the bag for, Wil?" Edwina asked.

Wil realized he was carrying the bag in his left hand. All he had to do was walk around his father, out the door, and never come back.

"I'll walk you downstairs, Edwina," Wil said.

"Like hell . . ." Keith reached out, yanked Edwina into the room, and slammed the door.

Edwina lay sprawled across the tile flooring. Wil dropped his bag and went over to lift her back onto her feet.

"What's gotten into your father, Wil?" she cried. "He gone demented?"

Edwina's whole body shook within Wil's grasp. Her nose began bleeding. Drops of blood fell onto his own hand. Wil's mouth watered and, unable to prevent himself, he brought the drops up to his own mouth and licked the back of his hand clean. Edwina pulled away from Wil, bringing her closer to Keith's wheelchair.

"I think you're both nut jobs. Pete outta throw you two out. And I'll tell him too." Slowing, achingly, she turned herself toward the door. "I'll tell Pete about your disgusting habits and your father's violent temper."

Wil felt the hunger pangs spread through his body. He hadn't fed in two days, and he was at his limit.

"Get out of my way, you peevish old man," she said.

Keith shook his head. "We're not going to let you go, are we, Wil?"

The glint in his father's eyes showed that he knew the agony his son suffered. Edwina turned back to Wil. Blood continued to slide from her nose and over her lips. He saw fear in her eyes, the first time he had ever seen fear in Edwina's eyes. And it wasn't caused by his father. She feared Wil. He moved closer to her. His own reflection would forever be stamped in her eyes. His hand touched the wrinkles on her face, the permed gray hair, finally the blood flowing from her nose. Like scared prey she waited, looking at death, feeling the coldness of death through Wil's fingertips. She had still not grown used to the idea of death. The pallor of her sagging flesh told him this.

"I can make it so easy for you, Edwina. Come into my arms and let me take away the pains and worries that clutter your life." Wil heard his own soft voice and knew he had no right to make his offer. "Get out, Edwina." Wil's sudden command broke the spell.

The woman blinked and turned back to the door.

"Hell, she's not going anywhere," Keith shouted.

Wil lunged at his father, toppling the wheelchair, giving Edwina time to open the door and run. Wil looked over his shoulder at the open door. He and his father should run, he thought. He and his father could be gone long before anyone understood the enormity of what had happened.

"Get the hell off of me, boy. Damn fool, you let her go. Stop her before she can tell anyone."

"She's not exposing us for what we are. You did when you killed on the elevator. She's innocent, Dad. We aren't."

"Suddenly you get guilty and want to confess. We'll both go to Hell whether you repent or not."

Wil shook his head. Repentance no longer had room in his vocabulary. No, he wanted to survive. His instincts gave him no choice.

"We have to leave," Wil said.

"Together?"

"Unless you think Sade is going to jump at the chance to give you shelter."

Wil stood, dragging his father with him. After righting the wheelchair, Wil remembered the open door. Too late. Pete stood at the threshold.

"What the hell you two doing scaring the hell out of Edwina? She's a skinny old scarecrow as it is. You guys have her so jittery she probably lost ten pounds. I certainly know she can be a pain in the ass, but trying to scare her to death isn't going to work. Far as I know, she's got a warrior heart there. Won't stop no matter how much fear you put into her. She's been living in that room of hers for thirty years. I've seen her go through hell and she hung in there.

"What's this filth on the floor? No wonder you guys refuse to let me have a spare key to the room. First thing you two guys did when you moved in was change the lock. Hell of a lot of nerve. Not supposed to do that, you know. Could toss you out for that."

"We're tossing ourselves out, Pete. Dad and I are packing up." Wil pointed to the duffel bag on the floor. "Edwina won't have to worry about us ever again." Wil looked over toward the bureau and saw that his father was trying to pry open the bottom panel of the bureau. When the panel sprang off the bureau, Wil viewed a secret compartment stuffed with cash, both in bills and change.

"Destroying my property. You gotta pay for that," yelled Pete.

"We'll pay the rent we owe, that's all. Goodwill wouldn't accept the shit you've got in this room." Wil took some bills from his own pocket and handed them to Pete.

When the elevator doors opened to the lobby, Wil immediately saw Edwina pacing back and forth. His father hissed at her as he passed her by. In return she raised her thumb to her nose just above the pinkish stain of blood and wiggled her fingers. Edwina seemed to have regained her courage.

Chapter Forty-five

"That woman deserved to be sucked dry. Not that she had much juice left in her anyway."

"Where do we go, Dad? Greyhound bus station?"

"To Mr. Sade's, of course."

"Maybe you do, but not me."

"What're you going to do, sit on some bench in a station and catch the first bus out of town?"

"Good idea, Dad." He began pushing his father along the street.

"Can't do that."

"Why?"

"Because Sade hasn't cured me yet."

"Did you ever think that he may not know how?"

"I figure he'll fumble into it somehow. He's

willing to try everything, and so am I. When you cross the street up ahead, take a right."

"Keep everything in the duffel. I'm taking my chances alone." Wil walked straight ahead, leaving his father ranting on the street corner. He figured he wasn't far from the station, and if he was lucky, there would be a bus waiting for him.

When he reached the end of the block, he heard a commotion coming up from behind him. A slender youth with a bandanna on his head ran past him, carrying their duffel bag. Will looked back to see that his father's wheelchair had gotten caught in a rut in the street.

Old man can't take care of himself, he thought, and set out behind the thief. People on the street gave them a wide berth. Wil caught up easily, sending the kid down to the ground with a flying kick. The youth threw the bag at Wil and got to his feet, but Wil lunged at the thief and caused him to take another spill. Wil straddled the thief's body until he had the kid pressed to the ground.

"That was my father you just robbed," he whispered in the thief's ear.

Wil pressed his hand near the thief's heart. So easy to reach in and pull out the pulsing mass of tissue. But dangerous. People stopped. If they saw blood . . . His fingers dug into the thief's sweatshirt, sliding the material inside the thief's chest. He thought he heard the thief say something, or perhaps it was an intake of air caused by the pain. Wil's hand eased off the thief's chest and traveled down to the man's solar plexus, where he did a quick shove with his palm. Wil looked around at the staring faces. His father sat quietly. Some stranger's hands rested on the handles of the wheelchair. The bag lay to Wil's right. He lifted the duffel and threw it at his father, who caught it on his lap.

Bystanders were asking questions, but he couldn't hear the words. He was so thirsty, and the breathing circle of blood around him couldn't be touched; nor could the dead body that lay beneath him. Shaking like a deprived addict, Wil got to his feet. Bystanders widened the circle they had formed.

"And you complain about me," his father said. He had moved to Wil's side. "Come on, let's get out of here before the police come. Come on, wake up." His father tugged on a pocket of Wil's jeans, leading him back up the block from which Wil had just run.

Wil turned and walked.

"Hey, mister, wait up. I just called the police."

"Don't worry, I saw it all. I saw him pull that bag off the invalid's lap."

"Must have knocked him out good. He ain't moving. Deserved what he got for trying to rip off an old man." Someone reached out and patted Wil on the back.

Wil took hold of his father's wheelchair and quickened his step. When they were twenty feet from the crowd, Keith mumbled almost under his breath, "How come you're a hero when you kill, and me, I'm lower than an ant with a hernia?"

Wil rushed down the block, and was able to

hail a cab at the corner. When Wil opened the cab's door, the driver popped the trunk. Quickly Wil lifted his father out of the chair and into the backseat of the cab. The wheelchair collapsed easily, and he put it away inside the trunk. His father gave an unfamiliar address to the driver, and they sped off.

And, when I am bored with these impious
    farces,
I will lay on him my frail and strong hand;
And my nails, like the nails of harpies,
Will dig a path to his heart.

The Blessing
Charles Baudelaire

Chapter Forty-six

"I'm not getting out of the cab."

"Someone's got to take *me* out, at least. Besides, I'm paying, and this is as far as I'm going." Keith reached into his pants pocket and pulled out some crushed bills. "Keep the change," he said, handing over several bills to the female cab driver.

The driver got out. Keith noticed she had the build of a man, even though her voice sounded high-pitched and sexy. She was tall, a good six-two, and broad-shouldered. She easily whisked the wheelchair from the trunk of the car, set it up, and came around to Keith's side of the cab. He opened the door.

"Used to work in a convalescent home as an aide," she said, reaching out with two large calloused hands to grip Keith's arms.

"Help the lady, son."

A totally unnecessary demand, since in a flash she had Keith comfortably seated in the wheelchair.

"It's all in the leverage," she said. "Your boy getting out here?"

Keith shrugged.

She leaned into the cab and looked directly at Wil.

"He looks shell-shocked. Hey, buddy, I charge rent if you wanta sit in the cab, and it ain't cheap." She snapped her fingers several times.

Wil reached into a pocket of his jeans and pulled out the few bills he had; shoving the money back into his pocket, he used his other hand to open the cab's door and stepped out into the street. A car honked at him, and he almost tripped into the path of a van.

Keith watched the driver of the cab lead his son to the curb. She couldn't get Wil to step up onto the sidewalk, but she obviously felt she had completed her job by simply getting him out of the way of traffic.

After the cab pulled away, Keith yanked his son onto the sidewalk.

"I'm not going into that house," Wil said.

"I always thought it looked kinda cute. All those little doodads decorating the porch. Needs a bit of a paint job. Wouldn't let anyone paint my house pink. And such a pink."

"It goes with the blue doodads."

Keith and Wil smiled at each other.

"I'm serious," Wil went on. "I'm not setting

foot in Sade's home. Did once before, and I promised myself I never would again."

"How do you know it's Mr. Sade's . . . Oh, all right, it is, but you have to stay somewhere. The worst thing you could do is sit around a bus station or even a train station. The cops will be looking for you. You did leave that damned thief dead, didn't you?"

"You feel better now that I'm the one who blew our cover?"

"I feel better that son of a bitch is dead. Goldilocks lives here."

"What the hell would I care if she does?"

"Never see her, though. I think she avoids me. I don't think she likes me."

"Neither do I."

"This is the safest place for you to be right now."

"I'm surprised Sade allowed you to find out where he lives."

"We had a bit of a shindig here. He even cooked me a meal once. Told me he would teach me the use of proper manners at the dinner table. Damn, the meal was good."

"What did he do, serve jugs of blood?"

"No, regular food like we used to eat, except I've never had artichokes before. They were good but a pain in the butt to eat. You roam the streets and you'll get picked up by the cops. If you're thirsty now, think what it would feel like in jail. Have a hard time slurping your blood there. Blow up like a balloon, Sade told me. If you don't get any blood, the gases inside from the slow decay will bloat you up. Come on, take me up those steps, and I'll ring the bell. It won't be so bad."

Wil lifted his father's wheelchair up the steps.

"I'm surprised he didn't give you the key," Wil said, "seeing that you two are such good buddies."

"I tried to get the key. I think the only reason he took me home was because he was embarrassed by my manners. He figured he'd smarten me up first before hanging out at the fancy restaurants. He likes good food, and this town is full of super restaurants." Keith rang the bell.

To Wil's surprise, Sade opened the door almost immediately.

"Get in!" Sade hurried the two men into the inner hall. "I have told you before, Monsieur Bridgewater, that I do not want you loitering on my porch."

"Wasn't. Just waiting for you to answer the bell. And you're pretty quick." Keith had to raise his voice above the sound of a booming overture. "Maybe you could turn it down." Keith found himself screaming over a light *glissando* of violins.

"Why, *monsieur,* is your son here?"

Sade glared at Keith, who spun his wheelchair around and entered the first doorway to which he could gain admittance. The shabby appearance of the room amazed Keith, who had only been in the kitchen and the basement of the house. Beanbag chairs didn't seem appropriate for any room in Sade's house. And the carpet must have been older than Sade himself.

Quenched

"I believe your son is fearful of leaving the safety of the vestibule, *monsieur*. Perhaps he would be happier in his own home."

"We don't have one," Keith said.

"Monsieur Bridgewater, there are many confusions in my life. Please do not add to them. You live in some *résidence, n'est-ce pas?*"

"Not anymore. Tell him, Dad." Wil had appeared in the doorway just behind Sade.

"My son killed a man in the street today. We can't go back; someone's liable to recognize him."

"I did not expect such impetuosity from you, Wil. From your father, yes. A brutal man, your father. One who does not think about consequences."

"That's exactly why we can't go back to our room," Wil said.

"You mean *ton père* . . . *Mais non*, I do not want to hear an explanation, for I am sure it is appalling."

"Mr. Sade, you promised to help me," Keith said. "I've done everything the way you say, and nothing has helped these legs. If only you could give me the cure, my son and I would leave you alone."

"There are several problems presented here, *monsieur*. First, the home soil."

Keith unzipped the duffel bag, reached in, and pulled out a fistful of soil.

"*Oui*. You have no . . . box to sleep in."

"You did promise to take me around to find a casket. Maybe we can pick up two."

"They don't have half-price sales at funeral parlors, *monsieur*."

"I have the cash to pay for them." Keith dropped the soil back inside the bag and pulled out a handful of money.

"*Un magicien*. You amuse me, *monsieur*. And you are lucky that you do." Sade turned to Wil. "On the other hand, Wil does not have your skills at entertaining me. What is it you can do, Wil, to earn your stay? Ah, we did make an attempt once before, but such a lot of tension in the room eliminated any of the joy we might have felt from our meeting."

"You set me on fire."

"Merely lighter fluid. If I had been serious, I would have used a much stronger igniter. Maybe we can start again. This time without the burden of satisfying a malevolent *sorcière*."

"No more," answered Wil.

"My son's retired from the profession," Keith said.

"*Grâce à* your experience with Marie. *C'est tragique* that she should have ruined the sport for you."

"Son, you go out onto the streets and cops will pick you right up," Keith told Wil. "Tell him about your experience as a vampire in jail, Mr. Sade. Tell how horrible and bloated you were. And you must have stunk too."

Keith watched Sade pull himself to full height. The sleeves of Sade's peasant shirt were rolled up to his elbows. The denim jeans were cut full for relaxing, and his bare feet were a gypsum color that contrasted with the dark stain of the wood floor.

"You are very lucky, *monsieur*, that at this

moment in time I need a diversion. Very lucky."
Sade turned away from both men.

"*Et, quand je m'ennuierai de ces farces
 impies,*
Je poserai sur lui ma frêle et forte main;
Et mes ongles, pareils aux ongles des harpies,
*Sauront jusqu'à son coeur se frayer un
 chemin.*"

"There he goes with the French again. I think
he does it on purpose so he can say things
behind my back," said Keith.

Chapter Forty-seven

His father and Sade had invited him down to the basement, but Wil refused to join them. Instead, he roamed the house, finding nooks and crannies that hadn't been dusted in years. Old spider-egg sacks clung to many corners of the rooms. This was certainly not in any way like Sade's former home. Except for possibly the basement, where he could imagine instruments of torture were stored.

"That's Louis's room."

Wil looked over his shoulder and saw the pregnant Cecelia. Her bald head shone under the ceiling light, her scrawny arms rested atop the bulge of her pregnancy, and her face seemed paler, shadows slipping under her eyes and indenting her cheeks.

"He's been careless. Doesn't lock the door as he used to in the other house."

Wil tried the door, but it was locked.

"I guess my visit a month ago smartened him up," she said. "It's so unnerving to wake up from the dead and find someone sitting near your coffin. Makes a vampire realize how vulnerable he or she is."

"Anyone would feel vulnerable around you. Whose baby? Tim's?"

"Do you care?"

"You killed that john Sondra had with her, didn't you? Why? You put Tim at risk. You could have left the apartment and found prey on the streets."

"He was so convenient and thankful, I believe, considering what he had lying next to him."

"You know Tim is in jail."

Cecelia nodded and walked toward Wil.

"But he has his mother," she said.

Wil shifted away from the locked door, uncomfortable with the knowledge that both Tim and Cecelia had been made orphans by his and his father's hungers.

"I wonder why Louis decided to lock the door now." She shrugged her shoulders. "I can still get in. This door is nothing to pull down."

"Why haven't you?"

"Attempted to get rid of Louis? Bad idea. I would be unable to raise my hand to him, since he created me. You're lucky the vampire who made you is dead and you're free."

"Sade's death won't make you free. You'll still need the taste of blood. Freedom is true death."

"Not what Liliana told me."

"Liliana?"

"She's in here," Cecelia whispered, patting her stomach. "I'm bringing her back to keep Sade company."

"He asked you to do that?"

"I just told you. She did. Two more months and she'll be born."

Wil thought about how much further along she looked in her pregnancy. She had difficulty walking, and he couldn't imagine how she climbed in and out of her coffin. The nails on her fingers were blackened. The whites of her eyes were clouded with a grayish-blue that was speckled with broken blood vessels. She reached out a hand to steady her balance.

"Why are you here?" she asked. "Did you break in? I didn't hear any alarm go off."

"I was invited in, sort of, by Sade."

Wil wondered whether he should grab hold of her before she fell. A gasp spilled out from between her lips.

"Do you want me to get Sade?" he asked. "He's down in the basement with my father."

"No, but I may need you to deliver Liliana."

"You said you were seven months gone."

"I don't know how long it takes for a half-vampire baby to gestate. I doubt you do." Her body wavered. Her lips seemed covered with a white foam that instantly dried.

"I'm getting Sade."

"Don't leave me!" she screamed. "Help me birth Liliana."

"I don't know anything about normal births, never mind how to deliver what you're having."

"I'm having a baby, Wil. A girl child. A girl for Louis to fawn over and coddle and take to bed as he did me. And she'll teach him. The lessons will break his heart, but he'll persist in loving her. My room is over there, Wil." She pointed. "Help me to get in there now."

Wil walked over to Cecelia and took her arm. The weight of her body surprised him, but he scooped her up and carried her to the room she had indicated.

Inside, a white coffin sat on the floor, covered with dust. She hadn't been resting. To his right was a thin scroll of material that seemed to be an exercise mat.

"Stretch out the mat for me, Wil."

When she seemed capable of standing on her own, he moved to the mat and unrolled it. The top half kept springing back up.

"Hold my hands, Wil."

He touched her fingers, and a blackened nail fell into the palm of his hand. Slowly she lowered herself down onto the mat.

"Have you been drinking blood?" he asked.

"As much as I can kill."

He turned away from her and headed for the door.

"There's no one that I want present except for you." She screamed and let the top half of her body fall back down. The rolled portion of the mat pushed against the midpoint of her back.

Wil rushed over and spread the mat flat on the floor so that she would be comfortable. Her right hand grabbed his shirt.

"She'll kill me to be born." Fear made her lips tremble and her eyes widened. "I'm her nemesis, Wil." Again she screamed.

She let go of his shirt and reached down to grab the gray silk skirt on which a dark stain was spreading. Wil pulled the skirt up to her waist. Blood turned her porcelain legs scarlet. Instead of spreading her legs to allow the baby to be born, Cecelia's body was folding into a fetal position.

"Cecelia, you're scared." So am I, he thought. "You have to open your legs and help push the baby out."

"She'll kill me, Wil! She's ripping my insides apart. Louis told me that vampire babies kill their mothers."

"But this baby is part mortal, Cecelia. Remember that. It's just trying to be born." Gently Wil managed to straighten and spread her legs.

"This isn't how mortals are born. The blood. The blood. There's too much blood."

"Push, Cecelia, get this thing out of you."

Wild-eyed, Cecelia comprehended his words and worked at expelling the baby she had fought so hard to produce.

Her screams filled the room with echoes. As the baby's head pulled from Cecelia, it caught its breath in loud hisses. Not a baby's sound, but a dark creature's pitiful complaint. Wil reached for the head, but hesitated when the baby brayed loudly. Cecelia was right; this was not a mortal baby. The scum-filled eyes opened slowly, revealing a shiny pulsating glaze of liquid that appeared to focus on him. A bloody tongue sprang out of the baby's mouth. The tongue had been chewed raw.

"Keep pushing, Cecelia," he yelled, wanting her to be rid of the monster.

A perfectly formed trunk with exquisitely delicate appendages slid into his hands. The baby hissed as he pulled her away from Cecelia. Cecelia drew herself up into a seated position. Wil immediately hid the baby from her view, but he need not have worried. Cecelia did not ask or look for the baby. Instead, she spread her hands through the blood and picked apart the placenta. Bringing her hands up to her mouth, she fed herself the bits of tissue, licking the drippings that flowed down her forearms with her tongue. Her translucent skin revealed veins that wallowed in her sagging flesh.

Trembling, Wil laid the baby on a small Chinese silk rug. The bright blues and yellows dimmed under the weight of blood. Wil went over to a closet and found a clean towel on the top shelf. He needed water, he knew, to cleanse the child. He remembered passing a bathroom right next door. He hurried for the bedroom door. Briefly he glanced at the baby and stopped. He turned to look at the baby and the new mother, who was licking blood off the baby's body. When he reached down to take the child from Cecelia, she struck out wildly with one hand. He threw the towel down next to mother and child.

Chapter Forty-eight

His mother drained of blood. Jerry drained of blood. The people on the elevator drained of blood. Tim touched his neck, recalling the healed bite Cecelia had given him.

"We don't know what happened to those two weirdos, but I believe they had something to do with all these deaths. That filthy old man is capable of worse than murder."

Tim tried to think of something worse than murder. He didn't bother to ask Edwina what would be worse. She had picked him up from the jail. The cops never did have any hard evidence against him, and now with another murder . . .

"Pete couldn't wait to rent out your apartment, of course. Hell, he tried to rent it to one of the cops. Can you believe? Cheap bastard has some pimp in there now. But don't worry, I took all of your and your mother's belongings down to my place. And you can sleep on the floor of my room until you get back on your feet."

"We didn't have anything," Tim mumbled.

"Yes, you did. Clothes and trinkets. I took the liberty of passing your mother's clothes on to the church. Thought you wouldn't mind."

"Money?"

"I looked through every drawer and closet, even checked under the mattresses, including the one folded up inside the couch. Nothing. I swear, Pete must have taken every penny he could find. Blames it on the cops, he does. Can you believe that?"

Tim fished through his pocket for the few dollars that had been returned to him at the station. He counted out the bills in the palm of his hand. Wouldn't keep him for very long, he thought.

"Don't worry." She patted his arm. "I get my Social Security check tomorrow. If we're careful, it'll feed the two of us for a while. We took up a collection in the building, even made Pete donate something. Not much money, but enough, we hope, to at least buy your mother a simple box. I have the address of the funeral home where she's at. I'd go with you, but the home happens to be the same place my last husband was laid out. He had been the best of them all."

Edwina remained silent the rest of the way back to the residence. No doubt pining over her fifth husband, Tim thought.

Pete looked up from his magazine when Tim and Edwina walked into the lobby.

"You bringing that kid back here?" Pete's face went sour.

"He's got nowhere else to go. He's living with me."

"That'll cost you more."

"Will not. You stole yourself enough money right out of Tim's apartment. And you know that. Don't you dare try to squeeze another penny out of this boy."

Pete rubbed his nose on the back of his left hand. "His mother was a failing prostitute. How much you think she could have had?"

"Enough for you to keep your mouth shut. And don't talk that way about Sondra. Not in front of her son."

"Just get him out of the lobby. I don't want to see his face more than necessary."

"People dying off like flies here." Jones had wandered into the lobby from the street. "Sure glad I ain't rooming here anymore."

"You're living on the street," Pete reminded him.

"Safer out there than in here."

"What do you want?" Pete asked.

"I got enough money to be able to rent that far chair over there for the afternoon. Getting nippy with that storm coming."

"I thought it was safer outside."

"But colder, Pete." Jones handed the money over to Pete.

"You're such a cheap bastard," Edwina commented. "Let's go upstairs, Tim, and I'll give you the money and the address of the funeral parlor. Neat little place. Old, still independent, which is unusual in this day and age. Might even have enough to lay her out for a single day."

"Nobody's going to visit her," Tim said.

He watched Edwina lower her head. She had no reply. He'd have his mother cremated. He wondered whether the funeral home would dispose of the ashes. He didn't want them. She was no good to him as dust. His lower lip shivered, and he forced himself to remember all the bad times he had had with his mother.

He began to feel nauseous on the elevator. The prison food had been lousy, and he had eaten sparingly. Not enough in his stomach to make much of a mess.

"I kept all your mother's jewelry because I thought you might want some mementos. You can take a shower, and I've got clean clothes for you to put on. I'll make some lunch for both of us. You eat ham, don't you? I have some cold cuts from down the block, and I got you a large Coke. I remembered your drinking that when we had last year's Christmas party. Your mother looked lovely that year. Her hair swept up in a fancy French twist and that dress . . . Your mother wasn't shy about showing herself off."

The elevator doors opened, and Edwina led Tim to her apartment.

"Come on in," she said. "Sit yourself down here." She patted an old wingback chair. The arms were threadbare, and the cushion on which he sat didn't match the faded pattern on the rest of the chair. In the far corner of the room a brass and iron bed stood covered with a hand-crocheted bedspread. A cluster of framed and unframed photographs had been placed on the night table. A guardian angel night-light peeked out from behind the table.

"Now, I have rye bagels and onion rolls. Which would you prefer?"

Tim shook his head. The prison food was erupting inside his stomach.

"They can't have fed you very good food down at the prison. What if you take a shower, and I'll make a couple of sandwiches while you're cleaning up. Maybe you'll feel like a couple of bites then."

Tim rushed to the bathroom and barely made it to the toilet before splattering the seat with vomit.

Curious souls who suffer
And are looking for your paradise . . .

Epigraph for a Condemned Book
Charles Baudelaire

Chapter Forty-nine

"She's a beautiful baby, isn't she? Look at those perfect toes and fingers. Itty-bitty nails." Cecelia bowed her head and kissed the baby's fingers.

Wil sat next to Cecelia, unable to take his eyes off the baby's face.

"Suppose she can see?" he asked.

"Of course she can. Two eyes, one nose, and two lips, all accounted for."

The baby suckled on a freshly killed rat that Cecelia had been keeping caged in her room. When Wil shifted his position, the baby seemed to follow his movements. Perhaps Cecelia was right, the baby could see, but the eyes were so . . . predatory, he concluded. He couldn't bring himself to call the baby Liliana. There was no resemblance at all to the beautiful woman he had known.

"How did you know the baby would drink the rat's blood?"

"That's what she liked. She avoided human blood, unless it was dead human blood."

"I can't believe this is Liliana."

"Did you know her?"

Wil nodded.

"Were you able to make love to her?"

"There was never any romance between us. She wouldn't allow it."

"She was too good for you, huh? Think she still is?" Cecelia asked, holding the baby up in front of Wil.

The baby stopped suckling on the rat, and Cecelia wiped away the few drops of blood that had slid down the baby's chin.

"You think you can find a fresh supply of food for Liliana?" Cecelia asked. "I'm sure in a few hours she'll be hungry all over again."

"I'll let her have some of my blood instead of a stinkin' rat's," Wil said.

"Liliana won't like it. She'll only drink animal blood. I don't want to see her go hungry. Please bring back a couple of small animals for her. You can try to feed her your own blood, but she won't accept it. She's very particular. Very self-righteous."

"You didn't like Liliana, did you?"

"I envied her closeness to Louis. I'm over that now. I want her to become a beautiful woman that Louis can't resist. I think she recognizes you, Wil. Look, her eyes are changing color."

The baby's eyes seemed to be flashing a green gold, unlike the muddled earth-tone that had been so liquid. The eyeballs appeared to be hardening. He reached out and touched the baby's cheek, but pulled away when the baby snapped at his hand.

"I'm not so sure she wouldn't go for my jugular if she could."

"It's Louis's jugular I want her to go for." Cecelia smiled at the baby. "We look a little alike, don't you think? We have the same lack of hair." Veins crisscrossed the baby's bald head, casting a pale blue shadow onto the child's skin. "Her eyes are changing color again. Do you suppose they reflect her moods?"

Again the eyes softened into a mud-like color. The baby's lids were closing slowly. The infant fought sleep, but lost the battle.

"I've bought some pretty little outfits for her. I can't wait to try them on her. Want to see them?"

"Cecelia, this isn't a doll. This is a real child. How do you plan on taking care of the baby?"

"Louis will take care of both of us. He'd never let Liliana do without."

"What about when you're resting? Who will care for the infant then?"

"Louis, of course. I'll always know where Louis is from now on. Cuddling, burping, changing smelly diapers."

"That's not Sade."

"I'll bet you a good lay that it will be. And if you lose, you can't run out on me like you did before."

"Do you want me to stay, Cecelia?"

"Were you going someplace? Oh! To fetch the food for Liliana."

"No, I was thinking about leaving, but I have a feeling you're going to need some extra support here."

"Can I give you some advice?"

"What?"

"Don't go down into the basement. You should never do that. It's Louis's playroom. By the way, your father seems to have taken a liking to the . . . basement."

"He and Sade are down there now."

"Don't let Louis have you. Please, Wil."

"I have no intention of getting involved in Sade's S and M practices."

"Good." Cecelia giggled. "Because I want you for myself." Her tongue slowly traveled her cracked and caked lips.

Wil pulled back when she reached out her bloodstained hand to touch him.

"Cecelia, I don't want the kind of relationship you want. I'll try to help you. You didn't ask to be made what you are."

"But I did. Weren't you aware of the consequences of drinking a vampire's blood?"

Cecelia brought her hand up to her mouth and covered a chuckle.

"You didn't know, did you?" she went on.

Wil shook his head.

"Here, hold Liliana for a minute while I set up a place for her to sleep. Here," she insisted when Wil didn't respond. "You say you want to help, but you won't hold her. I can't just lay her on the dirty floor."

Wil sat quietly, and Cecelia gently lowered the baby into his arms. The infant's body temperature was warmer than his own. The touch of the infant's skin scalded his arms.

"I think she has a fever," he said.

"She's normal temperature for a mortal. Don't worry, she won't die in your arms. She means to live again, and she's strong."

Cecelia set up a makeshift cradle for the baby in a corner of the room. After putting the baby in the cradle, Cecelia lifted the cage in which she had kept the rat.

"Here, bring back several rats. They become brazen around dusk and forage in the garbage cans in the alleyway."

"I was thinking about going to a pet store."

"Why?"

"Because . . ." He couldn't think of a reason, except that it seemed cleaner and less—he hated using the word in conjunction with Liliana—less disgusting.

"How are you going to present her to Sade?" he asked.

"I could yell 'surprise' and then walk into the room holding her. But don't you think it would be far better to just be feeding Liliana in the living room when he comes up from the basement? Quietly, mother and daughter bonding. Papa should beam with pleasure."

"He's not the baby's father."

"Liliana. Use her name."

"What if he physically attacks you while you're holding . . ." Wil could not call the babe by name.

"Liliana. He'd never hurt Liliana. And since I'll be holding her, I'll be safe." Cecelia smiled.

She was playing at being an adult, Wil thought, but was way too young, especially as a vampire, to take on the likes of Sade. He remembered how Sade had destroyed Marie. Chopping off her head, burning the head in the fireplace.

"Cecelia, maybe you should take the child and leave here. We could go someplace and . . ."

She shook her head. "I had this baby for Louis."

"You probably had the baby to spite Sade," Wil said.

"I didn't go through all this pain to run out. I want Louis by the balls. I want him under my thumb. And so does Liliana, although she may not quite understand that yet."

Wil looked over at the sleeping infant. Amazing how normal and truly lovely the baby looked with eyes closed deep in sleep.

"Hurry," Cecelia said, forcing the cage into his hand. "When she wakes up, she'll be very hungry, and as much as I'd like to taste your blood, I don't think it would appease Liliana."

Wil took the cage, walked out of the room, and down the stairs.

"Son, I was worried that you might have left. Where the hell are you going with that cage?"

Keith and Sade had just returned from the basement.

"Ah! I see you have been with Cecelia, Monsieur Wil. Has she sucked her pet dry already?"

"You know why she had the rat, Sade."

"Unfortunately I do. So the *bébé* has been born. It is up in her room, *je présume*."

"Don't go near her."

"Wil, Cecelia has had this *bébé* to flaunt it at me. She definitely wants me to see it and her together. *Vierge et l'enfant. Non?*"

"What the hell did you say? I hate it when you get into one of your French kicks," quipped an irritated Keith.

"Madonna and Child," Cecelia said from the top of the staircase, and slowly descended, carrying the infant with her. "And here we are, Louis. She's beautiful."

Wil watched as Cecelia pulled the blankets away from the baby's face. At the foot of the staircase she presented the infant to Sade with outstretched arms. Wil immediately stood in front of Sade.

"Don't you dare hurt them."

"You are easily manipulated by women, Wil. And this one," Sade said, indicating Cecelia. *"C'est une vraie garce."*

"Hell, you look like shit," said Keith, suddenly recognizing Cecelia. "That your kid?"

"You're so observant, Mr. Bridgewater. And yes, Liliana is mine and Louis's."

Wil vaguely recalled her seductive smile in the weak attempt she now made.

"You got her pregnant?" Keith asked Sade.

"Monsieur Bridgewater, she means my child figuratively. Alas, I could never take on such a burden."

"Will you throw us out?" Cecelia asked.

"Non, ma petite."

"You heard what I said, Sade. Don't you dare touch them," Wil reiterated.

"Wil, you do not make a good hero. You're

too . . . *Ce n'est pas votre affaire!* This family dispute will be settled quickly."

"Can we stay?" Keith asked.

"*Oui.* It is important that you stay. I need someone on my side, and I fear I am left with you," said Sade.

"Doesn't sound very welcoming," Keith grumbled.

"I think we can serve each other, Monsieur Bridgewater. A cruel man is always more exciting than . . ." Sade looked at Wil. "Than a weak one." Sade walked around Wil to head up the staircase, but Cecelia stood in his way.

"*Ma petite*, you look very tired and should rest," he said. "It has been months . . . Seven months, I believe, since you've truly slept in death's bosom. You should go rest. That is what I am about to do." He shrugged.

"Hold Liliana, Louis. I want you to feel how real she is."

"The thing you hold in your arms, I admit, is solid, unlike those voices that called to you. But as far as it being Liliana . . . *Non*, I do not agree with that presumption."

"You love her even as we stand here. You know Liliana is back and in my arms."

"You are desperate, *ma petite*. You now have a thing that needs to be nurtured, *mais* by whom? Perhaps by your *chevalier*, Sir Wil of the Tattoos."

"You would never allow anything to happen to Liliana if you could help it."

"Ah, *ma petite*, Liliana, *oui*, I could not bear to see her suffer. *Mais* this thing." His hands indicated the baby. "It does not belong in a human body."

"You know this is Liliana and you *will* accept this baby," commanded Cecelia.

"I could rip this thing from your arms!" shouted Sade.

Wil quickly moved closer to Sade.

"Ah, *le chevalier*. What do you think you could do to stop me?"

"I'll try."

Sade applauded. "*Mais* think of your father. I am the one he depends on."

"Son, I don't think you should involve yourself with this woman. She tried to stab you, remember. Let her and Mr. Sade work this out." Keith reached out and grabbed his son's arm.

Wil knelt down in front of his father.

"Dad, he can't do anything for you. Let's leave. Let's leave them all," he said, glancing over his shoulder at Cecelia. Wil flung the cage across the hallway. "Come on, Dad."

The infant woke, and the baby's wails almost deafened everyone in the room. The cries lingered in the air, ending with a vibrating hiss.

"Don't sound like a normal baby to me," Keith said.

"Please, Wil. I beg you for Liliana, please get her something to eat," shouted Cecelia.

Confused, Wil looked at his father, hoping he would agree to go, yet knowing that he himself could not totally desert Cecelia. His father turned his wheelchair around and headed for the main room.

"Please, Wil," she said.

"It would take me a while to find food for her."

"For *it*," Sade corrected.

Ignoring Sade, Wil offered to feed some of his own blood to the baby.

Sade roared with laughter. "The *bébé* will not live long enough to know true hunger, *mon chevalier*."

"She'll live, Louis. She'll live to make you kiss her feet," spat out Cecelia.

"Don't taunt him, Cecelia," Wil said. "Let him go upstairs. We'll feed the baby and then rest ourselves."

"Will you rest in Cecelia's casket? Or perhaps you have a collapsible casket that I somehow missed. *Mais* you do have the soil that your father showed me. Where do you sleep? Under beds? In closets? *La classe* of champion you have chosen is quite poor, *ma petite*." Sade ran the back of his hand along Cecelia's neck. "You used to be so beautiful. Have you looked at yourself? You have become a *soubrette* to a demon."

"The baby is no worse a demon than you are," Wil said.

The baby now whimpered. She was tired of being ignored, thought Wil. Or did the infant sense the closeness of Sade, perhaps even feel his touch through her mother?

Sade leaned forward and whispered in the baby's ear.

"Ame curieuse qui souffres
Et vas cherchant ton paradis . . ."

Chapter Fifty

Winnie always hit the streets at dusk. Sloop made sure of that. She rubbed her left side where he had last taken a potshot at her—for what, she couldn't remember. Everything seemed to be reason enough. "You're breathing, Winnie. I tell you to breathe?" Wallop.

Sloop would remain in bed until ten or eleven o'clock; then he would hit the clubs. Sometimes she'd take a break and go home around two in the morning just to be alone. Just to feel in charge again. She wasn't, though. She'd stay for an hour or so before returning to the streets. But that small amount of time was precious to her.

A passing driver honked his horn, not because he wanted to pick her up, but merely to feel superior to her. *Yeah, you fucks, you get to ride*

around in a car and laugh at me, but you'll be try-
ing to screw me later tonight, and I'll make sure
you pay high.

She wore a man's long shirt—long enough to
cover her naked behind, barely—and open-toed
sandals with thin five-inch heels. She had jelled
and spiked her strawberry-blond hair. Makeup
she had put on as an afterthought. Light lip
gloss, a hint of pink on her cheeks, and an eye
shadow to match the forest-green shirt. The only
jewelry she wore were gold stud earrings that
had been given to her on her sixteenth birthday.
Ages ago, she thought, unable to count back on
how many changes of seasons had passed since
she had lived at home. Was she twenty, twenty-
one? She couldn't be sure of the correct year;
her head was so fucked up. And she wasn't even
on drugs.

"Got any spare change?" asked the dirt-
covered bum sitting on the pavement.

Ritchie was her favorite. All the years she'd
been on the street he had been the only one she
could talk to. Not because he understood, but
because he remained silent while she talked. He
didn't interrupt to give advice or to whine about
his own life. He just instinctively knew that she
needed to talk.

Winnie slid her hand into the slit in the shirt
and pulled out a small velvet purse that she kept
on a silk string around her neck. Tonight she
could afford to give him a couple of bucks, since
Sloop had been generous with her evening's
allowance.

"Buy something good to eat this time. No

more of those awful candy bars. They're empty calories, Ritchie."

He looked up at her, and it took a moment for him to recognize who she was. When he did he smiled, showing gaps between his front teeth. He grabbed her hand and tried to get her to sit down next to him.

"Can't right now, have to get to work."

His greasy, dirty-blond hair covered his left eye, where he wore a patch. Ritchie had been beaten up on several occasions by youths out for a night of fun. The clothes he wore still retained some bloodstains from the last beating. The hospital hadn't bothered to give him new clothes that time, hadn't even taken time to see that he bathed. They'd just put a patch over his eye and told him to go. Hadn't asked him to come back for a check of the injury. Probably hadn't even done much to fix the eye. She wondered whether he'd be able to see out of that eye when the bandage finally fell off. He let go of her hand, allowing the dollars to fall into his palm.

"I'll see you at the end of the night," she said. "Maybe have a little spare cash to give you." She winked at Ritchie and moved on.

She made sure the velvet purse was settled between her plump breasts. Men didn't pay any mind to her breasts; usually they were interested in the holes on either end of her trunk. In her shirt pocket she kept a supply of condoms, the heavy-duty kind where the guy could barely feel anything.

She was about to cross the street when she noticed a potbellied man relieving himself on the tire of a Mercedes. A new expensive-model Mercedes, she noted. What had drawn her attention was the fact that the car seemed to be talking back to the man.

"You are too close to the car. Step back!" it kept repeating.

When the man finished, he zipped up and saw her watching.

"The yuppie freaks in this town think they can tell everybody what to do." When he moved away from the car the demanding voice ceased. "All I did was brush up against it when I was getting on the sidewalk. Damn thing starts yelling at me." The man kicked the tire for extra measure.

She figured if he carried a knife he would have slashed the tires.

"What's a honey like you doing out?" he asked. "Looking for work? Hey, I might have something for you." The man scratched his crotch.

"Depends what you want," she said.

"Some of that old mouth action would do fine."

"Seventy-five."

"Fifty, and if you're good, I won't complain about the price. Hey, why don't we go over here?"

She followed halfway down the street until they reached an alleyway.

"Hello," he called out in the alley. He checked the windows that faced the alley, and none had lights on. "This is as good as anyplace else. I'm not paying for any cheap hotel. Got one of my own I could use, but I'm in a hurry to get home and watch football. Come on, babe, let's get the action started." He moved farther into the darkness. She followed slowly, wary that it might be some kind of setup.

Winnie watched him quickly unzip his pants and search around for his equipment. She pulled a condom from her shirt pocket.

"None of that stuff, babe. I want to be able to feel something."

"How do I know you're safe?"

He laughed. "I have more cause to ask you that question. Let's tempt fate, baby."

Winnie turned away from the man, but he pulled her around by the hair and forced her to her knees.

"Don't even bother screaming, 'cause if the cops come I'll tell them you were soliciting, and I got the idea that they know you very well around here. Don't worry, I'll pull out when the time is right. Quit gawking and start the action."

He was soft and salty inside her mouth. Her tongue lapped quickly. He smelled rancid. She wanted this over. Maybe she'd get paid; maybe he'd only laugh in her face like some others had done. She hated these cheap bastards. He grew slowly, stretching out to touch the back of her throat. She prayed he'd come fast, and she increased her mouth action. When he did come, he held her head so that she couldn't slip him out of her mouth.

"Swallow, baby. Milk it."

He moaned and suddenly cursed. His grip in her hair loosened and she managed to pull away from him. While still on her knees, she turned her head to see a tall male with a cage in his hand.

"What the hell are you doing here?" the john asked, zipping up his pants.

"Looking for rats, Pete. Pay her, Pete. It looks like she did a good job."

"Yeah, okay." He threw a twenty down on the ground.

"What did you ask for?"

The man with the cage was looking at her. She jolted to her feet and said seventy-five.

"We agreed on fifty," Pete yelled.

"Then why do I see a twenty on the ground? Pick it up and pay her the seventy-five. I know you've got it."

"You should be minding your own business, Wil. The cops have been at the residence looking for you. Seems you killed some lowlife on the street, but I don't think they plan on giving you a medal for it. They messed up your room real bad too, not that you two hadn't left it a sight anyway. Where is your dad?" Pete looked beyond Wil.

Winnie edged further away from Pete. She'd run, except she wasn't sure whether one or both would give her chase.

"Pay her the seventy-five, Pete."

"Hell, she was going to try to use one of those industrial-grade condoms. Do you believe that?"

"I didn't," Winnie boldly said. "You were going to pull out and you didn't, so give me my money, you shit, and I'm outta here."

"You want a turn?" Pete said. "That what you want, Wil? I'll even spring for the cost."

"I'm not doing anyone else," she said. "I want as far away from you creeps as possible."

"She insulted us," Pete said.

"She is half-right," said Wil.

"The woman's not worth a penny. Skinny ass hanging out the back."

Winnie put her hands behind her and felt how the shirt had ridden up. With dignity she pulled it back down over her bottom.

The cage dropped to the ground and the man called Wil reached out and grabbed Pete's collar.

"Seventy-five. I got it. I got it. Don't get antsy." Pete counted out fifty-five. "Mind if I retrieve the twenty on the ground?"

Wil let go of Pete's collar, and Pete bent over to pick up the twenty.

"Here, bitch. Buy yourself some underpants. But I guess that'd slow you down on the job."

Pete laughed, and she saw that he looked to Wil for appreciation. None was shown.

"You drive a Mercedes, mister?" she asked Wil.

"No," he said.

"Too bad, 'cause if you did I'd have a real good story to tell you." She glared at Pete and started to walk away.

"I'd better be going," said Pete. "Wil, what's this, you going to hold me up here in the alley? Shit, I gave most of my cash to that broad you just let walk by."

"I don't want your money, Pete. But I am peckish."

The creeps deserved each other, she thought. Probably go around to some bar, have a few beers, a burger, and laugh at her expense.

Winnie didn't look back. She ran up to the curb and crossed, almost getting herself run over by a police car.

Chapter Fifty-one

In the morning Tim had found the bright sun beaming down on him and his bedroll disconcerting. Neither he nor his mother had been morning people. Edwina was. She kept the shades up. He doubted if they ever got pulled down. After showering and dressing in the clean clothes Edwina had ironed for him, he had sat down to a full breakfast. Sausage links, oven-baked biscuits, orange juice, coffee, and even a multi-vitamin.

"Now I'm only going to give you a portion of the money," she said. "You shouldn't have to pay the whole bill up front. Harry knows me." Edwina had a list in her hand and was checking each item off. "If you're going to cremate her there's no sense putting her in a fancy box. And he's going to try to sell you on embalming. They always do. Tell him you don't need it."

"Naw, it's my mother who would." Tim smirked in the mirror at himself.

"Remember, this is your mother. Show some respect. If he gives you any lip or tries to cheat, you call me and I'll give him hell. I'll be waiting for you to come back." She took a step back to assess him.

"I've never worn ironed jeans before." He looked down at the crease she had pressed into them. "Come to think of it, I don't recall seeing an iron in Ma's house."

"She was too busy—" Edwina caught herself.

"Too busy laying guys. I know."

Edwina reached up and slapped him on the side of his head.

"Don't you talk about your mother that way."

She walked him to the door.

"If Pete's at the desk, ignore him. He's got nothing good to say." She opened the door. "I'm sorry I can't go with you. A shame that at your age you have to be worrying about sending off your mother. Sure you don't want to buy an urn?"

"Where would I put it? Haven't got a home."

"Stop it. You have a place right here with me until you can find yourself a job. Guess they'll be willing to dispose of the ashes for you.

"Got a little plot waiting for me right next to my fifth husband, rest his soul."

Tim saw her eyes begin to glisten.

"I'd better go before these pressed clothes start wilting on my body," he said.

"Okay, but don't let Harry push you around." She stood on tippy-toe with pursed lips.

Tim leaned over so that she could kiss his cheek. He was surprised by the slap on his rear end after he had turned to enter the hallway.

Edwina had given him cab fare, but he walked. He could use the money himself, and besides, he didn't really want to arrive at the funeral home. But he did.

The outside decor of the building was Spanish colonial, with iron railings attached to each of the first-floor windows. The double doors looked as if they belonged to an old Spanish mission. The doors were heavily varnished, and the small window in one of the doors could allow some-one inside to check who was at the door. The buzzer button was located on the door frame to his right.

Tim wiped his palms on his jeans. He couldn't remember everything Edwina had told him. Snatches of sentences came back to him briefly, but none made sense. How hard can it be to ask to have one's mother cremated? he thought.

Maybe he shouldn't have eaten that last sausage. They were greasier than what he was used to. Mom's always turned out all dried out somehow.

The door before him opened.

"Young man, you cannot loiter in front of this door. Please move on." The man was dressed in a black suit, white shirt, and gray and black paisley tie.

"I'm here to get my mother cremated."

"Edwina sent you?"

Tim nodded.

"Then come in." The man's voice had changed from autocratic to consoling. "I'm very sorry, I didn't realize who you were. You're so young to be doing this. No other family members?"

"No, but I got the money."

"So Edwina informed me. No doubt you'll be wishing to make partial payment, the rest immediately on completion of services?" He didn't wait for an answer. "I've buried all five of Edwina's husbands. The last she truly loved. Not that I'm implying she didn't love the others, but the last was special to her. I assume he was the last. Has she . . . ?"

"She lives alone. Not exactly. I live with her now until I can find a place of my own."

"I'm sorry, I didn't introduce myself. I'm Harry Sanchez." Harry put out his hand to Tim, who grasped it tentatively.

Tim noted how warm the hand was. Did the funeral director keep his hand in an oven warmer for the next customer? he wondered.

"And you're Tim. May I call you Tim?"

"You already have."

"Yes. I'm sorry if I offended."

"Get on with it, Harry. I don't like this place."

Pastoral paintings hung on the eggshell-white colored walls. Wooden screens stood in each of the doorways, and the smell of fresh flowers was overpowering. A mahogany banister led up a flight of stairs, but a chain prevented access.

"Come back to the office," said Harry. "I've customers in the sample room." He pointed to a set of curtained French doors. "Probably trying out the merchandise. You wouldn't believe the kinds of requests we get. Some people want to plan ahead today. I've had customers come in a rented truck to take home their casket. Wanted to be prepared. Of course we will store, or should I say, make note that payments have been made. The caskets are usually ready on short notice. Have to be in this business. Take a seat, and I'll quickly go check on the other two."

Tim sat in a leather chesterfield chair. The arms looked polished from use. The rosewood desk in front of him was neatly laid out. Paper clips in a lucite box, a matching pen and pencil with white caps at the tip of the lids, a closed laptop computer centered on the desk, and a wireless telephone on the right side of the desk. A small printer sat on a two-drawer file cabinet next to a magazine called *Mortuary Science Monitor*. Unlike the hallway, the office walls were covered with framed photographs. Photographs from the twenties and thirties and all of San Francisco. A matching chesterfield chair had been pulled away from the wall and was next to where Tim sat. Incongruously, behind the desk was an ergonomic chair, the kind Tim had seen in one of the shop windows down on Market Street.

"They're still trying to make up their minds, so why don't we get started with the nitty-gritty details," Harry said, returning.

"Your mother was delivered to us two nights ago from the city morgue. The autopsy caused a bit of damage, but nothing we can't hide."

"No. She'll be cremated."

"I see. The embalming—"

"No embalming, don't need it." All the information Edwina had supplied was flooding back into his brain.

"Okay, then I guess it's just the casket we need to discuss. I have a few photographs of some models, and we can look at others in the sample room as soon as the other party is finished. We realize this is the last gift you will make to your mother and appreciate the care you wish to take before selecting her final resting place."

"I said she'd be cremated."

"Yes, you did. Let us start with the Dynasty line. Since you'll be using calcination we shall look at only the wooden models."

"Excuse me. I'm cremating my mother not calcin—whatever you said."

"Yes. Cremation and calcination are the same.

"Caskets in this line are a combination of craftsman's skill and fine natural wood. The woods used are oak, mahogany, and ash. Each casket is distinctively styled with rounded edges and moldings at the top and at the bottom. You have your choice in moldings as you do also with the lining. Satin is lovely, but velour runs a close second at this home. Now as far as the hardware—"

"Edwina said my mother doesn't need hardware. I'm having her cremated."

"Yes, you've mentioned. Now let's turn to urns."

"Don't want an urn. I have no place to put it."

"We happen to work with a very fine crematorium. A place where you can store your mother's ashes."

"I don't care what they do with the ashes. She's gone, and I'll never be able to conjure her back by storing her ashes."

"I guess what's left is to total up the cost and . . . Did you say you were paying by cash or check?"

"Don't have any savings account," Tim grumbled. "I'm paying by cash." Tim drew out of his pocket all the money Edwina had given him.

Without a bedmate, without intimate talk,
Old frozen skeletons worked over by
  worms,
They feel the winter snow dripping away
And the century melting . . .

The Warm-Hearted Servant
Charles Baudelaire

Chapter Fifty-two

"Lift me out of this thing. That guy Sanchez must think we're a pair of weirdos."

"*Monsieur*, do not trouble yourself with the help. Does it matter what he thinks of us? We are paying him good money, and if we wish to try out the merchandise, then it is not any of his business."

"I do kinda like this one. Feels real comfortable."

"He did say that this had an inner-spring mattress. However, when you sleep, *monsieur*, do you notice on what you are sleeping? For someone who has been sleeping on the floor under a bed—why you could not rest on top of the bed, I don't want to know—you are being overly choosy." Sade rubbed the side of the casket. "I'm not sure why you would need praying hands decorating the side of your casket. There are no prayers that can save us, *monsieur*."

"I hate those plain-looking things. Hell, when I got my wife's casket, they only had these grape-like things every few inches. She would have liked this one with praying hands and the angels at the corners guarding her while she slept."

"We are not attempting to make up for your poor taste by buying a casket in even poorer taste. This is far too busy." Sade waved a hand and moved across the room to view a plain rectangular casket. "This one has dignity."

"It's also way cheaper than this one." Keith waved Sade back to him. "Get me out of here, quick, before Sanchez comes back."

"Now that is something to consider." Sade raised his right index finger to his lips. "Hmm . . . How will you get in and out of your casket?"

"You said I'd have the use of my legs back. Otherwise, it would be the same way I've gotten under the bed and back out. Wil will carry me."

"Ah! But how will he feel when he must lift you into a rather *compliqué* casket and he must spread his nightly dirt on the floor?"

"We could buy him that cheap one over there."

"*Monsieur*, your son is someone I do not favor. I am only willing to pay for yours since we have agreed on a proper exchange."

"If you think it may bring back the use of my legs, I'm willing to go along with the deal. I must say it does give me the chills, though."

"Chills. *Monsieur*, you have killed many in

your *dément* quest. Why not do me the favor of eliminating one who should not exist?"

"Why don't you do it?"

"*Parce que* I am too close to the situation." Sade quickly lifted Keith out of the casket and dropped him into an even more elaborate one. "Solid copper, *monsieur*, with an inner-spring-mattress that tilts and lifts. Note the masculine but non-abrasive fabric." Sade touched the inner material. "Some sort of synthetic," he mumbled.

"I could be real comfortable in this one, huh?"

*"Sans compagnon de lit, sans bonnes
   causeries,
Vieux squelettes gelés travaillés par le ver,
Il sentent s'égoutter les neiges de l'hiver
Et le siècle couler. . . ."*

"I asked if you think I'd be comfortable, not for a French recital."

"Oui." Sade brought the wheelchair over to the copper casket. "Let us announce to this Harry Sanchez that we have made our choice."

Sade watched Keith's eyes brighten, and Sade knew this man would exist for eternity with the memory of what he was about to do. Sade lifted Keith out of the casket and slipped the invalid back into the wheelchair.

"Hope he comes back soon before you change you mind," Keith said.

"Why wait, *monsieur*? Let us make assault on his office."

But, in truth, I have wept too much! Dawns
  are heartbreaking.
Every moon is atrocious and every sun bitter.

The Drunken Boat
Rimbaud

Chapter Fifty-three

"She will be ready tomorrow morning." Harry stood, giving a hint that the arrangements had been completed. He moved around his desk while Tim remained seated.

"Seems you could have her ready in an hour," Tim said, getting to his feet.

Harry reached for the doorknob and Tim started for the door.

"I feel like something's missing," Tim said, standing in front of the door. "I've got little holy pictures from when my grandma died."

"They cost extra and are made in bulk." Harry opened the door.

Tim paused in the hallway.

"If you'll excuse me, I have other clients that need my assistance," Harry said.

Tim nodded at the man. The curtained French doors to his right were flung open.

"Lordy, it's that boy!"

Tim recognized the voice, and turned to see Sade with hands on his hips, standing in front of Keith and his wheelchair.

Tim lunged for Keith, but was deftly lifted into the air by Sade. Landing face-down on the floor, Tim felt a sudden burst of blood pour from his nose.

"Get out, you hoodlum," shouted Harry.

Tim rolled over onto his back and lifted his head to see the three men that stared down at him.

"*Le garçon* is mired in deep grief, Monsieur Sanchez. He needs only to think and recall the misery of the jail cell."

"He's a convict? Should I call the police?" Sanchez turned toward his office.

Dressed in a black fitted linen suit, a banded-collared white linen shirt, and a silky ascot decorated with tiny red fleurs-de-lis, Sade looked majestic walking toward the boy; crouching, he brought his hand in contact with the boy's blood. Tim saw Sade's eyes soften as he came close to bringing the blood to his own lips.

"I remember the taste," he whispered. He closed his eyes and bent his head back. "And the smell."

"Freak!" Tim yelled. "You're the freak from that club. You and Bridgewater were watching Cecelia and me making love."

Sade bent his head back toward Tim.

"It is never wrong, *mon petit garçon*, to watch love."

"We were . . ."

"Fucking?" Sade tilted his head. "Nothing wrong in that either, if you are careful about with whom you are fucking. Your cock was swollen and long with the weight of your juices and your ass. Ah, superb in its tightness." Sade allowed himself a lick of the blood on his fingers. "And the blood I will never forget."

"Shit." Tim scooted back away from Sade, but did not rise to his feet. Tim had the impression that if he now tried to escape, Sade would not let him.

"I really would rather not have any problems here, gentlemen. I prefer that you leave and take whatever dispute you may have with you," Harry hurriedly said.

"I want the all-cooper one," Keith interrupted. "The works, with the mattress and the tilty thing. And could I get the fabric in a pale sky-blue color?"

Harry took several breaths before answering. "I'm sure we can find a color similar to what you described."

"Sometimes I am lonely." Sade reached out a hand to touch Tim's cheek. He did not seem to be aware of the deal being discussed behind his back.

"*Mais, vrai, j'ai trop pleuré! Les Aubes sont navrantes.*
Toute lune est atroce et tout soleil amer. . . ."

Sade moved closer to Tim. "I knew immediately that Cecelia could not fill my loss, but you, *petit garçon*, you . . ."

Tim sat frightened but mesmerized, allowing Sade to caress his face.

"Where are you staying, *mon amour*? Tell me." Sade's thumbs separated Tim's lips.

Without a question, Tim immediately gave the address of the residence. "I'm staying with someone."

"*Alors*, you are trying to make me jealous."

"She's an old woman. In her eighties, I think."

Sade laughed heartily. "Would you meet me outside your residence tonight?"

Tim, confused, gulped, knowing what the answer should be, but not able to deny this man.

"He killed my mother." Tim pointed to Keith, who was looking at some folders Harry had brought from the office. "Everybody says he did."

Sade looked back at the invalid, then returned his attention to Tim.

"What do you want me to do, *mon petit garçon*?"

Tim remained silent, not wanting to call out for execution and not wanting to let the invalid go free.

"Meet me tonight, and I will prepare you so that one day you will know the answer to that question and will be able to carry out the action without any assistance." Sade licked his fingers several times.

The dried blood could not have been satisfying, thought Tim, for he noted that the stain did not fade from Sade's fingers. Geez, what the hell was he thinking? Worrying about some freak who wanted blood. Just like himself. Only the blood he wanted was Bridgewater's, and this man had promised to give him a way to claim it.

Chapter Fifty-four

"What are you doing out here?" Cecelia asked, stepping off the back porch of the Victorian house.

"Where's the baby?" Wil asked. His right hand held a photograph.

"Sleeping. Upstairs. I left the window open so I could hear her cry."

"Can sure as hell hear that baby when she cries. Did I ever show you an old photograph of my father when he was young?"

Cecelia shook her head.

"Get a load of this." Wil presented her with the photograph. "A dapper sort."

Cecelia held the photograph and thought how amazingly similar father and son looked at about the same age.

"Do you have one of your mother?" she asked.

"Yeah, left it back in the house on the East Coast. I was in such a hurry I didn't have a chance to pack it."

"But you took your father's photo?"

"Stupid, isn't it? Don't know why I did that. We left the house in a hurry after we . . ."

Cecelia looked at his face and saw terrible pain. Fleeting but deep, she thought.

"Dad was supposed to be comatose, and he would have had to remain housebound had we stayed there. Otherwise, doctors would have been amazed at his recovery and would want to prod him with all kinds of equipment and tests. We ran. We fed and ran. I'm so sorry, Cecelia." Wil squatted. "I'm going home. Dad doesn't need me. He's managed to form some sort of symbiotic relationship with Sade.

"I killed a man last night."

"Certainly that's not unusual," said Cecelia.

"I killed a man I knew and hated. Not because I hated him, but because he reminded me of all the damnable things Dad and I have done here in San Francisco. I looked at Pete and saw my father rip open a young prostitute. I saw him drain a mother who would do anything to gain her son's freedom. Know what else I saw?"

Cecelia knelt next to Wil. "An alien being that in no way seemed related to you," she said.

"No, I saw that my father and I are one. I share his taste for blood. I share his anger about what we are. And I share his loneliness, since we both are truly without the love of a family. I don't have a father, Cecelia. I have a vulture that clings to me, biting my body, chewing me up, until only the vulture will exist." Wil turned his head toward Cecelia. "I'm leaving. I have to go alone."

Cecelia, sensing that he was making a point of including her in his farewell, smiled and kissed his lips.

"I didn't ask to go with you. I have Liliana, and Louis will buckle," she said.

"I've been out here wondering whether I should tell you a secret. Would it be fair to leave you not knowing? Can the knowing change anything for you?"

"Why you couldn't make love to me?"

"Guilt. You're a beautiful woman."

"Even now with the bald head, the withered body, and the tattoos?"

"You'll recuperate. Even now I see that the shadows have passed from your face. Your body will blossom into the luscious, sexy woman I hooked up with at a club."

Cecelia almost reached out to embrace him— to molest him, she admitted to herself. But couldn't. He didn't want it. And some sixth sense told her that he had done something so horrible that she would regret ever wanting to be his lover.

"You can't go home, Cecelia."

"I already know that." She tried to smile but couldn't.

"My father and I didn't know how to feed. We tried to survive on each other's blood, but we grew weaker. I went to Sade's house to seek help."

"Louis and I never returned to the house after

Liliana's death. He had halflings, people who were not vampires, but were not completely human, fetch the caskets for us."

Wil nodded. "Your mother was there."

Cecelia's body ached. A shiver seemed to crawl through her flesh. She had fantasized about bringing the baby home to her mother, proudly showing the beautiful baby she had birthed. Although that never could be, she enjoyed the blessing of knowing her mother still existed. Someday maybe she could go back, cuddle in her mother's arms and . . . No, she would never have done that. But this man squatting in front of her had stolen the dream. She knew that before he confirmed her fears.

"You know what the hunger is like," he said. "The blind hunger."

"You didn't make her a vampire?"

"I wouldn't have known how."

"Share your blood. Take from her but give a little back. A few drops. All she needed was to swallow a few drops."

"I doubt a few drops would have been enough. Besides . . ."

"Your father ripped her apart."

"Oh, shit! Cecelia, I just didn't want you to go back and expect to see her."

"Will I be able to see a headstone?"

"I buried her on our property. I . . . There's a tree, an old willow. I sat under it as a boy to dream of a different life than what I had. It's quiet. I love that spot."

"You made the right decision in not fucking me."

"I'm sorry, Cecelia. Since I've been with my father, everything seems out of control."

"I think your father was always in control, whether you lived with him or not. And when you leave here, you still won't be free of him. It's what you deserve, Wil."

Cecelia stood and walked away from him. She fussed with bagged soil and pottery that had been left on a splintery wooden table, gray with age and weather. He never said another word to her, but minutes later when she turned round he was gone.

Nothing is dead but what has never
  been. . . .

Cortege
Guillaume Apollinaire

Chapter Fifty-five

"We must do this *rapidement*," Sade said, carrying Keith up the flight of stairs to Cecelia's room.

"What if she's there?"

"*Non,* she is not. I saw her from the hall window. She is in the backyard talking to your son."

"Don't they make a lovely couple?" Keith chuckled.

Sade kicked open the door to Cecelia's room. The baby lay in a cradle Cecelia had brought home from an antique store. The wood cradle had been newly finished, and the linen was fresh, unused. The baby could be rocked to sleep, and the designs on the head and footboards were mainly made up of stick figures. The kind a child would draw. Sade set Keith on the floor next to the cradle. The baby slept. Her lips sucked air as she dreamt.

"You know, with its eyes closed, it's a damn cute baby."

"Get on with it, Monsieur Bridgewater." Sade wrung his hands. They itched for the touch of Liliana. "I have kept my part of the bargain. A first-rate casket will be picked up and delivered by my associates. Now you must complete your part. After all, I believe you still have something to gain, since your actions will cure the malady you experience."

"Damn, I really want to walk again." He reached out for the baby. "Reminds me of Wil when he was small. I hated him and loved him and wanted to protect him, and wanted no part of him. It was such a jumble when his mother died giving birth to him."

"Don't think of your son, *monsieur*. This is not a human *bébé*. This is your salvation."

Sade watched Keith's hands pull down the blanket from the baby's neck.

"Quietly, *monsieur*. Do not wake *le bébé*."

"Don't want to bring this to the mother's attention yet, huh? She is going to know."

"You will be walking when she learns of this."

"I hope so. She can be a fiery bitch when she's mad." Keith's hands began to shake. He pulled them back from the baby.

"Your son is in the yard with Cecelia, Monsieur Bridgewater. It has been a long time since he lay in a cradle."

"Never had a cradle. Just a crib. White crib.

Mary Ann Mitchell

Spanking new. Everything was spanking new. Emmeline, my wife, wouldn't have it any other way. People offered to lend us things, and she turned them all down. Her baby wasn't going to have any hand-me-downs. We knew it would be a boy, so all these little blue outfits started showing up in the nursery. Every day there was something new. I thought of the money, but couldn't tell her to stop."

Sade yanked Keith's head back by the hair.

"Do you want to walk again, *monsieur*? Or do you wish to crawl your way down the stairs to your wheelchair, for I will leave you here."

"I want to walk."

Sade released Keith and watched as the invalid reached into the cradle and carefully lifted the baby out. The baby stopped her mouth motion and slipped her tongue out. The chewed tongue had begun to heal, and yet still retained the scars of its own making. Keith cradled the baby and slipped one hand over her mouth. Slowly he brought the tiny neck up to his lips. Sade watched as Keith bit into the flawless flesh. The old man sucked so hard that Sade could see the ribbons of flesh parting. Tears ran out of the baby's soft, murky eyes, wetting the hand that silenced its cry. The wide eyes began to close. A peace came upon the baby's body. He saw the arms and legs stop their flailing and rest. Blood marred the white undershirt in which the baby was dressed. The stain spread across the shirt, drawing attention to the fading breaths.

"Rien n'est mort que ce qui n'existe pas encore."
Keith's lips were red when he raised his head.

He placed the dead infant on the floor and wiped his mouth with the back of his hand.

"I feel different. Don't know what it is, but it's nothing like when I've fed before." Keith reached down and rubbed his legs through the fabric of the pants. "Damn, I think I feel something."

Sade watched Keith stretch out his legs.

"They're moving. They're moving." Keith excitedly shook his legs out. "Feels like they've been asleep. You know that old tingling feeling you used to get when you were mortal? Feels the same as that. Shit, I can't believe it. I knew you'd find a way." With difficulty Keith stood. "Look at this!" He tried to take a step but stumbled, catching himself on a near wall. "Think I'll have to learn to walk all over again? How embarrassing. A man in his seventies taking his first step, so to speak." He attempted another step, and this time was able to stand on his own. "Thank you, Mr. Sade. I owe it all to you and your beautiful niece. She was a real kind lady. I guess in a way she lives inside me. You know, like when people get transplanted hearts and all. Her spirit's been transplanted into me, giving me the strength to walk again."

"My Liliana cannot live inside of you," Sade said.

Keith took another step. With more confidence he took several steps. He appeared proud, almost haughty in the renewal of his legs.

"Suckers are starting to work as well as they ever did. Damn, it must be your niece. Hey, and I'll keep her safe, don't worry about that. Long as she's good to me, I'll be good to her."

Mary Ann Mitchell

"She cannot live joined to you," said Sade.

"She's doing a damn good job of living." Almost completely recuperated, Keith did a careful jig. He laughed and waved his arms in the air to soundless music. "Wanta dance?" Keith reached out to grab Sade's arm, but Liliana's uncle quickly backed away.

"Liliana was never soiled by the baseness you have allowed yourself to experience," Sade said.

"If you're talking about that kinky sex stuff, most of it was your idea. I went along for the ride, so to speak."

To Sade, Keith's laughter sounded crass and cackly. Keith's movements were lewd, and his face could be confused with Satan's.

"Let us celebrate, *monsieur*. I have prepared a surprise for you in the basement."

"One a redhead, the other a dark-haired beauty." Keith winked. "Won't they be surprised when I come struttin' in giving the orders."

Keith led Sade to the basement door.

"How do I look?" Keith asked, pulling in his belly. He spat on the back of his hand and used the saliva to clean off his mouth.

"Il n'y a pire imbécile qu'un vieil imbécile."

"I hope imbecile in French don't mean the same as it does in English."

"Monsieur, we are delaying much too long. I am sure you are ready to relax after our long day."

"Relax? Nah, I'm raring to go. Bring on the girls." Keith flung the door open, switched on

328

the basement light, and stepped onto the top step.

Sade took hold of Keith by the collar and seat of his pants, lifted him into the air, and flung him down onto the floor of the basement. Stunned, Keith tried to get to his knees, but Sade used a knife to open the old man from gut to collarbone. Keith fell onto his back. The fear in the man's eyes drove Sade on to reach inside the opened belly and pull out the intestines. Keith's body shivered uncontrollably. Sade glared down into Keith's still-open eyes, holding a portion of the intestines in front of him so that the old man could view them.

"Slowly you will wither, *monsieur*. I will take you apart as you did to others, as you did to Liliana. Don't shake you head; even you admit that Liliana lives inside your foul body. I will cut her free, open each crevice of your body to send her spirit back to the earth's bosom. She will never be tortured by one such as you." Sade split Keith's face in half with the tip of the knife. The nose gaped open, while the rest of the skin began to slip apart. "I could not murder her myself, but I knew you could. You would have drunk your own son's blood long ago to have the use of those ruined legs of yours." Sade ripped open each pants leg and cut notches in the flesh underneath. "Now that you have feeling in your legs, *monsieur*, tell me about the pain each wound brings. Here are your intestines, *monsieur*." Sade tossed the intestines down on the widening cut of the chest. "Shall we read your entrails and see what your future holds?" The knife worked at gutting its victim, an old hopeless man forming a single word upon his lips. The syllables Sade put together for him and gave voice to. "Wil-bur."

Chapter Fifty-six

Cecelia gathered a bunch of wildflowers. Weeds, she guessed; still, they were a pretty, golden yellow. They would brighten Liliana's room. Sade would buy a rocker so that Cecelia could sing to his favorite niece. There would be myriad stuffed toys. Giraffes with long necks, elephants with long trunks, pigs with flattened snouts. Lady bugs, bright red and somber black. A huge teddy bear that will sit upon the floor, and that as a toddler Liliana will climb all over. Of course there would be dolls. All kinds of dolls. Infant dolls, dress-up dolls, and fancy French porcelain dolls. A dollhouse. Cecelia had always wanted a big dollhouse; instead her parents had given her a simple cardboard house that didn't even have a closure to the back or front. Liliana would have a mansion, so many rooms and so many different eras of furnishings that she'd not be able to use them all.

And the room needed to be painted. No, they needed newer quarters. Something in Pacific Heights. Louis had refused to take Cecelia to France; she surmised it was because it would remind him too much of his dear niece. However, now the niece was back. They could afford a castle surrounded by vineyards. She would be sure that Liliana would learn English well, unlike her uncle, who often slipped back into French when the English did not come quickly enough. How like a child he was, with his tantrums and inability to wait. They would be three children growing up together—except that Cecelia doubted Louis would ever mature.

Cecelia sighed and looked back at her flowers. Mustard flowers, someone had told her once. Maybe, maybe not, but they were pretty and bright. Perfect for an infant's room.

She was glad Wil had left. All he seemed to do was irritate Louis. The sight of him soured Louis's disposition. If only Wil had taken his father with him. That old man would not be going to France with them, else she'd threaten to go off with Liliana and never allow Louis to watch his young niece grow up a second time. That old man was filthy anyway. Wouldn't trust him around Liliana.

Amazing how long Liliana had been quiet. Once she had awakened, she would remain alert for a long time. Louis would have to share in the care. Cecelia smiled, certain that Louis wouldn't mind, for finally he had been reunited with his love.

She sat on the porch steps, enjoying the salty San Francisco breeze. A hummingbird flitted about some slender red bell-shaped flowers. Suspended in the air, the bird paused at certain flowers, wings almost impossible to see in their speed. A neighbor's cat jumped up on the deteriorating wooden fence that separated the two properties. The cat paused, poised to jump, mesmerized by the tiny bird.

"Shoo," Cecelia called out, and stood.

The cat caught her movement and jumped back down into its own yard. By then, though, the bird had exhausted the nectar and moved away, out of sight.

Suddenly Cecelia wanted to look at her baby. Watch the infant sleep. See the little chest rise and fall. Hear the giggles, as Cecelia interpreted the noises the infant made in her sleep. If Cecelia poked her finger inside her child's little fist, the baby would grasp hold without awakening.

Thanks to that pathetic boy Tim, Cecelia had what she wanted. She had read about his being freed from jail. The case would be reopened. The hunt for her would become more intense. She didn't care, for they would soon leave for France. Louis must flee to protect his beloved niece.

Cecelia went back into the house and climbed the stairs leading to her daughter's room. She surprised herself with the thought that she did love the baby. The baby was not only Liliana, but also a part of Cecelia, a living being that came out of her belly. She no longer had her own mother. She would exist for her daughter, who would block the pain of losing her mother.

The door to the baby's room was open. Cecelia could have sworn she had closed it. She didn't want that old man to go near her daughter, or to even see her daughter, for that matter. Liliana would never be exposed to such crass stupid people.

Softly she entered the room and closed the door behind her. She looked across the room at the cradle and found it empty. The blanket had been swept back over the foot of the cradle. All that was left was a tiny indentation where her daughter's head had rested on the pillow.

She was about to set her hand on the doorknob when a faint smell surrounded her. Blood. A small amount. The odor existed in the confines of this room. It did not waft in on the San Francisco breeze. The scent did not press itself into the room from behind the door. Cecelia walked closer to the cradle. A beautiful cherry-wood cradle with which she had immediately fallen in love, a cradle meant to hold her child, sturdy enough to protect the babe from falls. She had made sure of that, testing it before she even took it home with her. The breeze was becoming chillier; she would have to close the window to protect her half-mortal baby from the cold. She moved to the window, but stepped on something. A tubular-shaped object that gave quickly under her weight. Cecelia lifted her foot and looked down. Her daughter slept with eyes closed at her feet, the bald head twisted into an uncomfortable position, the little fists partially opened. She knelt and tried to reposition her daughter's head, only to find a gaping hole in the neck—shredded, the same as that damned old man would do to his prey.

He would never touch the baby, she thought to herself. He feared Louis too much. Louis would have to have given his permission.

"Sade!" she screamed out only once. He did not come. Her daughter did not awaken and never would.

Cecelia would forever be alone with Sade as her keeper.

Cecelia sprang to her feet and hurried to the locked door to Sade's room. With hands out in front of her she rushed the door, splintering the wood. She used her fists to break the door down completely.

In the room was the pretentious white marble altar with the pinkish-hued lamb in the center of the front piece. Resting atop the altar was Louis Sade's coffin, the burled wood polished so smoothly, the solid gold etching between the strong brass handles depicting his coat of arms. She touched the lid and did not sense his presence. Decay did not seem to foul the air around the casket. She lifted the lid. Empty. Only soil and yellowed white silk that carpeted all of the interior.

Cecelia walked to the bay window and looked through the wavy glass at the ground below. A short time ago she had been on that grass talking to Wil, totally unaware of the wrath that had taken her daughter's life. Cecelia raised her fists and hit the glass, spraying the air with sharp shards.

The coffin moved easily within her grasp. She hoisted the coffin up to rest upon the window's ledge. With one push the coffin fell to the ground, the lid flying free from the bottom. She stepped off the window ledge and allowed her body to fall two stories. From a crouched position, Cecelia sprang onto the coffin, emptying the dirt and ripping the lining, until she hit an object. A scorched skull had been sown into the lining where Sade's feet would rest. His infamous mother-in-law's skull. The woman he despised above all. Perhaps, Cecelia realized, not above herself, not after Louis Sade had seen the damage she had inflicted on his safe harbor. The skull she set aside, and she continued to rip the coffin apart, breaking the wood into splinters, blending the soil in with the San Francisco dirt, so that Louis could not tell which was his own.

When there was nothing left of Louis's coffin except unrecognizable firewood, Cecelia looked about the yard. An old paint-splattered tarp lay in a ball by the pottery and bagged soil. Quickly she tore off a piece of the tarp and wrapped up the scorched skull. If there was any way she could bring this woman back, she would. The skull had to have had an important significance, or Louis would not have bothered to hide it so well. This was all she would take with her. Let Louis deal with the shell of his niece. Her baby was gone.

Cecelia ran around to the side of the house. As

she neared the street, her movements became more cautious. He would never let her flee if he knew what she carried· away with her. Once he had seen the remains of the coffin, she would probably not be allowed to even survive. Her own skull and the mother-in-law's skull would become a pair of footrests.

He would not stay long in San Francisco without his home soil, she knew. Never would he allow his body to wither as she had for her baby. *He'll return home tonight,* she thought. Much later he might look for her, or he might want to wipe her from his memory. She felt the tarp that she gripped close to her. Was it wise to take the skull along? Would he allow Cecelia to go free if he at least retained the skull?

But the skull held some sort of magic, or he would not have kept it so close to him. Someday she might need that magic. Someday she might meet Louis again. The skull, in some way, would prepare her for that encounter.

A man walked his sleek greyhound. A teen slouched on the steps of the house across the street. He was smoking a cigarette and drinking a can of soda. There was no sign of Louis or his invalid protégé.

O my little lovers,
How I hate you!
Plaster with painful blisters
Your ugly tits!

My Little Lovers
Rimbaud

Chapter Fifty-seven

Sade ripped off his ascot as he walked through the hall. He had already removed his jacket and was about to take off his blood-splattered linen shirt when he stopped at the foot of the staircase. He remained still for several seconds, trying to sense whether Cecelia had come back into the house. The stillness prickled his flesh. He unbuttoned his shirt and decided to stop for a glass of Pinch before he had to deal with the girl.

The kitchen was bare, except for one cluttered counter where he kept his various liquors. A table had been centered in the room until Keith had arrived to stay. He had complained about it hindering his movements. Wil had moved the table into the empty dining room. Inconvenient for a cook like Sade, who needed lots of counter space when preparing some of his elaborate dinners—fewer, now that he did not have a servant.

Sade took a crystal goblet from a cabinet and half-filled it. His taste buds seemed to have sharpened over the years, and the cutting taste of the Scotch made his tongue tingle. Thank God he had soundproofed the basement so well. Wil rushing in to help his father would have caused so much confusion and might have shortened the time he required to destroy Keith.

Wil. Perhaps he could keep him as a pet. One that would need to be muzzled on occasion. Sade felt tired, and wasn't sure he wanted to make the effort.

Sade would rest after he destroyed Cecelia. She had disobeyed too many times, and certainly the young Tim would be a far better companion. He was not as strong-willed, not as likely to strike a bargain with either Liliana or with Sade's mother-in-law, Marie.

Would he have enough time to rest before meeting Tim tonight? he wondered. After all the action he had seen today, no doubt he would sleep deeply. Better to take the boy after destroying Cecelia. The idea already had started to invigorate him.

Now, where was that girl? Still talking to Wil in the backyard? He would snatch Wil's life quickly and extend that kindness to Cecelia. She was willful, but Sade didn't believe her to be malicious.

Sade placed the empty glass back on the counter. The liquor did not give him a high, but did remind him of when he was mortal, the taste of the Pinch so different from the sweet, coppery blood on which he survived.

Sade walked to the kitchen door and decided that it was time to face the fools. He opened the door and saw no movement except for the turning of the head of a calico cat sprawled across the top of the far fence. As he stepped onto the porch, the cat leaped back onto his own territory.

There were shreds and ribbons of a yellowish-white material stuck to bushes, blown there by the San Francisco breeze that had picked up briefly into a gust of wind. He stepped off the porch and onto the grass, feeling the flutter of his open shirt around him. Suddenly his hair was whipped up by another gust of wind, and he found that he could not see clearly through his white strands of hair. Yet he thought he recognized something. Bits of wood covered the ground, and shining in the midst was his crest. The very crest that had marked his coffin.

Another gust of wind, and a ribbon of material slipped from some shrub and wound itself around his linen pants leg. He reached down, grabbing the material, lifting it close so that he could see better. With the other hand, he brushed back his white hair. Silk. Fine, old silk, such as he had demanded to line his coffin.

Obviously Cecelia had already found her babe, and the girl was probably nowhere near the house. Too smart not to flee, but then she would have had to be an imbecile like Keith to think he would allow her to survive.

He looked down at the dirt upon which he walked. Raked over. He could not tell his own soil from this damp hellhole he had mistakenly allowed himself to settle in.

Very good, Cecelia; I cannot follow you now, he thought. Immediately I must return home. This day and the previous ones have been trying. My body needs rest.

And then he remembered, and began wildly searching the debris, looking for signs of a smashed skull. Marie and Cecelia would not be as powerful or as wise as he, but they could cause him serious harm if they worked together to defeat him.

Why hadn't he pulverized the skull into dust? His ego had not allowed that. No, he'd wanted her at his feet for eternity, her spirit recoiling from the image. He'd needed even in her destruction to flaunt his victory.

"O mes petites amoureuses,
Que je vous hais!
Plaquez de fouffes douloureuses
Vos tétons laids!

Chapter Fifty-eight

Tim stood outside the residential hotel. Several feet away, Jones crouched up against the building, as if hugging his mother's breast. It was late, and even the street people were making their beds. Most cars sped by; a few slowed down so that the driver could have a good look at him. He ignored them and turned his back.

Jones sneezed and shifted under the worn covers that protected him from the San Francisco dampness.

Pete hadn't relieved his afternoon man, who'd waited all of fifteen minutes before throwing on his coat and leaving. No one manned the desk. Jones didn't know. Tim wondered whether he should tell him. He hated to hear Pete bawl out Jones, but if Jones could warm up for just a short time, maybe he could avoid coming down with pneumonia.

"Jones," Tim called.

The man under the mountain of fabric didn't respond. Tim walked over to Jones and shook the man's shoulder. Jones, startled, skittered away from Tim.

"It's okay, it's only me. Tim. Remember me?"

"What you want? Pete send you out here?"

"No, haven't seen Pete. Matter of fact, no one's sitting behind the desk. The lobby was empty when I passed through a while ago."

"So?"

"Why don't you go in and grab and few winks? The worst that can happen is Pete shows up and tosses your ass back onto the street. Until then, you've got a warm place to bunk out."

"Can you warn me when he comes?"

"I may not be here. I'm meeting a . . ." Tim wasn't sure what to call Sade, certainly not a friend. Then why in hell was he waiting? "A man. A weird kind of guy. Knows the man that killed my mother. Maybe I can get him to help."

"Let that ride. Nothing you can do for your mother now. Next thing we know, they'll be taking up a collection for your pine box."

"Didn't get my mom a pine box."

"I gave Edwina some coins I had found when she came around asking for money. Didn't directly ask me, but why shouldn't I be included? I had something to add. People think I got no heart because I got no change in the pocket. But I had a mother. A good lady not like, excuse my saying it, but not like your mother. She didn't go off with no men, rest her soul."

Tim understood that getting into a "my mom's better than your mom" argument was useless. About the only thing Jones had to hang on to was the ideal he had built around his mother. Whether she was as good as Jones said didn't matter. Like Tim, Jones needed the image, the fantasy that something had been good in his life; otherwise, why go on?

"Go in and warm up, Jones. Nobody but Pete will throw you out."

Jones attempted to stand, but needed Tim's assistance to get on his feet.

"I'll walk you in and get you settled."

"What about that man you were talking about?"

"I'm sure he'll wait a couple of minutes for me. Hell, I've already been out here fifteen minutes. He's so damn late he can't say anything about me."

There was a chill in the lobby, but at least there was no wind. Jones settled in an old threadbare wingback chair. Tim helped cover him up with the blankets and coats Jones dragged around with him.

"If I told Edwina you were down here she'd probably bring you some soup. Want me to tell her?"

"No, don't want to bother her this late at night. Maybe if I'm still here in the morning, someone could bring down a little coffee and maybe a buttered roll."

"I might not be here. I'm sure anyone who lives in the building and sees you in the morning will think of sharing their breakfast."

"Where you going?" asked Jones.

"I told you. I'm meeting someone who can help kill my mother's killer."

"Can't take the law into your own hands, Tim. Why not go to the police and give them the name? Edwina could go down to the station with you. I'd go too, but I don't think bringing me would help your case." Jones yawned, pulling the blanket up to his chin.

Tim smiled. Sometimes Jones was insightful.

"Why don't I dim the lights a bit," Tim said.

"I don't want people hurting themselves because of me. Some people in the building have bad eyesight as it is without making it harder for them to walk through the lobby."

"Don't worry. I know how the lights work. I can turn the light over your head off without dimming the walkway area." Tim went behind the desk and opened the box containing the lighting controls. On the first try he shut off the lighting fixture over Jones's head.

"Sweet dreams," Tim called out as he opened the lobby door.

Jones grumbled some words Tim could not understand, and then went silent except for his heavy breathing.

Back on the street Tim looked up and down the block for Sade. He wondered whether Sade would come with Bridgewater.

A well-dressed businessman dressed in charcoal-gray wool and carrying a leather briefcase walked across the street in Tim's direction. He cursed loudly at a car that had just honked at him. His salt-and-pepper hair was stylishly cut, his features firm, puppet lines drooping down from each end of his mouth. As he stepped up onto the curb, he spoke.

"I think you're waiting for me."

The businessman was too tall and tan to be Sade, and the hair color and features were not the same.

"You're looking for a date, aren't you?" the businessman asked.

Tim pushed his hands into his jeans pockets and shook his head.

"You state the price and I'll pay it," the businessman insisted. He put his free hand inside his jacket pocket and pulled out a roll of bills held together by a silver money clip, flat, smooth, no design.

"I'm waiting for someone I know."

"Been here a while, I noticed. Perhaps your regular's not going to show tonight. A shame to waste the evening." The businessman placed his briefcase on the ground, counted out five hundred dollars, and offered the money to Tim. "For the night."

Again Tim shook his head.

"Name a price then, don't keep me waiting."

"I'm not keeping you waiting. You're harassing me. I could call a cop."

"You can't afford to call a cop, kid. Think you're pretty ass is going to pull in more than this?" The businessman waved the money in front of Tim's face.

Mary Ann Mitchell

"I'm not selling myself to you or to anybody else. Go home and jerk off in front of the mirror if you want company."

Tim turned around and climbed the steps to the residence.

"Punk kid!" the businessman yelled.

Tim opened the door and walked into the lobby. Jones snored loudly. The desk remained unmanned, and the elevator didn't work. He climbed the stairs, thinking about Sade. What would Sade do for him? Introduce him to bisexual orgies with women who were capable of killing? Sade didn't want to help; he wanted to use him just the same as that businessman in the street. *I'd slip deeper and deeper into the same circle of shit my mother did.*

Tim gently knocked on Edwina's door.

"Come in," she called.

He tried the knob and the door opened.

"Should keep that door locked," he told her.

"Figured you'd be coming back and didn't want to get up. Tomorrow I'll see if I can have a key made for you."

An old movie from the era when Edwina was young was on the television. She had a cup of tea and a bag of cookies next to her. She lay sprawled across the crocheted bedspread, two pillows bunched up behind her shoulders.

"Saw this movie on my first date with my first husband. Such a character. Cheap. Used to bring a brown bag of goodies to the movie theater so he wouldn't have to pay the higher price at the theater. I loved ice cream and told him wso. Next movie date he hands me a melting

Klondike Bar. Wonder why I married him." She appeared to be attempting to answer that in her own mind.

Tim sat on the floor, his back up against the wall. "Remember you told me you could get me a job interview?" he asked.

Edwina perked up. "I sure did. Wouldn't be much of a job, but it'd be a start. Larry's always short on kitchen help. I don't know whether it's the money he pays or his disposition, but he can't seem to hold on to help for very long. I'd speak to him, though, and make sure he treated you decent, also do a little negotiating for you in the salary department. Get yourself a few dollars to buy a nice suit, and you'll be able to find yourself a real job."

"What's a real job?"

"One that you can have pride in. Someone asks you what you do, you can look that person in the face and tell him."

"Yeah, that's what I want. A real home too, not sleeping in dives like this with the rats outnumbering the people."

"Sometimes the people are the rats."

"I know." Tim laughed. "My mom tried, didn't she?"

"Yes, Tim. But you have to try harder," Edwina replied.

"Think you could give your friend a call tomorrow?"

"How about tonight?" Edwina muted the television and picked up the telephone receiver.

"Isn't it too late?"

"Hell, he's probably still at the restaurant

cleaning up. I'll make an appointment for you for tomorrow afternoon. Say about three o'clock. That would be in between the lunch and dinner crowds. Like Italian food?"

Tim nodded.

"Then you'll love this job."

"Speaking of food, think we could spare some coffee and a roll for Jones tomorrow morning?" Tim asked.

Chapter Fifty-nine

Cecelia sat cross-legged on the ground. The tarp-wrapped skull rested in her arms as her baby once had. This was no baby, she knew; the skull could potentially conjure up the most hated woman in Sade's life. Slowly Cecelia unwrapped the tarp, laying the scorched skull bare. Her hands worked the texture of the skull, feeling the bumps and a solitary patch of glacial smoothness.

She recalled Sade telling her of Dr. Ramon, who was his last treating physician. The doctor had been eager to perform an autopsy on Louis. Claude-Armand, Louis's younger son, refused to permit the procedure and had a Mass quickly said at Charenton. Louis was supposedly buried in the Charenton asylum cemetery with a stone lowered over the grave. The stone had no inscription; only a simple cross marked what most believed was Louis's final resting place.

Dr. Ramon continued to insist on an autopsy, and many years later he managed to have a body exhumed from Louis's grave, a body of a simple monk who had lived his life in prayer, dedicated to the service of God. Therefore, when Dr. Ramon studied the skull within the confines of phrenology, he found that the skull belonged to someone who had "a complete lack of ferocity." A skull consistent with "a Father of the Church." How Louis had laughed when he told the story, deception being his favorite pastime.

What would a man like Dr. Ramon say about the skull she held in her hands?

She held the skull high in the air over her head. A quarter moon flashed briefly in one of the eye sockets.

"I need your help, Marie. I have revenged Liliana and left a victor. For now. If he comes for me, I don't know how I could defeat him. Help me, Marie, and I will avenge what he did to you."

An owl hooted, and she heard the soft rustle of nearby shrubs. Prey escaping? Or attracting its predator?

Cecelia looked around the small cemetery in which she sat. Most graves were marked with simple headstones. An occasional angel rose above the monotony of tombstones. An elaborate stone Bible lay open upon a stone pedestal.

Lowering the skull, she studied its uniqueness; the cavities, the scorch scars that defaced the structure. It was very difficult to believe this skull had any powers. Perhaps it was only a token of a war now over. But Louis had been assiduous in the keeping of this memento. There had to be a reason.

A figure drew her attention to the far end of the cemetery. A lone male bundled in black walked the cemetery. His flaxen hair fell forward, covering most of his face. He carried flowers: roses, carnations, and lilies. Every few feet he would lay a flower in front of a tombstone. He skipped the angels and didn't even go near the Bible. He centered his attention on the simplest markers.

Quickly Cecelia wrapped the skull and jumped to her feet. Holding the skull under her right arm, she pulled away from the approaching figure. Still he came closer, his long white fingers tipped with nails shaped in the likeness of claws.

The man could not be Sade. His gait was different, less frenetic. A good deal taller than Sade, he towered above the markers, bending his knees slightly to drop a lily or a carnation or a rose.

Ready to run, she turned toward the ramshackle gate that no longer protected its inhabitants. She would have fled, except she did not know where to go. Her soil and her coffin remained at the Victorian house, but she dared not return. Even if she found the house empty and her own coffin still in one piece, she would not trust Louis not to tamper with her soil. He could now be filling her coffin with San Francisco dirt after having disposed of her home soil. Irked by the thought, she kicked a stone at her feet. Not that she had believed he would take no vengeance, but she was sorry she hadn't thought the matter out more; she rued the fact that she had missed her chance to exchange Louis's soil. Instead she had acted wildly, tossing the coffin out the window, destroying the trap she could have set.

So engrossed in her thoughts, she had almost forgotten the figure that now stood several feet from her. The straight flaxen hair hung in strands in front of the bowed head. He seemed to be blocked by her presence. Finally he took a lily from the bouquet he carried and offered the flower to her.

She stood tall before the figure and asked, "Who are you?"

He raised his head, and she saw green pools where his eyes should be. The whites had been drowned out; only a rich, deep green colored the eyes.

"The flowers are for the dead," he said. "This one is for you."

"Do I look like I just crawled up out of one of these graves?" she asked indignantly.

He tilted his head to the side, causing some strands of hair to spread apart, revealing parts of his face. His features were even, his lips neither fat nor thin, his nose neither long nor stubby. His eyes round with anguish.

"I know what you are," he said.

"You know me from the clubs?"

"We have never met before. Please take the lily. I want to bring you peace."

Cecelia stepped back several paces. "You still have not told me who you are."

"You would flee, but are afraid to turn your back on me. Wise."

"I'm not afraid. There is nothing you can do to me."

"I am a child of yours."

"Please. You're years older than I am."

"I can't move on until you have accepted the flower." His hand still held the lily before him.

"Then you'll just have to back up."

"I can't go back. I can only go forward."

"Okay. Throw the flower at my feet."

His eyes darkened into muddied earth. He tossed the lily on the ground before her.

"You're half-vampire, aren't you? Your eyes change the way Liliana's did."

"I do not know Liliana."

"Do you live here in the graveyard?" she asked.

He nodded, turning to point in the direction of a cluster of trees. Beyond the trees, almost hidden from view, was a weathered shack.

"That's just the caretaker's shed," she said.

"And my home."

"You're the caretaker here. You do take care of the dead." Cecelia moved past the man, trying to obtain a better view of the shack. "And your name?"

"I am whoever you want me to be."

She immediately turned her head toward him.

"I want a name. Don't play with me."

"Call me Justin, then."

"Justin, I'm Cecelia, and I want to see your

home. You see, I find myself homeless right now and may need a place to . . . to meditate. I have to make a long journey. I must go home, to where I was born."

Justin nodded. "You are without home soil. That is why you sit here alone in a cemetery."

"You say you help the dead, Justin. Show me mercy."

Justin took the bouquet and placed it at the foot of the oldest and most decrepit headstone.

His gait grew stronger as he led her across the cemetery to his home.

The windows were covered with cardboard. The wood was gray from age, and the door seemed to be fastened with a thin wire. He walked past the shack, and in the distance she could see a lone mausoleum. Marble spiraled in columns on either side of a metal door. Rust covered the very bottom of the door, but the rest of the door had obviously been scraped and painted recently. The body of the mausoleum was made of stone that had been stained by rain and moss. Justin reached for the door handle, and the metal squeaked with age as he pulled it back.

"You live here?" she whispered. She walked past the man and entered the mausoleum.

A number of small rectangular doors lined the walls on either side of her. She assumed the ashes of a family member lay behind each door. Before her was a well-kept wooden casket, polished to shine; a painted portrait was centered just below the lid's closure. She moved closer, and saw a beautiful woman dressed in seventeenth-century attire. She heard the door squeak closed. The light dimmed, but not her eyesight.

On the floor to her right was a horsehair mattress covered with a rough-textured blanket. A wooden recorder lay next to the bed.

"You play?" she asked.

"Mother taught me when I was a child. She loved music."

"You still play for her?" she asked, turning once again toward the casket.

"Yes," he answered.

"Your mother lies in the casket. You stand guard over her. She was mortal?"

"No," he answered. "She is like you."

Wary, Cecelia moved closer to the door. "Then she's only sleeping."

"Both my parents are sleeping. Only my father sleeps deeper and in peace, for he was mortal."

Justin went to the casket and opened the lid; at the same time Cecelia placed her hand on the handle of the door. He threw the lid back and invited her to view his mother.

Cecelia let go of the handle and with small steps approached the casket. Eventually she saw shriveled, mummified remains laid out on a pinkish-yellow satin. A stake pierced the chest where the heart should be.

"Who did this to her?"

"I did."

"To your own mother."

"And creator," he said.

"Why?"

"To give her peace from the rampaging to which she was shackled. She wounded, killed, and sometimes replicated, but not without conscience. Mother missed Father desperately when he died. You see, he did not want to live her life, and she, causing her own unhappiness, honored his wish. Sometimes I would go hunting with her, but I do not thirst for the blood. Ordinary food can nourish my body. And unlike you, I will grow old."

"And die?"

"I have met no one like myself, so my future is a mystery to me."

"You're the only human child she birthed?"

He nodded.

"Why stake her?" she asked.

"To give her and myself time to be quiet. Time to think over the way we each live."

"And someday you'll yank that dreadful wooden stake out of her heart?"

"I don't know," he answered.

"How long have you been alone?"

He shrugged. "I no longer count the years."

"I need help, Justin. Will you help me?"

Slowly he closed the lid on the casket.

"I had a baby like you," she said. "She was half-human, but someone killed her. Drained the blood from her tiny body."

"The person did her a favor," he mumbled.

"No, he didn't. She wanted to live. She begged for life, and a man refused to allow her to have one. I . . . did something to the man for which he will never forgive me. Now he too must return home. Home for him is Europe. He will probably leave tonight. I need you to go back with me to where he and I had lived so I can take what-ever remains behind."

"Your coffin with your home soil."

"The soil may be tainted, but there may be money to help in the journey I have to take. Will you go with me tomorrow morning?"

"I take care of the dead."

Cecelia meditated throughout the night, keeping the tarp-wrapped skull close to her body. Justin slept, but not peacefully. Sometimes he would jerk awake and would appear almost relieved to find Cecelia guarding the premises. Who, she wondered, did he fear? His mother, or perhaps those that would come to destroy her?

In the morning he left Cecelia to go down to a nearby stream that ran just past the cemetery. She followed, curious about the man on whom she was basing her fate. He stripped the clothes from his body, revealing a well-molded form, perfect as Liliana's body had been. He scrubbed his body clean while she watched. In the chill water he had no erection. His pale body did not have the glow of a vampire. She could see no scar, no blemish, no visible network of veins. Body hair was minimal.

She thought about joining him in the stream; however, she had no time for play. The taste and feel of his body would remain a mystery. She needed him not as a lover, but as a companion.

He stepped out of the stream and vigorously rubbed his body with the pale lilac towel he had carried down with him. He saw her, and his erection began to flower. Turning her back to him, she walked back to the mausoleum. Once she was inside, the darkness felt good, the bareness soothed. When she spotted the tarp-wrapped skull, she knew she must hide it before Justin returned. She would not return to the Victorian house with the skull in her possession. Spying the casket, she moved closer and opened the lid.

Justin's mother waited for her son to get over his snit. Cecelia could not make out the features, since the folds of the skin had dried into paper-thin slices. The woman's hands were merely skeletal bones with flakes of a dark tissue paper lightly spread across them. The dress was over-large for the body, and the burgundy cloth had grayed. The style of the dress could be dated a good twenty years back.

Cecelia hurried to the tarp-wrapped skull and picked it up. She returned to the casket and sought a safe spot for the skull. Why not? she thought, placing Marie's skull next to the mummified head. She placed it against the backside of the casket, feeling the features through the tarp and placing the skull face-up.

"You'll probably feel more comfortable here than where you came from," she whispered.

After closing the lid, she became aware of her hunger. She would never make do with petty animals. Soon she would need to make a human kill.

The door squeaked open behind her.

"I'm ready to go," Justin said.

Chapter Sixty

Justin wore a dark-brown flannel shirt, well-worn jeans, and Birkenstock sandals. Most of the buttons on his shirt were open, allowing the sleeves to hang over the back of his hands and his smooth chest to be partly exposed. The broad, black sunglasses he wore hid his green eyes.

Cecelia, still in her clothes from the day before, felt unclean and couldn't wait to at least change her clothes once she reached the house.

Cecelia saw the mothers walking with their small children to school buses. Some children looked half-asleep, others looked miffed at the inconvenience, and only a few gloried in the challenge of the day.

"How were you taught, Justin?"

"I went to a private school. A school where the

children didn't make fun of the fact that I had to wear dark glasses all the time."

"Do you ever walk around without the glasses?"

"When alone or with a person who understands." He looked at Cecelia, and she remembered that she hadn't seen the dark glasses until they were about to leave for the house.

"I'm famished," she said. "What are you going to do for food?"

"I'll have a bagel and coffee when we're through at your house."

"You never drink blood?"

"Only in small amounts. I have never killed anyone."

"Except for your mother," she reminded him.

"My mother cannot truly die."

A man dressed in a green T-shirt and matching green shorts ran with his black Labrador. Rich in swollen blood vessels, his hand held tightly on to the leash.

She paused as the man ran by her. Justin's hand touched her shoulder, forcing her to recall the task she had to perform.

"I don't know how you can wait for that bagel and coffee, Justin."

"Because it will taste better when I don't have a distasteful chore to accomplish."

"Two more blocks and we make a right. Our house is the fourth one on our side of the street."

The next two blocks were empty of people except for some teenagers sitting on the steps of a dilapidated house, sharing drags of marijuana.

Justin and Cecelia made their turn, and she

saw several people standing where the Victorian house should be. She pulled Justin across the street, and both slowly wandered down the block.

The house had been burned to the ground. Louis had made sure he had left nothing for her. Her casket as well as the body of her child were ashes. The houses on either side still stood, but were not inhabitable. The raw gaping hole on a neighbor's house testified to the heat and strength of the fire. The other house had an exposed inner wall, with Mother Goose characters sprinkled across the wallpaper.

"Maybe you no longer have to worry about this man." Justin had turned toward her to study her reaction, she knew.

"This is his doing. He exists."

She walked closer to the curb. Her attention was distracted by a neighbor who whispered and pointed in her direction. Several people had turned to look at her.

Cecelia grabbed Justin's hand and led him down the block.

"He will come back for you, won't he?" Justin asked.

The smell of burnt wood receded as they walked. The hunger increased. Justin escaped from her grip and placed his arm around her shoulders.

"I know where you can feed," he said.

"And afterwards I have to return to home soil."

She was very tired and needed to rest. She needed to plan her future without Louis.

Sips of Blood

MARY ANN MITCHELL

The Marquis de Sade. The very name conjures images of decadence, torture, and dark desires. But even the worst rumors of his evil deeds are mere shades of the truth, for the world doesn't know what the Marquis became—they don't suspect he is one of the undead. And that he lives among us still. His tastes remain the same, only more pronounced. And his desire for blood has become a hunger. Let Mary Ann Mitchell take you into the Marquis's dark world of bondage and sadism, a world where pain and pleasure become one, where domination can lead to damnation. And where enslavement can be forever.

___4555-9 $5.50 US/$6.50 CAN

DRAWN TO THE GRAVE — MARY ANN MITCHELL

"A tight, taut dark fantasy with surprising plot twists and a lot of spooky atmosphere."
—Ed Gorman

Beverly thinks that she has found something special with Carl, until she realizes that he has stolen from her. But he doesn't just steal her money and her property—he steals her very life. Suddenly she is helpless and alone, able only to watch in growing despair as her flesh begins to decay and each day transforms her more and more into a corpse—a corpse without the release of death.

But Beverly is not truly alone, for Carl is always nearby, watching her and waiting. He knows that soon he will need another unknowing victim, another beautiful woman he can seduce...and destroy. And when lovely young Megan walks into his web, he knows he has found his next lover. For what can possibly go wrong with his plan, a plan he has practiced to perfection so many times before?

___4290-8 $4.99 US/$5.99 CAN

BLOODLINES

J. N. WILLIAMSON

Marshall Madison disappeared the night his wife committed suicide. She saw the horrible things Madison did to their son, Thad, and couldn't deal with the knowledge that their daughter, Caroline, was next. Caroline is taken in by a kind, hardworking family, and Thad runs off to live by his wits on the streets of New York. But Madison means to make good on his promise to come for his children. And as he gets closer and closer, the trail of bodies in his wake gets longer and longer. No one will keep him from his flesh and blood.

___4468-4 $4.99 US/$5.99 CAN

SPREE

J. N. WILLIAMSON

Mix equal parts Charles Starkweather and Bonnie and Clyde and you've got Dell and Kee, a couple in love and out for fun—their kind of fun. When Kee casually suggests they murder her parents, that's just the beginning of their grisly road trip. After all, there's a long highway in front of them… and a lot of people to kill before they're through.

___4370-X $5.50 US/$6.50 CAN